# Also Available by Mike Resnick

Ivory: A Legend of Past and Future

New Dreams for Old

Stalking the Dragon
Stalking the Unicorn
Stalking the Vampire

Starship: Mutiny
Book One

Starship: Pirate
Book Two

Starship: Mercenary
Book Three

Starship: Rebel
Book Four

Starship: Flagship
Book Five

# MIKE RESNICK

THE BUNTLINE SPECIAL

A WEIRD WEST TALE

an imprint of Prometheus Books
Amherst, NY

Published 2010 by Pyr®, an imprint of Prometheus Books

Cover illustration and interior illustrations © J. Seamas Gallagher.

Inquiries should be addressed to
Pyr
59 John Glenn Drive
Amherst, New York 14228–2119
VOICE: 716–691–0133
FAX: 716–691–0137
WWW.PYRSF.COM

14 13 12 11 10    5 4 3 2 1

Library of Congress Cataloging-in-Publication Data

Resnick, Michael D.
    The Buntline special : a weird west tale / by Mike Resnick.
        p. cm.
    ISBN 978–1–61614–249–0 (pbk.)
    1. Edison, Thomas A. (Thomas Alva), 1847–1931—Fiction. 2. Inventors—United
States—Fiction. 3. Tombstone (Ariz.)—Fiction. 4. Earp, Wyatt, 1848–1929—Fiction.
5. Holliday, John Henry, 1851–1887—Fiction. 6. Ringo, John—Fiction. I. Title.

PS3568.E698B85  2010
813'.54—dc22

                                                                              2010030361

Printed in the United States of America

To Carol, as always,

and to my good friend
(and a fine writer)
Kevin J. Anderson.

# PROLOGUE

*From the September 7, 1881, issue of the* Tombstone Epitaph

## THE BRIGHTEST LITTLE TOWN IN THE WEST
### BY JOHN P. CLUM, PUBLISHER

*T*ODAY MARKS ONE FULL YEAR *since Tombstone became the first city, not just in America but in the world, to be illuminated by artificial electric light, thanks to our two resident geniuses, Thomas Alva Edison and Ned Buntline. The* Epitaph *thinks it's time to salute these two gentlemen, without whom life in our fair city would certainly be less bright.*

*Ned Buntline moved to Tombstone from Dodge City three years ago, and since that time he has invented a type of brass that cannot be penetrated by bullets. Most of the outlying ranch houses and barns are now covered with this remarkable material, and of course those who live in town daily pass buildings constructed of Mr. Buntline's brass, which was also used in the construction of our lovely and ornate lampposts.*

**7**

Mr. Buntline invited his friend, Mr. Edison, to immigrate to Tombstone exactly one year ago today, and it is Mr. Edison who is responsible for the harnessing of electricity to power not only the streetlights, but also the Tombstone Territory Stage, which has since been renamed the Bunt Line. Remarkably it is now impervious to attack by highwaymen or Indians.

Perhaps the pair's most remarkable creation is Mr. Edison's artificial arm. The original had to be amputated after it was shattered by a bullet during a failed assassination attempt, and Mr. Buntline, under Mr. Edison's direction, crafted the appendage that is now attached to Mr. Edison's shoulder. According to Mr. Edison, it is stronger and works better than the original—and of course is immune to pain. This principle has since been used by Mr. Buntline in other experiments, while Mr. Edison has just completed work on the phonograph and is working on something we have not yet seen which he calls the "telephone."

When asked what they plan to create next, Mr. Buntline merely shrugged and said, "The sky's the limit."

Mr. Edison then added, only half smiling, "There's no reason why it should be. Leonardo didn't accept that, so why should we?"

Whatever they come up with next, Tombstone is proud to have it invented right here. Happy first anniversary, Mr. Edison!


## FIGHT AT THE ORIENTAL

There was another disturbance at the Oriental Saloon last night. No shots were fired, and according to Marshal Virgil Earp, both Curly Bill Brocius and One-Armed Kelly will be spending the next forty-eight hours as guests of the county jail, as the city jail is currently being outfitted with Mr. Buntline's brass bars.

## LOCAL LADIES PROTEST

*Sheriff Johnny Behan's office has received a petition signed by seventeen local ladies demanding that Mr. Buntline cease and desist certain unspecified experimental work. According to Sheriff Behan, Mr. Buntline has broken no laws, and he is dismissing the petition. Mrs. Eleanor Grimson has told the* Epitaph *that if Mr. Buntline continues his activities, her group plans to picket his office.*

## CLANTONS BEAT CHARGE

*In a trial that lasted less than fifteen minutes, all charges were dropped against Ike, Fin, and William Clanton, who had been arrested for stealing horses and cattle. The case was dismissed when none of the prosecution's witnesses showed up to testify.*

## CLAIMS AND MINES

*Three new silver mines were opened this week, and claims were filed for fourteen more at the Assay Office.*

## ANOTHER TRAGEDY IN THE COUNTY

*Morgan Earp reports that, acting on a tip from a cowboy who was looking for strays, he found the burned remains of a covered wagon at the eastern end of Cochise County. There were no survivors. It is assumed they were killed for their horses by local Apaches. As Geronimo has never declared war on Tombstone, it is likely that they were renegades who acted independently.*

## SOCIAL NEWS

*Actress Josephine Marcus, a close friend of Sheriff Behan, has announced her intention to remain in Tombstone and become a resident here when the rest of her theater company moves on to California next week. Miss Marcus is, we believe, the first person of the Jewish faith ever to live in Tombstone, and we welcome her.*

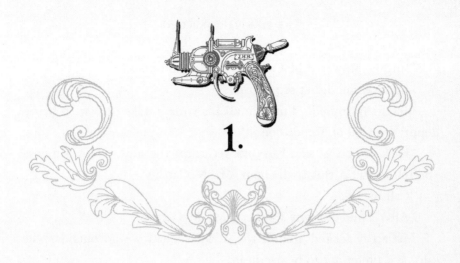

# 1.

THE TALL, LEAN MAN with the thick, droopy mustache entered the saloon and looked past the faro dealers and poker players, past the portrait of Lillie Langtry, until his gaze fell upon a well-dressed lone man seated at the side of the room. The man smiled and waved a hand. The tall man, oblivious to the stares and whispers of the patrons, walked over.

"Mr. Earp?" said the seated man, and the newcomer nodded. "I'm so glad you agreed to come."

Wyatt Earp seated himself, filled an empty glass with whiskey from the open bottle in the middle of the table, took a swallow, and wiped his mouth off with the cuff of his black jacket.

"All right," he said. "You sent for me, Mr. McCarthy. You do the talking."

The man extended a hand. "I'm pleased to meet you," said McCarthy. "Your reputation precedes you, and of course your brother has informed me of your current activities."

"Which brother?" asked Earp. "I've got a lot of them."

"Virgil," answered McCarthy. "He's a good man."

"I notice you didn't send for *him*."

McCarthy smiled. "I'm sure all his time is taken up with being deputy marshal of Tombstone."

"He keeps busy," said Earp, not returning the smile. "Now suppose you tell me what this is all about, Mr. McCarthy."

"Call me Silas."

"After I find out why I'm here, Mr. McCarthy."

McCarthy looked around the saloon. "Shall we go outside?" he said. "I'd prefer not to be overheard."

Earp shrugged. "Suit yourself."

They got up from the table, walked through the swinging doors, and out into the street of Deadwood, Colorado.

"That's a magnificent animal," said McCarthy, gesturing to a roan that was tied to the hitching post in front of the saloon. "He wasn't there when I arrived. Yours?"

Earp shook his head. "We don't have much use for horses in Tombstone, not anymore."

"Yeah, I've heard about that."

"I suppose word gets out."

"Chilly, isn't it?" said McCarthy, as they turned a corner and began walking down a side street.

"I've seen worse," replied Earp. He stopped and turned to McCarthy. "I've come a long way at your request, Mr. McCarthy," he said. "I'm hungry, and I'm tired, and I've got a blister on my left foot, and I'll be damned if I'm inclined to walk all around town until you're sure no one can hear your voice or read your lips, so why don't you just stand still and tell me what's on your mind?"

McCarthy nodded. "Might as well. It's a legitimate request." He took one last look around. "Mr. Earp, your country needs your help."

"I was born too late for the War between the States, and I'm not aware that we're fighting another one," said Earp.

"You're wrong," said McCarthy adamantly.

Earp looked mildly surprised. "England? France? Maybe Mexico?"

McCarthy shook his head.

"I'm not real good at guessing games, Mr. McCarthy," said Earp.

McCarthy studied him silently for a long moment, and then spoke. "Why do you think the United States ends at the Mississippi River?"

Earp shrugged again. "Nothing much on this side of it. Couple of gold and silver mines, a few ranches, maybe a couple of hundred settlements, and a bunch of Indians."

"It's the Indians that we're at war with."

"Dumb," said Earp firmly. "You go to war with the Apaches and the rest, you're going to lose. They'll kill you all."

"I notice they let *you* live," noted McCarthy.

"I'm not at war with them," answered Earp. He pulled out a tobacco pouch and began rolling a cigarette. "Tombstone is a silver-mining town, and they have no interest in silver. We haven't got anything they want, and they haven't got anything *we* want."

"Well, they have something the United States wants," said McCarthy, swatting a fly away from his face.

"What?" said Earp, lighting the cigarette.

"The Western half of the continent, of course."

"Why?"

"It's our destiny to reach the Pacific Ocean," said McCarthy with absolute conviction.

"I've heard that manifest destiny crap before," said Earp. "If you want all that land, why don't you just buy it from them?"

"We haven't bought one square inch of the United States!" snapped McCarthy. "We're not about to start."

"Seems to me you bought New York from the Indians. Twenty-four dollars, wasn't it?"

"That was a totally different situation," said McCarthy defensively. "The government of the United States didn't do that, because there *was* no United States at the time."

"Okay, it's your destiny to own all the land from one ocean to the next," said Earp. "Good luck taking it from them."

"That's where you come in, Mr. Earp."

Earp looked amused. "You think *I'm* going to scare the Apaches and Sioux and Cheyenne and the Western tribes into giving you their land and hightailing it to Canada or Mexico?"

McCarthy returned the smile. "That was never our intention."

"Well, then?"

"Let me explain. The reason that we stopped our expansion at the Mississippi was not that the Indian armies were too much for us. No, Mr. Earp, we defeated the British, and we can defeat the Indians, tribe by tribe or all together, on a field of battle." He grimaced. "But what we can't do is defeat the magic practiced by the medicine men of the Western tribes. We may have the cannon and the Gatling gun, but the Southern Cheyenne have got Hook Nose, and Goyathlay of your local Apaches is almost as powerful."

Earp frowned. "Goyathlay?"

"You know him as Geronimo," said McCarthy. "Those two, and scores of less well-known medicine men, have used their powers to keep us on our side of the Mississippi."

"You're wrong," said Earp. "They haven't kept me and my brothers there, or a hell of a lot of other men."

"You're allowed in the West on sufferance," continued McCarthy. "You represent no threat to them. You don't make war on them, you don't hunt the game they need for food, and while there's not much water there's enough for them and the small handful of whites they allow to live in their territories."

"They let more than white men come out here," noted Earp. "Damned near every tribe has got an escaped or freed slave as a translator. That way they don't have to learn our language, and we don't have to learn theirs." He paused. "Okay, so now you've explained why the United States stopped at the Mississippi, but you still haven't told me what you want of me. I hope you don't think I'm about to wage a one-man war against the Apaches."

"No, of course not," said McCarthy. "We're taking steps to counteract their magic."

"Then why the hell did I travel all the way from Tombstone to Deadwood?" demanded Earp irritably.

"You and your brothers own the Oriental Saloon in Tombstone, do you not?"

"Two of them."

McCarthy seemed surprised. "Two saloons?"

"Two of my brothers: Virgil and Morgan. We'll be sending for James and Warren when the saloon's a little more prosperous."

"What would you say if I offered to let you keep running the Oriental while you and your brothers work for me, and paid you double whatever it makes, month in and month out?"

"I'd ask who you wanted me to kill—Geronimo or President Garfield?"

McCarthy uttered an amused chuckle. "I hope you won't have to kill anyone."

There was a momentary silence. Finally Earp said: "I'm waiting."

"First I want your agreement that anything I tell you will be kept confidential."

"It's been nice knowing you, Mr. McCarthy," said Earp, starting to walk back toward the saloon.

"*Wait!*" cried McCarthy.

Earp stopped and turned. "I don't make blind promises, Mr. McCarthy. I probably won't tell anyone what you want to tell me, but I won't promise it until I know what it is."

McCarthy considered the statement. "Fair enough," he said at last. "What do you think of Tombstone?"

Earp looked puzzled. "I like it fine. Certainly better than Dodge or Wichita."

"As well you should. You know, New York's and Boston's streets are still illuminated by gas, and our main form of transportation is by foot: either our two or our horses' four."

Earp stared at him. "This has got something to do with Tom Edison, right?"

"He is the most brilliant scientific mind the country has yet produced. Ben Franklin proved there was awesome power in electricity, but it took Thomas Edison to harness it. The potential in this electricity of his is limitless. Yes, Mr. Earp, this has got *everything* to do with Thomas Edison. Why do you think he moved to Tombstone? He could make ten times the money in New York or Baltimore." McCarthy didn't wait for a reply. "He's in Tombstone because we paid him to go there, to secretly study the medicine men and see what he could concoct to counteract their magic."

"You want me and my brothers to protect him," said Earp. It wasn't a question.

"That's right. Outside of Sheriff Behan, whose reputation is, shall we say, *questionable*, you're just about all the law there is out there. I know how you cleaned up the criminal elements in Dodge and Wichita, and Virgil was just as successful in Prescott."

"You've got to understand," said Earp. "Virgil is the Tombstone Territory marshal. We don't have any US marshals out here. His authority isn't very well defined; the mine owners invented the position because Behan still has two years to serve and nobody trusts him. The truth of the matter is that Virgil's more of a private lawman than a public one."

"Details," said McCarthy impatiently. "You've *got* to protect Edison!"

"Against who?"

McCarthy shrugged helplessly. "We have no idea. As more and more whites have settled in the West, some of the tribes have started to feel threatened. We've kept it quiet, but five towns have been destroyed, burned to the ground, every citizen slaughtered. Tombstone's getting to be a popular destination, thanks to its silver strike—"

"And to Edison and Buntline's improvements," interjected Earp.

"That, too," agreed McCarthy. "Mr. Earp, we *can't* lose Thomas Edison. He is our best hope, maybe our only hope, of fulfilling America's destiny. This land was put here for us, and nothing is going to keep it from us."

"And you don't know who's planning to kill him, or even if anyone is?" said Earp.

"We're hearing rumors," said McCarthy. "We can't pinpoint them, but Edison's too important for us to ignore them. It will be your job to protect him. It could be the Indians, or a jealous rival, or an entrepreneur who wants to steal his secrets and get rich off them. It could be a hired killer, working in the employ of any of those I just named. We don't know who will try, just that *someone* will, and you have to prevent it."

"That's a tall order, Mr. McCarthy."

"I know. To that end, I've contacted William Masterson."

Earp frowned. "William Masterson?" he repeated, puzzled.

"The two of you brought law and order to Dodge City."

Suddenly Earp smiled. "You mean Bat Masterson."

"I guess I do," said McCarthy. "At any rate, he has accepted our offer and is on his way to Tombstone even as we speak."

"It'll be good to work with him again," said Earp. "You couldn't ask for a better lawman."

"Well, that's four lawmen—you, your two brothers, and Masterson," said McCarthy. "Hopefully that will prove sufficient against any threat that may arise."

"I need one more," said Earp.

"Another lawman?"

Earp smiled grimly and shook his head.

"A medicine man from a friendly tribe, perhaps?"

"This man makes his own medicine—with his gun."

"Is he willing to face death for you?"

"He looks death in the eye every morning," said Earp.

"Every morning?" repeated McCarthy, puzzled.

"When he looks into the mirror."

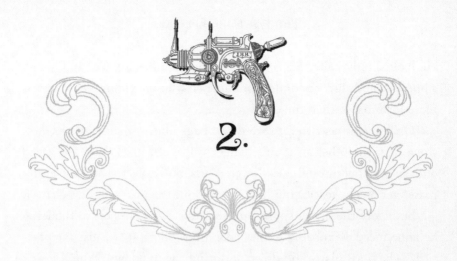

# 2.

THE BRASS STAGECOACH rolled across the flat, dusty countryside. In most parts of the West—and all of the East—it would have been pulled by a team of horses, but out here, in Tombstone Territory, it was propelled by an interior engine filled with whirring gears and powered by electricity. The driver sat in an armored cage atop the coach and directed it with a very simple accelerator and steering mechanism. A speaking tube allowed him to converse with the passengers. The sign on the door proclaimed to one and all that it was a vehicle in the Bunt Line, and the brass Gatling guns atop the roof discouraged both Indians and highwaymen from attacking it.

Which was probably just as well, because seated inside it was an emaciated man with ash-blond hair, a thick mustache, and piercing gray, almost no-color eyes. He was dressed in an expensive gray suit coat and dark pants. Hanging down from his neck, on a very thin string that could be easily broken, was a wicked-looking knife. He had a small pistol tucked into his vest pocket, and a lightweight pearl-handled Colt revolver rested in the holster he wore around his waist.

He looked only half alive, a couple of inches under six feet and barely a hundred and thirty pounds—but anyone who knew him knew he was more formidable than the Gatling guns.

On the seat next to him were two bags, one a small leather Gladstone bag, the other an even smaller, well-worn black bag. He gazed out the window through half-lowered lids, oblivious to the bald, aging passenger on the seat facing him, tuning out the man's endless chatter.

Suddenly the driver spoke into the tube. "Apaches off to the left," he announced. "Probably gonna take a few shots at us, just for practice." The brass plates slid down, covering the windows. "You'll hear a couple of bullets hit, and maybe some arrows will bounce off, but they're just playing with us. If they meant business, they'd have put a bunch of boulders down where the road narrows. So there's nothing to worry about."

"Are you quite sure?" asked the balding man.

"Mister, if they knew who was inside this rig, they'd hightail it in the opposite direction."

The bald man stared at the emaciated man curiously.

"Is he referring to you, sir?" he asked.

The emaciated man shrugged. "Could be," he said with a Southern drawl. The hint of a smile played on his lips as he added, "In the absence of anyone else."

"May I ask who you are?"

"My name is John Henry Holliday." He patted the black bag. "I'm a practitioner of dental science. If you need a cavity filled or a tooth pulled, come and see me when we get to Tombstone."

"John Henry Holliday, John Henry Holliday," repeated the balding man, flinching every time a bullet struck the coach. "The name is vaguely familiar, but I don't believe I've—" Suddenly he froze. "Oh, my God—you're Doc Holliday!"

"At your service," said Holliday, inclining his head slightly.

"I hope I haven't said or done anything to annoy or disturb you, Mr. Holliday, sir," said the man nervously.

"Just Doc will do."

"Those Indians don't know how lucky they are!" said the man fervently at the sound of an arrow careening off the door. Then: "Have you ever killed an Indian, Mr. Holliday?"

"Doc," repeated Holliday.

"Doc," corrected the man. "Have you?"

"It's possible."

"You don't want to talk about it?"

"You noticed," said Holliday.

The man pulled out a cigar and lit it, trying to ignore the war cries of the Apaches as they raced alongside the stage, screaming and shooting. "Do you mind?"

Holliday shook his head.

"Where are my manners?" The man offered one to Holliday. "Care for one?"

"No, thanks."

"They're very good. I picked them up in Cincinnati, just before I came West."

"I don't smoke," said Holliday.

"I thought everyone out here did," said the man.

"Not quite," said Holliday. He suddenly pulled a handkerchief out of his pocket and coughed into it.

"That doesn't sound good," said the man. He saw traces of blood on the handkerchief.

"You'll get no disagreement from me," replied Holliday sardonically.

"Does my smoking bother you? I can put it out."

"You can't toss it out a window until we're free of the Indians, and if you try to put it out in here you'll probably set the carpet or the seat cushion on fire. Just smoke and don't worry about it."

"You're sure?"

Holliday gave him a look that said he was sure and he was tired of talking about it, and the man busied himself straightening his jacket, brushing off his sleeves, and pulling out a comb to run through the fringe on the sides of his balding head.

They heard another bullet thud home into a brass window plate, and a few more arrows bounced off the doors. A moment later the driver's voice came through to them again: "They're all through playing, and going home to refresh their squaws. I'll be opening the windows when the last of them is out of rifle range."

The windows opened less than a minute later, and the balding man tossed his cigar out and asked how far they were from their destination.

"We'll reach Tombstone in another thirty minutes or so," came the answer. "That's another reason I knew they weren't in earnest. If they were, they'd have attacked before we got this close to town."

Holliday pulled a small bottle out of a pocket, opened it, and took a deep swig.

"My medicine," he said with a self-deprecating smile. "Would you care for a swallow, Mr. . . . ?"

"Wiggins," said the man, taking the proffered bottle. "Henry Wiggins. And thank you." He lifted the bottle halfway to his mouth, then paused. "No offense, Mr. . . . ah, Doctor . . . Doc, but is it safe?"

Holliday shrugged. "*I've* never caught anything from it."

Wiggins stared at the bottle, decided that returning it unused would be more dangerous to his health than drinking from it, and took a small swallow.

"Very good," he said, returning the bottle.

"Well, it's wet, anyway."

"We've been hearing and reading about you back East," said Wiggins. "Is it true that you killed all those men?"

"Probably not."

"I have a sister who lives in Dallas. She wrote me about you a few years ago. You were famous even back then." Wiggins looked suddenly nervous. "She said you left one night in a hell of a hurry."

A wry smile crossed Holliday's face, which was not the reaction Wiggins had expected, but one he was relieved to see.

"Yeah, I guess you could say that," said Holliday with a chuckle.

"She said you killed a man," ventured Wiggins.

"She's right."

"And that the court found you innocent, and ruled it was self-defense."

"It usually is," replied Holliday.

"And that you left town in the middle of the night just a few hours after you were exonerated."

Another smile. "I'd had a few scrapes down there, and even though I was a free man with a clean record, the sheriff decided that Dallas would be a lot more peaceful if I left, so he came to me late that afternoon and told me I had until sunrise to get out of town or he and his deputies would take it as a personal insult."

"He had no right," said Wiggins.

"Right or wrong had nothing to do with it," answered Holliday. "He had seven guns on his side, and two of them were Cole and Jim Younger, so I made up my mind to leave. But about four hours later, he came to my office as I was packing the last of my equipment. Seems I was the only dentist he could find at that time of night, and he had a very painful abscessed tooth." Another smile. "So I sat him in my chair, put him under with laughing gas, pulled every tooth in his head, and left town before he woke up."

Wiggins threw back his head and laughed. "I like your sense of humor, Doc!"

"It was my sense of justice," answered Holliday, "but the two aren't that far apart."

"I hope you'll let me buy you a drink when we get to town," said Wiggins, finally comfortable in Holliday's company.

"Sounds good to me," said Holliday. "I don't know it for a fact, but I've long suspected that the world will come to an end if I ever refuse one."

"Where will I find you?" continued Wiggins.

"I don't know where I'll be sleeping, but I expect I'll spend most of my waking hours in the Oriental Saloon."

"I'll find it," said Wiggins. "I'm staying at a boarding house on Allen Street."

"What's your line of work?" asked Holliday.

"I'm between jobs at the moment."

"You plan to try your hand at silver mining like most of the people who come to Tombstone?"

"I wouldn't begin to know how," replied Wiggins. "I've been a salesman all my life. I sold corsets up and down the Ohio and the Mississippi, candy in Chicago and Detroit, branding irons all over Texas Territory, even sold some firearms for Mr. Colt. From what I hear, Thomas Edison and Ned Buntline have a lot of stuff that the public will spend good money on. I thought I'd see if I could make a deal to start hawking it back in some of the new settlements that have sprung up on this side of the Mississippi, places like St. Louis or Tulsa or even Dallas."

"Sounds interesting," said Holliday, with no show of interest.

"I might even find something that *you'd* be interested in," said Wiggins. "They say Buntline has created a pistol-sized Gatling gun."

"If you're in a gunfight and you need more than one barrel, you're a dead man," commented Holliday.

"Well, maybe that's not so commercial, but everyone talks about how Tombstone is filled with his and Edison's inventions."

"So they say," agreed Holliday. "But mighty few men are going to buy electric streetlamps, or stagecoaches like this one."

"True," said Wiggins. "Still, there must be something the average man can use."

"I suppose so."

"Too bad they can't make a mechanical mine worker," continued Wiggins.

"I'd settle for their making a pair of mechanical lungs," replied Holliday.

"I wish you luck," said Wiggins.

"I've had my share. Just not in the lung department."

They rode the rest of the way in silence.

"Entering Tombstone," announced the driver.

"So where are these electric lights I've heard so much about?" asked Wiggins.

"They're there lining the streets. We don't turn 'em on 'til it's dark," answered the driver. "Where can I drop you gents, or do you want to get off at the depot?"

"Fourth and Allen streets," said Wiggins.

"You staying at Mrs. Oswald's?"

"Yes."

"Watch out for the beef stew," said the driver with a chuckle. "How about you, Doc?"

"The Oriental."

"We'll be there in just a minute."

"Remember," said Wiggins, shaking Holliday's hand, "I owe you a drink."

The coach slowed down and came to a stop. The metal door swung open, three brass stairs appeared, and Holliday, a little shaky on his feet after the long ride, climbed down to the ground.

"Hand me my bags, will you, please?"

"Happy to," said Wiggins, handing them to Holliday, who had some momentary difficulty managing the larger of them.

"I'll take that," said a deep voice, and Holliday turned toward its source.

"Hello, Wyatt," he said as the door closed and the brass coach began rolling down the street.

"Good to see you again, Doc," said Earp. "You hungry after that long trip?"

"Thirsty," replied Holliday. He stood, hands on hips, and surveyed the exterior of the Oriental Saloon. It was a large, sturdy building, the wood had thus far escaped dry rot, unlike the neighboring buildings there was no brass on it—possibly, thought Holliday, because the Earps were all the protection it needed—and there was a pair of large glass windows so that passersby could see the interior. "You're doing right well for a small-town lawman."

"I hear you're not doing all that badly for a consumptive dentist," answered Earp.

"Not doing badly at poker and faro," answered Holliday. "I think my days as a dentist are just about through. Hard to keep a practice going when you cough on all the patients."

"Come on in," said Earp, heading toward the Oriental's swinging doors. "Virgil and Morgan are anxious to see you, and maybe we can find a little something at the bar that will help that cough."

"If not, just point out the bad guys and I'll cough on *them*," said Holliday with a smile.

"It's going to take more than a cough," said Earp grimly.

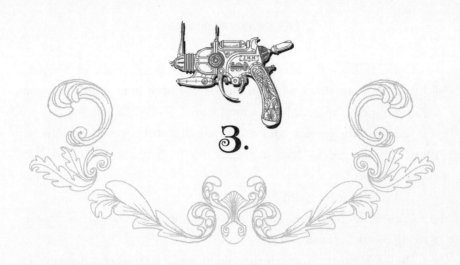

## 3.

"**W**HAT THE HELL is that thing you got on your hip, Wyatt?" asked Holliday as they entered the Oriental.

"My gun."

"Man and boy, I've never seen a gun take up that much space."

Earp smiled and gently withdrew his weapon. It was made from super-hardened brass, the same as the stagecoach, and it had four rotating barrels, much like a Gatling gun, though the barrels were only six inches in length.

"May I?" asked Holliday, reaching for the weapon.

"Be my guest," replied Earp.

"Doesn't have a lot of bullets for so many barrels," noted Holliday as he examined it.

"It holds twelve bullets now, but Ned is working on it."

"Ned?"

"Ned Buntline," answered Earp. "Same guy who built the stage that you rode in on, and the electric lampposts, and a bunch of other things you'll see."

Holliday frowned. "I thought all that was the work of Thomas Edison. At least, that's what all the papers have been saying. Maybe we're being paid to guard the wrong man."

"Edison's the genius who thinks all this stuff up and designs it. Buntline's the genius who manufactures it. We don't want to lose either of them."

"I'd like to meet them."

"You will," promised Earp. "But first there are a couple of people waiting to say hello to you."

He led Holliday through the saloon, amid a series of whispers: "*Is that him?*" "*Look how skinny he is. It's the Doc, all right.*" "*How many men has he killed?*" "*What's he doing here?*"

The two men ignored them and soon passed through a doorway leading to a back room, where two more tall, mustached men were sitting at a table.

"Hello, Doc," said the older of them. "Good to have you here."

"Hello, Virg," said Holliday, shaking his hand.

"Killed anyone today, you refugee from the gallows?" asked the younger man.

"Not since lunchtime, Morg," answered Holliday with a warmth he hadn't displayed toward the other two Earps.

Morgan Earp got to his feet and threw his arms around Holliday. "Damn! It's good to see you again, Doc!"

"It's good to be off that stagecoach, I'll tell you that," answered Holliday. "Horses have enough brains to avoid the worst parts of the road. The guy who was driving this rig sure as hell didn't."

"No trouble, though?" asked Virgil Earp.

"Some Indians a few miles out of town," said Holliday. "The driver assured us that it wasn't a serious attack." A pause and the hint of a smile. "I assume they were firing very unserious bullets and arrows."

"Same old Doc!" laughed Morgan. "Doesn't anything ever bother you?"

"Losing at cards and being stone-cold sober," answered Holliday. "Where the hell's a chair?"

Morgan got up, walked to an adjoining room, and returned a moment later with a chair.

"In Dodge they had cushions," remarked Holliday as he seated himself.

"Damn!" said Morgan. "We're washing 'em all today, along with the doilies. You'll just have to rough it, Doc."

"All right," said Holliday, seating himself. "So now that I'm here, suppose you tell me what I'm here for."

"To protect Tom Edison," said Virgil. "I thought Wyatt told you that."

"He did. But to protect him from *whom*?"

"That's quite a list," said Virgil. "A lot of Indians want him dead, ever since he invented the stagecoach and some of our handguns and rifles. Some of the locals want him and Buntline dead for making the jail escape-proof with those super-hard brass bars . . . and believe it or not, Edison invented a lock that doesn't have a key, just like a bank vault. Rival inventors probably want him dead, and there's more than a few towns back East that would love to kidnap him and set him to work on *their* lights and such."

"But no one is more likely than the others?" persisted Holliday.

"They're *all* motivated."

"Four of us might not be enough."

"Bat Masterson's on his way here," said Morgan. "Didn't Wyatt tell you?"

"He's no gun for hire," noted Holliday. "I thought he was coming to help with the marshal business, not to guard Edison."

"Comes to pretty much the same thing these days," said Virgil.

"Well, as long as I'm going to be here for some time," said Holliday, "I want to take a look around. And I want to see the guy I'm being hired to protect."

"Yeah, it's early enough."

Holliday got to his feet. "Might as well go right now while there's still some light."

"In this town that doesn't make any difference," said Morgan.

"Might as well go before all the card players show up," amended Holliday. "If Wyatt will point his place out to me—"

"I'll take you there," said Earp.

"It's not necessary."

"Sure it is. Can't have the notorious Doc Holliday walk into the wrong building and scare some innocent man or woman out of twenty years' growth."

"No sense carrying your gear all over town," said Morgan, opening a cupboard and putting Holliday's bags into it. "Come back after you've eaten and lined up a place to stay. The tables heat up about nine o'clock."

"I'll be here," promised Holliday, following Earp through the saloon and out into the street. After a moment he turned to his companion. "It feels strange, with hardly any horses hitched out here."

"It'll feel even stranger in two or three hours, when the sun goes down and Johnny Behan throws the switch that turns on all the streetlights."

"Johnny Behan?"

"He's the sheriff. Tom gave the lights to the city, so the sheriff's in charge of turning them on and off."

"I've heard some bad things about him."

"All of them true," said Earp. "Come on, let's start walking. It's just a couple of blocks away."

They walked past four saloons, a greengrocer, a pair of dry-goods stores (one of which was being fitted with the omnipresent brass siding that almost all the other buildings possessed), a photo studio, a boarded-up stable and an abandoned corral, and finally they came to a pair of small brick buildings, connected by a hardened brass passageway.

"Very unprepossessing, except for the brass," noted Holliday.

"For the reigning genius of the nineteenth century, he's a pretty unassuming man."

"Is that building next door Buntline's?"

"Yes," said Earp.

"I figured as much," said Holliday. "And that's why they're connected."

Earp nodded. "Right."

"What's Edison working on now?"

"He'd damned well better be working on some way to counteract the medicine men's magic," said Earp. "I'm getting tired of hearing about this fluoroscope thing that he's been obsessed with this past month."

"Fluoroscope?" repeated Holliday.

"Some kind of machine that lets you look right through a man's skin and see his insides. Can you believe that?"

"Sounds like magic to me," said Holliday. He stared at the building that housed this wonder and sighed. "Maybe the Indians don't have a monopoly on it. Let's go on in."

Earp knocked at the door, and a man in his early thirties opened it. The first thing Holliday noticed about him was his prosthetic arm. He'd seen artificial limbs after the War between the States, lots of them, but they were usually wooden, and the few that weren't were ivory. But this one was an intricate concoction of brass plates and pieces, with a pair of whirring little motors inside it, and an impressive-looking pincer at the end of it.

He wore a one-eyed goggle, and Holliday could see that it acted as an enormous magnifying glass.

"Tom," said Earp, "I'd like you to meet an old friend of mine, a friend who will be working to keep you alive and inventing—Doc Holliday."

Edison extended his metal hand, and Holliday took it carefully. "I've heard a lot about you, Mr. Holliday."

"Most of it wrong, I'm sure," said Holliday. "And call me Doc."

"If you'll call me Tom."

"Happy to, Tom."

"You should also meet Ned Buntline," said Edison. "I just dream all these things up. He's the man who gives them life."

"We'll go next door as soon as we leave here," promised Earp.

"That won't be necessary," said Edison. "Follow me."

He led them to a small office. A bookcase was crammed to capacity, with piles of books on the floor next to it. There was a wooden desk covered with notebooks and scraps of paper. A brass table was home to a motley collection of test tubes, beakers, and vials, as well as a pair of very small motors. There was a single stool by the wooden table, plus a small chair next to the bookcase, with still more books piled atop it. A single overhead light cast its electric luminescence throughout the room.

"Do you see that little machine on the desk, Wyatt?"

"Yes."

"Pull the switch atop it."

Earp reached forward and pulled it. "Like this?"

"Precisely."

"What happens now?"

"It just rang a bell in Ned's office, and he should be here any minute, wondering why I've bothered him," answered Edison with a smile—and sure enough, a pudgy, balding, clean-shaven man in his midsixties entered through a different door a few seconds later.

"What's the problem?" he asked of Edison, then noted the two visitors. "Ah! Wyatt! And you don't have to tell me who this is. I'm an admirer of yours, Doctor Holliday."

"Doc," Holliday corrected him. "I just arrived on one of your stagecoaches, Mr. Buntline."

Buntline smiled. "My pride and joy. You never have to feed it, it never breaks a leg, it can go hundreds of miles without resting, it's faster than any horse, and it's immune to bullets and arrows. Did you find it comfortable?"

Holliday nodded. "And safe," he added.

Buntline looked like a proud father. "Someday I'll span the continent with them." He turned to Earp. "I meant to tell you: I've been getting some more threats from the Cowboys."

"Ike again?" asked Earp, frowning.

"And the McLaury brothers, and Curly Bill Brocius," said Buntline. He turned to Holliday. "It seems my stagecoach will damage their business if I start mass-producing it."

"What's their business?" asked Holliday. "Wells Fargo?"

Buntline laughed. "Horse stealing. They steal them across the border in Mexico and sell them here—and I may kill a large part of their market, if they don't kill me first."

"Just point them out to me," offered Holliday, "and I'll take care of that little problem before I sit down at the gaming tables tonight."

"You can't just shoot them, Doc," interjected Earp. "You're on the law's side now, and working for the government."

"The government didn't ask for me because of my winning smile."

"I'll be all right, Doc," said Buntline. "I'm working on designing some lightweight body armor right now. If it works, I'll make some up for you and the Earps as well."

"Tell you what I'd really like," said Holliday. "That eyepiece you made for Tom here. I could use it in my dentistry work."

"No problem," said Buntline. "Come by tomorrow afternoon and I'll have it for you. And a gun like Wyatt's."

"No, thanks," replied Holliday with a self-deprecating smile. "I need one I can lift and aim."

"Well, if you ever do need a weapon, Doc, I'm the man to see about it."

"I'll bear that in mind," said Holliday. "Now that we've met, I won't keep you any longer. I just wanted to know what you look like. And it's probably a good idea that you know what I look like as well, so you don't think I'm loitering with intent to kill or kidnap if you see me hanging around here."

Edison stepped forward and extended his artificial hand again. "It's a pleasure to meet you, Doc—and feel free to come by any time you want."

"The same goes for me," added Buntline.

"I expect to be here night and day for the next week, working on this new invention," said Edison.

"Is that the thing you told me about, where you can look at a man's insides?" asked Earp.

"That's the one. It's going to save a lot of lives."

"Finding a way to fight Hook Nose's magic will save a lot more," said Earp pointedly.

"I'm working on it," Edison assured him.

Earp turned to Buntline. "Will we be seeing you tonight?"

"I don't think so," answered Buntline. "I believe they're delivering another young lady after dinner."

"Well, we'll be on our way now."

Earp and Holliday left the house and walked out into the street.

"Given a choice of the two lifestyles, I'll take Buntline's," remarked Holliday with an amused smile. "Imagine having a girl delivered right to your office. Nice work if you can get it."

Earp looked amused. "It's not what you think, Doc."

"Oh?" said Holliday, arching an eyebrow. "Suppose you tell me what it is."

"You'll find out soon enough, if I know you," replied Earp with a smile. "And if not, Morg will get more of a kick telling you about it than I will." He paused. "Coming back to the Oriental with me?"

"I need to find a place to stay," answered Holliday. "I'll be along later."

"See you then," said Earp, walking off toward the saloon.

Holliday went down a side street, looking for a welcoming building where he could take up residence.

He found one—but it wasn't what he was expecting.

# 4.

OLLIDAY REACHED THE END of the side street, turned past a few nondescript shops sporting new brass siding, turned again, and found himself on Fremont Street. He saw a couple of signs advertising rooming houses at the far end of the street, and began walking toward them when a voice called out.

"Hi, Doc!"

He stopped and turned, and saw Henry Wiggins hurrying to catch up with him.

"Didn't think I'd see you again so soon," said Wiggins.

"It's not *that* big a town," answered Holliday, "and from what I can tell, all the permanent residents are at the other end of it."

"What do you think of all these streetlights?" said Wiggins. "It's like daytime."

"I've seen streetlights before, but they were always lit by oil. These things are brighter, there's no flame inside them, and they don't smell."

"By the way, where are you staying?"

Holliday shrugged. "I'm just starting to work on that."

"There's a nice hotel on Allen Street," offered Wiggins.

Holliday shook his head. "A rooming house is fine for me. It's cheaper than a hotel."

"Surely a famous man like you could afford a hotel."

"I can," answered Holliday. "But I'd rather spend the difference at the tables."

"There's more to spend it on than gambling, or so they tell me," offered Wiggins with a wink.

"There usually is."

"They say this particular bawdy house is unique."

"Every bawdy house says that," said Holliday with an amused grin. "And they all lie."

"Not this one, from what I hear."

"What has it got that's so special?" asked Holliday. "Chinese girls? Indian girls?"

"Metal girls," answered Wiggins.

"I'd heard a rumor about that, but I didn't really believe it. An hour ago I'd have bet it was a lie. But I just saw the arm Ned Buntline made for Tom Edison, so maybe there's some truth to it."

"It's supposed to be on Fifth Street, not too far from here," said Wiggins. "I was thinking of trying it out. Care to come along?"

Holliday shook his head. "First I have to find a room, then some dinner, and then there's a game waiting for me at the Oriental."

"Too bad," said Wiggins. "Metal girls or real ones, these places are no better or worse than their madams, and they say this one's got the best madam this side of the Mississippi. Course, she's been running bawdy houses from Dodge all the way out to Tombstone, so she figures to know her stuff."

"Give her my felicitations, and tell her I'll be by to sample her offerings in a day or two."

"Will do," promised Wiggins, starting to head off toward Fifth Street. "Weird name—Older. Older than what, I wonder?"

"*What?*" said Holliday, so sharply that Wiggins froze in his tracks. "Older."

"Could it have been Elder?" asked Holliday.

Wiggins frowned. "Maybe."

"Kate Elder?"

"Yes! That's the name!"

Holliday walked over to join him. "Let's go."

"You know her?"

A bitter smile crossed Holliday's lips. "I know her."

Wiggins was suddenly nervous, and they walked in silence until they reached their destination, a large two-story frame house.

"Well, here we are, Doc." He suddenly stepped aside. "You go first."

"You've led the way here," said Holliday. "Go on in."

"I'd rather not."

"You suddenly decided to be shy around women?"

"No, it's that expression on your face when I mentioned Kate Elder," said Wiggins. "I spent hours with you in the stagecoach, and you never looked like that. If you're going to kill her, I don't want to get in the way."

"I'm not going to kill her," said Holliday.

"You're sure? Because I can come back later, or hunt up some other bawdy house. It isn't like Tombstone doesn't have its share of them."

"It's all right," said Holliday. "Nobody's killing anyone. Go on in."

Wiggins took a deep breath, then knocked on the oversized wooden door. A young woman in a dress and apron—Holliday assumed she was a maid, but you could never be sure in a place like this—opened the door and ushered them inside.

They soon found themselves in an elegantly furnished parlor, filled with stuffed chairs and a buffalo-hide couch. There was a bar at one end of it, and a bartender, possibly Indian, probably Mexican, with a brass ear and a set of goggles that helped whatever vision problem he had. Four men mingled with half a dozen girls, and Holliday studied the girls closely. Two, clad in corsets and silk stockings, looked perfectly normal. A third had a prosthetic left leg, made of the same brass and gears that powered Edison's arm, a fourth had a pair of prosthetic arms and a brass jaw, and suddenly Holliday knew what Buntline had meant when he spoke of another girl being delivered to his office.

The last two "girls" weren't girls at all, but were metal constructs built to resemble women, at least in the areas the men frequenting the establishment were paying for. They didn't have a shred of clothing between them. They possessed large, perfectly rounded breasts, broad hips, tiny waistlines, more artistic but less practical arms and legs than the prosthetically equipped girls, and their faces, possessed of unblinking eyes and permanently puckered lips, lacked all expression. A brass panel covered their genitals, but Holliday assumed they possessed some semblance of them or they wouldn't be working here.

"By God, it was all true!" exclaimed Wiggins.

One of the normal girls approached him, but he waved her off. "I may never see another metal chippie again," he announced, "so I might was well try her out while I can." He pointed to one of the metal woman, who walked over, less awkwardly than Holliday would have expected, and, taking Wiggins by the hand, led him down a corridor.

"You see anything you like, Mister?" asked the girl who had approached Wiggins.

"I like everything I see," replied Holliday. "But I came here looking for someone in particular."

"What's her name, and I'll let you know how long before she's available."

"Her name's Kate Elder, and you tell her she'd better be available right now."

The girl looked surprised. "Who shall I say is asking?"

"Her dentist."

"That's all? Just her dentist?"

"That's all," said Holliday.

The girl left the room, then reappeared a moment later. "Come with me, please."

Holliday followed her to the very end of the long corridor that Wiggins had entered, and came to a door. He looked at the girl expectantly.

"Go right in," she said. "She's waiting for you."

Holliday entered the room. It had been a bedroom once, but was now an office, with a large brass-plated desk, a rack of clean towels, a washstand with a metal basin and a pitcher of water, and a very substantial safe. Two oil paintings of voluptuous nudes graced the walls. The windows were shuttered, but the room was illuminated by two of Edison's electric lamps with delicate shades and ornate brass stems.

Seated behind the desk was a tall, buxom woman of indeterminate age, possibly as young as twenty-five, perhaps as old as forty. Her hair was brown, her eyes gray, her nose rather prominent, her chin firm and jutting slightly.

"I was wondering when you'd show up," said Kate Elder.

"You ran out on me while I was in jail back in Jacksboro," answered Holliday bitterly. "What made you think I'd come looking for you?"

"I didn't. I figured you'd come looking for Wyatt, or more likely, he'd get in over his head and send for you to save him." She stared at him pugnaciously. "Besides, I broke you out of jail in Fort Griffin. Just how the hell many times was I expected to do that?"

Holliday made no answer, but merely stared at her.

"I was right, wasn't I?" she said. "Wyatt sent for you."

"You should be happy, Kate. I'm here to protect the guys who supply you with ready-made whores."

"Ned and Mr. Edison?"

Holliday grinned. "Well, now I know which one is a customer."

She looked at him dispassionately for a long moment.

"For better or worse, you're back," she said at last. "Have you got a place to stay?"

"I'm working on it."

Another stare, as if she was making a decision. Then: "You'll stay with me. I've got the whole upstairs to myself."

"I suppose I've stayed in less inviting places," replied Holliday. "Some of them weren't even jails." Holliday paused. "The consumption's gotten worse, Kate. I don't have the staying power for all-night fights anymore. I'd never admit it to Wyatt or the others, but I've always been honest with you."

"How much worse?"

"It comes, it goes." He grimaced. "Mostly it stays."

"We've got to reach an understanding on one thing," said Kate. He looked at her suspiciously, but said nothing. "I'm a madam now."

"You always were," said Holliday. "Well, all the time I've known you."

"But I was also a whore, and now I'm not."

He frowned, trying to guess where this was leading. "Okay, you were and now you're not. I used to be a dentist and now I'm not."

"I don't sleep with the customers," she continued, staring at him, "and *you* don't sleep with the girls. Are we clear on that?"

Holliday seemed lost in thought.

"Well, *are we?*" she demanded.

Finally he shrugged. "What the hell," he said. "One woman's pretty much like another."

"Watch your tongue," she said ominously. "You may not live long enough to enjoy me *or* the girls."

"One man's pretty much the same as any other too," he said. "We're all racing hell for leather to the grave."

"Try not to be so cheerful," said Kate.

"Pour me a drink and I'll make an effort."

She went to a cabinet, chose a bottle, got a glass, and brought him a drink. "You want anything else?" she asked seductively.

"Yes."

A smug smile crossed her face. "You never could keep away."

He returned her smile. "Where's your kitchen? I haven't eaten all day."

She swung a sledgehammer blow at him that he barely ducked.

"Four minutes," said Holliday, looking at an imaginary watch. "I think we just set a new record for not fighting."

Her anger evaporated in a peal of laughter.

"What the hell," she said, walking him to the door. "Come along, Doc, and I'll fix you a steak."

"Sounds good," said Holliday. "And I'll take this"—he held up his glass—"to wash it down."

"Where are your bags?" she asked as they walked down a corridor to the kitchen.

"At the Oriental," said Holliday, surveying the large kitchen. There was a wrought iron wood-burning stove, a chopping block, a few cabinets for holding dishes and silverware, a pair of electric lamps, and a scarred wooden table that had seen better days and doubtless better decades, surrounded by beat-up chairs. "Not much of a kitchen," he noted.

"I don't need much of one," she replied, tossing a steak into a skillet. "Most of my girls eat out, and some don't eat at all." She paused. "You want me to send for your bags?"

"Beats the hell out of carrying them. But I'm still going to the Oriental."

"That figures," said Kate.

"Anyone I should pay attention to?"

"Other than the ones Wyatt will point out to you?" she asked as the steak began sizzling. "Probably the best poker player is Johnny-behind-the-Deuce."

"I've heard of him."

"And watch out for Rattlesnake Bill Clement."

"Good card player?"

"Terrible," said Kate. "But he's got a bad temper, and he thinks that any time he loses he was cheated."

"Thanks," said Holliday. "I'll remember that."

"Just remember where you're staying—and with whom," she said.

"Absolutely," said Holliday, idly wondering what a night with a totally metal woman might be like.

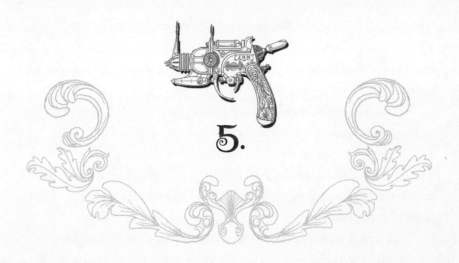

# 5.

HOLLIDAY BROKE EVEN AT THE ORIENTAL, found his way back to Kate Elder's establishment despite consuming close to a fifth of whiskey, took her to bed as best he could in his condition, and slept until two o'clock in the afternoon, par for the course for him.

He got up, dressed, shaved, and poured himself a shot from Kate's bedside bottle just to get his blood circulating. He climbed down the stairs, saw the light peeking out from under Kate's office door, decided he didn't need a repeat of the previous night's arguments or its sex, and walked past it. He tried to smile at three of the whores—one human, two brass—and couldn't quite bring it off. Then he stepped outside, winced at the sunlight, and began walking to the Oriental.

When he arrived he found the place almost entirely deserted except for the Earps, and four men at the bar.

Wyatt and Virgil nodded to him, but past experience had taught them not to speak to him early in his day until they saw what kind of mood he was in.

"Good morning, Doc," said Morgan, who seemed to always be

brash and good-humored around Holliday. "You look like you've had a hard time of it."

"Wait 'til you're as old as me, youngster," rasped Holliday, collapsing on a wooden chair, "and then see how well *you* hold up."

"Is *anyone* as old as you?" asked Morgan with a smile.

"You're *all* kids," said a grizzled, gray-haired old man at the bar. "I ain't never seen a gunslinger over thirty, and I don't expect that to change in the future."

"We're not gunslingers, we're saloon owners," said Morgan.

"Right," said the man. "That's why people keep gunning for your brothers."

Morgan smiled and looked around the saloon. "I don't see any."

"You never see the one that plugs you in the back," said the old man. "Besides, you ain't likely to see any for a while, now that Doc's here."

"You make me sound positively antisocial," said Holliday.

"Just telling the truth," said the man. "Ain't no one can stand up to you in a gunfight except maybe Johnny Ringo, and he's hundreds of miles away."

"Never met the gentleman," said Holliday.

"He's as sweet a feller as you'll ever run into," said the man. "When he's sober, that is, which ain't all that often. When he's drunk, he's vicious pure through, and every bit as good with a gun as you are."

"I heard he has a college degree, and reads the classics in the original Greek," said Holliday. "I'd like to meet him sometime. Those of us who can read Greek and Latin are pretty rare out here."

"Well, just catch him when he's sober, that's all I can say."

Virgil walked to the door. "I'll leave it to these guys to terrify you, Doc. It's time for me to take a walk around town. It's a cinch Johnny Behan will never patrol the streets."

"I might as well go with you," offered Morgan. "It's too early to start drinking and gambling."

"Bite your tongue," said Holliday with mock severity.

"See you later, Doc," said Morgan, walking out the door with his oldest brother. "I'll take north, and you take south."

Holliday turned to Wyatt Earp. "You're not going with them?"

"It doesn't take three men to make the rounds," answered Earp. "Besides, Bat's due to arrive this afternoon. I sent for him a week ago, but he had some business to take care of first."

"I assume they're burying what's left of his business?" said Holliday.

"No, actually he was writing a bunch of articles for a New York newspaper."

"Ringo, Masterson, and me—a scholar, a writer, and a dentist," said Holliday wryly. "It's a strange crop of shootists we're growing this year."

"No stranger than being a couple of blocks away from a guy who makes electricity and another who makes women," answered Earp. He paused. "I assume you saw some of Ned's handiwork at Kate Elder's last night?"

"Now, Wyatt," said Holliday with a smile, "what makes you think I was at Kate's?"

"First, because she's here and she's alive," answered Earp. "And second, because a salesman named Henry Wiggins was in here last night telling us about it."

"Talking about *me?*" said Holliday, surprised. "I figured he'd talk your ears off about his metal whore."

"He tried," said Earp. "But just about everyone here has already been with one of them, so he gave up and talked about you instead." Earp paused and stared at him. "Did you really pull that sheriff's teeth?"

"As a matter of fact, I did," said Holliday.

"I was wondering why you can never go back to Texas. That explains it."

"The whole of Texas wants me? I only pulled his teeth in Dallas."

"I think it's more that the whole of Texas *doesn't* want you. The warrant and the 'Wanted' posters are for your benefit, to keep you away."

"Not a problem," said Holliday. "There isn't anything back there except more of Texas. Dry ugly country." He paused and grimaced. "Just like here, in fact."

"I'll vouch for that," said a voice from just inside the swinging doors. They looked up to see a dapper young man with a neatly trimmed mustache. He was immaculately clad, wearing a derby, an expensively tailored jacket, a silk vest with a gold watch chain hanging from a pocket, dark gray pants, and custom-made leather shoes instead of boots. He had a barely discernable limp, the result of a bullet to the pelvis three years earlier, and in his right hand was a polished black walking stick with a silver knob at the top of it.

"Well, look who finally made it," said Earp by way of greeting.

"Hello, Wyatt," said Bat Masterson. "I'd have been here sooner, but the *New York Morning Telegraph* waits for no man." He nodded to Holliday. "Hi, Doc."

"Hello, Bat," said Doc. "Spinning some fictional yarn about how you cleaned up Dodge all by yourself, I presume?"

Masterson chuckled. "Actually, I was writing about the greatest gunfighter in the West."

"Let's change the subject," said Holliday.

"Why?" asked Masterson, surprised.

"Because John Wesley Hardin is in jail, and if you named Johnny Ringo I just may shoot you myself."

Masterson threw back his head and laughed. "Ringo's pretty good with a gun from what I hear, but they say he's a very nice fellow when he's sober, so I certainly didn't want a procession of young guns seeking him out just to prove they were faster, so"—a smile—"I named you, Doc."

Earp laughed aloud, and Holliday at least smiled.

"Now," continued Masterson, "who are the bad guys and where are they holed up?"

"We don't know who they are yet," said Earp. "Right now our job is to protect the good guys."

"Guys?" repeated Masterson. "I thought it was just Thomas Edison."

"And Ned Buntline, too," said Earp.

"It's kind of like the Yankee president and Congress," added Holliday. "Edison proposes and Buntline disposes, which is to say, Edison figures out what to make, and Buntline makes it."

"The Yankee president is the only one we have, Doc," noted Masterson.

"Until Tombstone Territory becomes a state he's not *my* president," said Holliday.

"Did you fight in the War between the States?" asked one of the men at the bar.

"I was nine years old when it started," said Holliday. "What do you think?"

"Sorry. I was just asking."

"How the hell old do I look anyway?" muttered Holliday.

"Not a day over eighty," said Masterson. "Wyatt, why don't you take me over to meet Edison and this Buntline? If I'm to help keep them alive, I ought to know where they live and what they look like."

"Let's go," said Earp, heading toward the doorway.

"You don't mind if I don't accompany you," said Holliday, making sure it didn't sound like a question.

"No, just sit there and guzzle Wyatt's whiskey," said Masterson. "We'll be back when you're halfway drunk and ready to lose at poker."

As the two men walked out into the street, Holliday ordered a bottle, lit a cigar, and poured himself a drink. He asked the bartender to bring him a deck of cards, and he spent the next hour playing solitaire and nursing his liquor. Then Earp and Masterson returned to the saloon and sat down at his table.

"I trust you had an enlightening visit," said Holliday.

"Very," answered Masterson. "Edison gets all the credit, but if Buntline never did anything but invent that lightweight super-hard brass he'd go down in the history books. He's made a vest of the stuff that can't weigh five pounds, and I guarantee you'll never take a bullet to the heart or even be gut-shot if you're wearing it."

"I'll remember to aim for your head next time I'm annoyed with you," said Holliday, downing another drink.

"I've got to rent a room and stash my suitcase at the Silverstrike Hotel over on Safford Street," said Masterson. "And I haven't eaten all day, so I'd like to grab a late lunch or an early dinner. But then I think I'll go out to Geronimo's camp and have a talk with him."

"You know him?" asked Holliday, surprised.

"Never met the man," replied Masterson. "But if we're going to protect Edison, it makes sense to find out if Geronimo was behind the attack that cost him his arm."

"I'll go with you," said Earp. "And we'll have to go on horseback. The Apaches don't like Ned's coaches."

"Don't be stupid, Wyatt," said Holliday. "If he *did* order it, he's not going to admit it to a lawman." He turned to Masterson. *"I'll* go with you."

"That's not necessary, Doc," replied Masterson. "I can go alone."

"Can't lose a promising journalist taken in the bloom of youth," said Holliday. "I'll ride shotgun."

"I'm as old as you are," replied Masterson.

"Perhaps," acknowledged Holliday. "But my bloom faded years ago." He paused. "Still, there's seven or eight saloon owners who just might kill themselves if anything happens to me. So we'll protect each other."

"Okay," agreed Masterson, getting to his feet again. He walked to the swinging doors, then stopped briefly and turned back to Holliday. "No sense putting it off. Shall we meet here at nine o'clock tonight?"

"That would cut into prime gambling time," replied Holliday.

"Sunrise tomorrow, then."

"I have never seen a sunrise at the beginning of a day," said Holliday. "We'll leave when I wake up."

"When might that be?" asked Masterson.

"You'll have finished digesting lunch by then," said Earp with an amused smile.

# 6.

K ATE HAD BEEN more sexually demanding than usual, Holliday had been more inebriated than usual, and as a result he slept until three o'clock in the afternoon. He walked to the Oriental, where Masterson was waiting for him, and the two men rode out of town.

"It's probably going to take us to twilight to get there, from what Wyatt told me," remarked Masterson.

"Did you remember a white flag?"

Masterson looked surprised. "No," he admitted. "It never crossed my mind."

"Well," replied Holliday, "hopefully they're ignorant savages and won't know what a white flag means anyway."

"The ones I've run into haven't been all that ignorant *or* savage."

"Same here," agreed Holliday. "But when you're riding into Geronimo's camp without a flag of truce, you've got to hope for the best."

Masterson threw back his head and laughed.

"Let's hope they find it as funny as you do," continued Holliday.

"Have you ever met Geronimo?" asked Masterson.

Holliday shook his head. "Not a lot of white men live to tell about it. But I figure if just two men ride into his camp with their guns in their holsters, he's got no reason not to talk to us before he starts using us for target practice."

"He's got more of a reputation than that Cheyenne, what's his name? Hook Nose," remarked Masterson.

"Hook Nose just performs magic. Geronimo is a hell of a general as well. That's one more arrow in his quiver, so to speak."

Masterson looked at Holliday, unable to tell if he was making a joke or not. It was a problem he often had, depending on the amount of liquor his companion had consumed.

They rode across the barren landscape for two more hours, and the sun began dropping lower in the sky.

"Movement off to the right, behind those bushes," said Masterson softly.

"I saw it," answered Holliday, bringing his horse to a stop. "Do what I do."

Holliday unbuckled his holster and slung it over his shoulder, then raised his hands and urged his horse to begin walking again, and Masterson followed suit.

"So where are they?" he asked after another minute.

"Probably riding ahead to see if Geronimo wants to talk or have us killed right here."

Masterson grimaced. "Maybe this wasn't the brightest idea I ever had."

"I'd rather face him outnumbered a few hundred to two than on even footing," said Holliday. "Whatever else he feels about our invading his territory, he won't feel threatened."

Masterson was about to answer when they heard hoofbeats up

ahead, and a moment later they saw half a dozen Apache warriors riding toward them, each carrying a rifle.

"Someone's selling them weapons," noted Masterson.

"Or else they took them off the bodies of the men they've killed," said Holliday. "Just as likely, maybe even more so."

The Apaches slowed down as they approached, and quickly surrounded the two white men.

"Who are you and why have you come to Goyathlay's land?" asked one of them in reasonably good English.

"We wish only to speak to him," said Masterson.

"Give us your guns, and we will take you to him."

Masterson and Holliday handed over their holsters. One of the Apaches stared at the knife hanging around Holliday's neck, then held out his hand for it. Holliday jerked it, breaking the string, and gave it to him.

The Apache then pointed to Holliday's vest, and with a sigh he withdrew his tiny pistol and relinquished it.

"Now we will go to Goyathlay," announced the first one.

They broke into a slow, easy canter, and in another mile they could see campfires burning in the distance. As they approached, they saw that the camp was composed of about fifty huts that could be broken down quickly, so that the entire camp could be moved on just a few minutes' notice. They rode up to the largest of the huts, dismounted at a signal from their guide, and waited for instructions. Finally a burly man in buckskins emerged from the hut and approached them. He wasn't tall, he wore no special emblems, but something in his bearing immediately convinced them that he was Geronimo. Accompanying him was a tall, lean black man.

"Greetings," he said. "My name is Obidiah. I will be Goyathlay's translator."

"Been with him long, have you?" asked Holliday.

"Long enough to know that he treats me better than you ever did."

"I had no slaves," said Holliday.

"But you come from the South, do you not? I can tell by your accent."

"Georgia."

Obidiah studied him closely. "You were just a child. But your family had slaves, did they not?"

"We're here to talk about the present, not the past," interjected Masterson.

"And to Geronimo, not to his . . . translator," added Holliday.

"Goyathlay wants to know who he is facing," said Obidiah.

"Bat Masterson and John Henry Holliday," replied Holliday.

"*Doc* Holliday?"

"The very same."

Obidiah turned to Geronimo and spoke to him in the latter's native tongue. Geronimo stared at Holliday and then said something to Obidiah.

"He wants to know if you really killed seven men in a card game in Mexico."

"Probably not," answered Holliday.

Obidiah repeated Holliday's answer. Geronimo's face remained expressionless. At last the medicine man spoke.

"He wants to know if Wyatt Earp sent you."

"He's a sharp old buzzard," acknowledged Holliday.

"Tell him we come on our own," said Masterson. "Wyatt Earp does not know we are here, and would be angry if he knew we came without his permission."

Obidiah translated, and Geronimo turned to Masterson. As with Holliday, he studied the young man's face for a long moment, then spoke.

"Goyathlay has heard of you," said Obidiah.

"I'm flattered."

"He wants to know why you are called Bat."

"I picked up the name early in my career," answered Masterson. "I teamed up with Baptiste Brown, who everyone called 'Old Bat,' and pretty soon I was known as 'Young Bat.' I didn't like the 'Young' so I got rid of it."

A brief translation, and Obidiah spoke again. "He says it is a fool's name."

Masterson smiled. "I'm not about to argue when he's got a couple of hundred braves backing him up. Tell him he can call me William or Bill if he likes."

"He wants to know why you are here."

"I'm glad he asked," said Masterson. He spoke to Obidiah, but looked Geronimo in the eye. "We have a man, a newcomer to Tombstone, who was ambushed one night about a year ago. His arm was shattered by a rifle bullet. Nobody knows who fired it. But the man has decided he wants to stay in Tombstone, and he wants to know if he'll be safe there, or if the Apaches have a grudge against him. Nothing happens here without you knowing it, so I am asking you, not as a lawman, but simply as the man's friend: did one of your braves shoot him? His name is Edison." Masterson pulled a photograph out of his shirt pocket. "This is what he looks like."

Geronimo listened impassively to the translation, then looked at the photo. Finally he looked up and spoke.

"You are the man's friend," said Obidiah. "Why is Doc Holliday here?"

"Mr. Masterson gets lost in the dark," answered Holliday before Masterson could speak. "I'm here to make sure he can find his way back to Tombstone."

Another translation. "Goyathlay says he doesn't like you."

"He's got a lot of company," acknowledged Holliday with no show of concern or surprise.

"Does he also dislike Thomas Edison?" asked Masterson.

Obidiah put the question to Geronimo, who uttered a brief answer.

"No," said Obidiah. He turned to Masterson. "He says your friend was not shot by an Apache."

"He's sure?" asked Masterson.

Obidiah didn't bother translating. "He is Goyathlay," he answered.

Masterson nodded toward Geronimo. "Thank you." Then, to Obidiah: "That's what I wanted to know. I guess we'll be going now."

He and Holliday began walking toward their horses when a pair of warriors stepped forward and blocked their way. Masterson stopped, smiled, and gestured for them to walk past. They stood where they were.

"I thought we were done here," muttered Masterson. "What the hell is this about?"

"Probably a test to see if we're as peaceful as we claim," answered Holliday.

"Are we?" asked Masterson, studying the two braves.

"*I* am," answered Holliday. "They've got both my guns and my knife. I'm not going to be much help without them."

"Then we'll be polite," said Masterson.

He smiled, tipped his derby, bowed, and began walking around the two in a wide semicircle. Once again they moved to block his way.

He turned to Geronimo. "I don't supposed you'd like to call them off?" he said, but Obidiah was nowhere to be seen, and Geronimo merely stared at them impassively.

"It gets cold in the desert at night," said Masterson to Holliday. He looked at the last rays of the setting sun. "I don't know about you, but I don't plan to stand out here until morning."

He feinted left, the braves responded, and he trotted quickly to his right, accompanied by Holliday.

The assembled warriors broke into laughter at their fellows' discomfiture, and one of the two braves lost his composure. He screamed and hurled himself at Masterson, throwing him to the ground.

Masterson was up in an instant, and felled the warrior with a left to the belly and a right cross to the chin. But as the warrior fell, he reached out with his legs, entangled Masterson, and a second later both men were on the ground, face to face, pummeling each other.

The two rolled over and over, the warrior's knife suddenly appeared in his hand, they rolled once more, and now Masterson had somehow gained possession of the knife. He brought it down into the warrior's chest. The man screamed and squirmed to get away, and Masterson, now kneeling astride him, plunged the knife into him again and again until it was clear the warrior was dead.

"On your feet," said Holliday softly, and Masterson got up quickly to find himself facing Geronimo, who had walked over and now stood some ten feet away, accompanied by Obidiah.

"Geronimo saw it," said Masterson to Obidiah. "Your man started it."

Geronimo spoke to Obidiah, who translated. "You have come to Goyathlay's domain and killed one of his warriors."

"He attacked me," said Masterson. He held up the knife. "I came in peace, but I'll mete out the same to any other brave who thinks he can keep me here."

Another brief exchange between Geronimo and Obidiah, and the black man turned back to Masterson.

"Goyathlay will not stop you from leaving, and he will order his braves to let you pass."

"Good," said Masterson. "*That's* settled."

"But you have come here and killed an Apache brave, and there must be retribution."

Suddenly Geronimo stared at the sky, where the full moon was framed by a million stars. He lifted his hands above his head, and began uttering an almost hypnotic singsong chant. It lasted almost a full minute, and then he stopped and stared at Masterson, a grim smile on his face.

A wave of dizziness swept over Masterson. He fought it back and focused his eyes on Obidiah. "I've got *this* now," he said, holding up the knife. "Nobody had better lay a hand on me!"

"You will only have it for a few more seconds," said Obidiah expressionlessly, and as the words left his mouth the knife fell from Masterson's hand and his fingers began curling up into his palms.

"What the hell is wrong with me?" he mumbled.

"You have killed an Apache, and Goyathlay has pronounced your punishment," announced Obidiah. "From nightfall to dawn, for as long as you live, you shall not only be called a bat, but you shall *become* a bat. You will have a bat's thoughts, and a bat's hungers, and a bat's body. Goyathlay has spoken."

Masterson tried to reply. Nothing came out but a high-pitched screech. He held his arm up, and watched in horrified fascination as it morphed into a wing. The other arm followed suit, his clothes dropped away as his legs all but vanished, and a moment later he took flight, a bat with a six-foot wingspread and huge canines reflecting first the firelight and then the moonlight. He circled the camp, higher and higher, emitted a series of ear-shattering shrieks, and took off in the general direction of Tombstone.

"You look like you cannot believe it, Doc Holliday," said Obidiah in amused tones.

"You'd be surprised what I believe when I've got enough liquor in me," replied Holliday. He watched Masterson until he'd flown out of sight. "He will become a man in the morning?"

"If no one kills him before then," answered Obidiah. "And he will be extremely difficult to kill, I assure you."

"Ask Geronimo what it will take to lift this curse from him," said Holliday.

"He will not lift it."

"Ask him anyway."

Obidiah spoke to Geronimo, listened to the brief answer, and turned back to Holliday.

"He will lift the spell if you bring him the head of Hook Nose."

"I'm sure glad he didn't ask for anything difficult," said Holliday sardonically. "And now, if you'll return my weapons to me, I'll be on my way."

"They remain here," said Obidiah.

"That's his final decision?"

"It is."

Holliday shrugged. "Have someone bring me my horse, please. I don't want to run the same gauntlet that Mr. Masterson did."

Obidiah nodded and gestured for a warrior to go retrieve Holliday's horse. Holliday mounted it and turned it to Geronimo. "Am I going to have any trouble leaving your camp?"

Obidiah relayed the question. "He says there will be no trouble—this time. But now he knows what the famous Doc Holliday looks like, and he will know it is you if you ever dare to return."

Holliday flashed a very insincere smile of gratitude at Geronimo, then turned his horse and headed back to Tombstone.

"And I know what you look like too," he said so softly that no one else could hear. "Let's see who acts on his knowledge first."

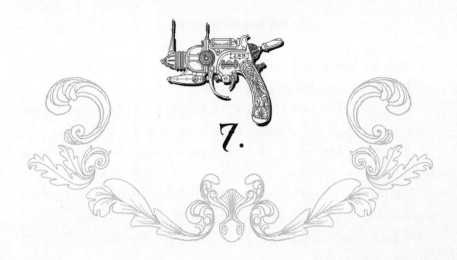

# 7.

OLLIDAY REACHED TOWN just as the last faro game was break-ing up. He went to the whorehouse, fell asleep on a couch in the parlor—such was his reputation that no one except Kate Elder would have dared to disturb him, and she was sleeping off a quart of whiskey in her own room—and he woke up when the last pair of patrons were leaving just after sunrise.

He realized that he hadn't eaten since early afternoon the previous day, and that he was famished. He knew better than to wake Kate from one of her alcohol-induced stupors, so he got to his feet, told a robotic whore to inform Kate that he had indeed spent the night under her roof and alone, then went off in search of some breakfast.

There were a couple of restaurants near the Oriental, and since he was still learning his way around town, he headed in that direction. As he approached the Oriental, he saw a small crowd gathered around something in the street.

"What's going on?" he asked.

"See for yourself," replied one of the men, with a smile. "Old Bat, he really must've hung one on."

Holliday shouldered his way through the circle of onlookers and saw Masterson lying naked on the street.

"He's all right," said Holliday. He turned to the two closest men. "Help me get him to his feet and into the Oriental."

"Doc?" said Masterson, trying to focus his eyes. "What am I doing here?"

"I'll explain it once we get you inside," said Holliday, leading the way into the saloon. The two men deposited him on a chair.

"Thanks," said Holliday. "One of you, wake Wyatt and tell him to get his ass down here."

"I don't know about that," said one of the men. "Word has it he's sleeping with Johnny Behan's girl—that actress from back East. I don't want Wyatt Earp getting mad at me."

"If you don't get him, *I'll* be mad at you. Figure out which of us is more likely to do something about it."

The man looked into Holliday's eyes, swallowed hard, and left the saloon, followed by the second man.

"What happened?" asked Masterson when they were alone.

"You really don't remember?"

Masterson shook his head. "The last thing I remember is getting jumped by one of Geronimo's braves. Next thing I know I'm lying naked in front of the Oriental." He shook his head in puzzlement. "I've never gotten that drunk before."

"You didn't take so much as a sip," said Holliday.

Masterson stared at him disbelievingly. "What are you talking about?"

"Let's wait for Wyatt and I won't have to explain it twice," replied Holliday. He suddenly remembered why he was up and around at daybreak. "You hungry? We could wait for Wyatt next door."

Masterson frowned. "I feel full. Stuffed, almost. Besides, I'm stark naked. I need to borrow some clothes."

"You've got a point," agreed Holliday. He walked out the swinging doors and faced the crowd, which hadn't yet broken up, then pulled a couple of bills out of his wallet. "We're going to need some clothes for Mr. Masterson," he announced. "I've got twenty dollars here. The man who buys them can keep whatever's left over."

Three men volunteered, Holliday chose one, and was about to go back into the Oriental when a man at the back of the small crowd spoke up. "Are you officially the law, Doc?"

"Bite your tongue, sir," answered Holliday.

"Damn. I guess I'll have to wait for one of the Earps."

"What's your problem?"

"Something killed one of my cattle last night," replied the man. "Wasn't a wolf, neither. It was like nothing you ever saw."

"Oh?"

The man nodded. "Throat was ripped out. Wasn't near as much blood as you'd think, neither."

"Interesting," said Holliday noncommittally.

He walked back into the saloon, went behind the bar, pulled out a bottle of whiskey, and poured himself a glass.

"Isn't it a little early in the day for that?" asked Masterson.

"It's not the first breakfast I've ever drunk," replied Holliday. "I think you can be sure it won't be the last." A pause. "How are you feeling?"

"A little fuzzy."

"Fuzzy?"

"Disoriented. But it seems to be passing."

They sat in silence for a few minutes. Then the man Holliday had sent shopping for clothes arrived, and Masterson started getting dressed.

"They don't fit too well, and they look like shit," he complained.

"If you'd rather sit around naked, give me back my twenty dollars and be my guest," said Holliday.

Masterson grimaced. "They'll do until I can get to my hotel and change. What the hell happened to my gun and my cane?"

"Geronimo's got them."

Masterson nodded. "That's right. I remember handing the gun over." He frowned. "But not the cane."

"It's with your horse."

"Good. Where is he? Back outside my hotel?"

"With Geronimo."

"You're not going to try to tell me I *walked* home from his camp!"

Holliday shook his head. "No, Bat—you didn't walk."

Wyatt Earp entered the Oriental just then.

"I hear someone had a little too much to drink," he said with a smile. "And not quite enough clothing to wear."

"Ask *him*," said Masterson, jerking a thumb at Holliday. "I don't remember a damned thing."

Earp turned to Holliday. "Well?"

"Geronimo put a curse or a spell on him."

"What kind?"

"As we were getting ready to leave—he swears his people had nothing to do with attacking Edison—a young brave tried to stop us, and Bat killed him."

"In Geronimo's camp?" asked Earp, frowning.

"He had no choice," answered Holliday. He paused. "Geronimo knows a little more English than he lets on."

"What are you talking about?"

"He knows what Bat's nickname means," said Holliday. "So to punish him, he's put a spell on him. Every night, from sunset to sunrise, he actually *becomes* a bat."

"The hell I do!" said Masterson.

"I was there," said Holliday. "I can testify to it. Biggest damned bat I ever saw. Your clothes fell away as you changed shape. You had maybe a six- or seven-foot wingspan, and you flew off into the night. I guess some part of you that was still human knew to come back to Tombstone. I don't know when or where or even how you landed, but when they found you it was sunrise and you'd changed back into yourself, minus your clothes."

"Do you believe that fairy tale, Wyatt?" demanded Masterson.

Earp shrugged. "Doc's never lied to me yet . . . and if the medicine men can keep the United States east of the Mississippi, I suppose one of the most powerful of them can change a man into a bat." Suddenly he looked out the door. "You know, when I got here, one of the ranchers told me something ripped the throat out of one of his cattle. Hasn't been a wolf in this area for years, and no twenty-pound coyote could do that."

"Bat says he's not hungry," added Holliday, "and the man said there was a lot of blood missing. I don't know what a vampire bat looks like, but I know what it feeds on."

"This is crazy!" growled Masterson.

"There's an easy enough way to find out," said Earp. "Ned Buntline has installed those super-hard brass bars in the jail. We'll take you there an hour or two before sunset and lock you in. If you're still yourself after the sun goes down, we'll turn you loose then and there. If not, we'll let you out in the morning and lock you in each night until we can figure out what to do about it. If you get hungry enough, or thirsty enough, and there's no cattle handy, you might go after a man or a woman, and then we'd have to kill you."

"I must still be drunk," muttered Masterson. "Things like this don't happen."

Holliday pulled a handkerchief out of his coat pocket and handed it to Masterson.

"What's this for?"

"I thought you might like to wipe a little of the blood from your chin," said Holliday.

# 8.

"**Y**OU'RE SURE YOU BELIEVE HIM?" asked Earp.

He and Holliday were sitting in the back room of the Oriental, munching on some sandwiches the bartender had sent out for.

"Geronimo had no reason to lie, Wyatt," said Holliday. "I mean, hell, if he looked us in the eye and said, 'Yes, I ordered one of my men to shoot Edison,' what the hell could we have done about it?"

"Hook Nose?" mused Earp. He shook his head. "No, he's too damned far away."

"I wouldn't be so hasty to write him off," said Holliday.

"You know something?"

"No, but you're talking about medicine men who can stop the United States from expanding across the Mississippi, who can conjure up a fire that can wipe out a town from hundreds of miles away—so why *couldn't* Hook Nose be responsible? He's supposed to be the most powerful of the lot."

Earp frowned. "I hadn't thought of it that way. And of course, he wouldn't even have to use a Cheyenne. He could make a deal with a white man or a Mexican right here."

"Anything's possible," replied Holliday. "You notice anyone whose luck has changed for the better since Edison got shot?"

Earp stared off into space for a long moment without answering. "We've got a bunch of ranches a few miles out of town. Most of them supply us with beef, but there are a few that deal in horses, and they can't be too happy about the Bunt Line. I suppose it's a possibility."

"Then why didn't they shoot Buntline instead of Edison?"

"Ned invented the lightweight bulletproof brass, but it doesn't go anywhere without Tom's electricity powering it. You kill Ned, someone else will take over and come up with brass or iron or something else—but kill Tom and none of those coaches moves an inch."

"So none of the horse ranchers figures to weep bitter tears if Edison dies," said Holliday. "I suppose the next step is to find out who among them is doing a lot better than he ought to be."

"Well, it's a start, anyway," said Earp.

"There are people who won't talk to a lawman," said Holliday, pushing away his half-eaten sandwich. "As long as I'm here, I might as well start asking some questions."

"No shooting, Doc," said Earp.

"Shooting's too quick," said Holliday with a smile. "Maybe I'll just strap the recalcitrant ones in my dental chair and go to work on them."

"Remind me never to tell you if I have a toothache."

Holliday chuckled and began leaving the back room. Suddenly he stopped and turned back to Earp.

"Wyatt?"

"Yeah, what is it?"

"Bat's not here."

"He's shopping for some new duds," replied Earp. "He'll probably take them back to his hotel."

"If I were you, I wouldn't let him out of my sight for too long. He doesn't really believe it's going to happen again, and you don't want a bloodthirsty hundred-and-seventy-five-pound bat wandering around Tombstone after dark."

"I told him to report to the jail half an hour before sunset," answered Earp. "I'll go over there myself and see if this spell really works."

"I told you it did."

"Once, in Geronimo's camp. Let's see if it works in Tombstone."

"According to Geronimo, it works wherever Bat is for as long as he lives," said Holliday.

"If so, we'll make his cell as comfortable as we can until we find a way to take the hex off."

"Comfortable to a man isn't the same thing as comfortable to a bat with a thirst for blood," said Holliday. "If Buntline's bars aren't strong enough to hold him, you'd better be prepared to shoot him before he starts killing the townspeople."

"You're overreacting, Doc," said Earp. "Even if it happened, and I still don't believe it, it doesn't mean it'll happen again."

"Maybe not," said Holliday expressionlessly. "Let's see what you think about it tomorrow morning."

## 9.

OLLIDAY SPENT THE NEXT FEW HOURS visiting half a dozen saloons, trying without success to find out who would benefit most from Edison's death. Finally he decided to go back to the Oriental, and he took a shortcut down an alley between Second and Third streets.

He had traversed half the distance when he suddenly found his path blocked by a snake that was some fifteen feet in length, black as coal, with glowing ruby eyes. He came to a halt and let his fingers rest lightly on the gun in his holster.

"Don't startle me like that," he said. "I could just as easily have blown your head off."

"Then you know who I am?" hissed the snake.

"No," answered Holliday. "But I sure as hell know what you aren't, and I can guess who sent you."

The snake seemed to coil and gather itself, and suddenly morphed into an Apache brave.

"Goyathlay has a message for you, White Eyes," said the brave.

"My eyes are bloodshot," said Holliday. "They haven't been white for years."

"You are *all* White Eyes."

"Okay, we're all White Eyes. What's the message?"

"He says you are an honorable man, that you did not try to shoot him or any of his warriors when he visited the bat man with the curse. He has returned both your weapons, and the bat man's clothes."

"Where are they?"

"In the wagon without horses."

"Thank him for me. I'll retrieve them as soon as you tell me why you're here." He stared at the brave. "You didn't have to tell me where our goods were. Our guns and Bat's cane are so distinctive that who-ever unloads the coach would recognize them."

The brave smiled. "Goyathlay told me you would say that."

"Then let's get down to business," said Holliday. "Why *have* you sought me out?"

He suddenly heard some high-pitched laughter behind him, and turned to see the cause of it. Two girls from one of the saloons had just walked out of the frame building and entered the alley, on their way to another destination. He looked back, but the brave was gone, replaced by a mangy dog sniffing for scraps of garbage.

The girls passed Holliday, still talking and giggling. He tipped his hat to them, and watched until they reached the end of the alley and turned to their right. The instant they were out of sight the dog was gone, replaced by the brave.

"That was pretty close," said Holliday. "What would you have done if they'd seen you?"

"I?" said the brave. "Nothing."

"All right," said Holliday. "Let me amend that: what would Geronimo have done?"

"You would have to ask Goyathlay," came the reply. "If he wanted them dead, he would probably have killed them with your weapon and left you to explain it to Wyatt Earp. Goyathlay is not without a sense of humor."

"Hilarious," said Holliday.

"You disapprove?"

"It's not up to me to approve or disapprove," answered Holliday. "Now suppose we get back to business. Why did you seek me out?"

"You have an interest in common with Goyathlay."

"I do?"

"You want to know who shot the man Edison. He wants those same men eliminated, because we have been blamed for their crimes."

"Yes, I'd call that a mutual interest," agreed Holliday, pulling out a thin cigar and lighting it. He offered one to the Apache, who refused it. After he'd taken a couple of puffs, without inhaling and began coughing anyway, he stared at the brave. "Well?"

"Goyathlay says that there was a thriving business stealing horses from Mexico and selling them here. Now, thanks to Edison, that business is all but vanished."

"If Geronimo knows about it, so do the Earps," said Holliday. "Why didn't they arrest these men?"

"The crimes were committed in Mexico, which is beyond their jurisdiction."

"Makes sense. Who ran the biggest horse-stealing operation in these parts?"

Suddenly Holliday was talking to empty air. He looked around and saw a drunk staggering down the alley.

"Come on," said Holliday. "He's probably used to seeing snakes and Indians whenever he's on a bender."

The drunk got to within twenty yards of Holliday, then sat down and started singing.

"I haven't got all day," said Holliday. "Where the hell are you?"

"I'm right here," said the drunk. "Come sing with me."

Holliday waited another minute and when the Indian didn't appear as himself or any of his magical guises, he announced that he'd get the answer elsewhere and walked between buildings and out onto Third Street.

"You're up early," said a familiar voice. "It's not even noon yet."

"Hello, Morg," said Holliday. "Got a question for you."

"How much do you need?" asked Morgan Earp.

"Not that kind of question."

"Good. I'm tapped out anyway. Ask away."

"Who runs the biggest horse-thieving outfit around here?"

"That'd be the Clantons," answered Morgan. "Old Man Clanton and his sons—Ike, Fin, and Billy."

"Where are they located?"

"Maybe two miles south and west of town. Why?"

"I thought I'd call on them and pay my respects."

"I'll come along," said Morgan.

Holliday shook his head. "These particular respects are better paid without the law hanging around."

# 10.

OLLIDAY'S FIRST STOP was at Thomas Edison's combination house and laboratory. He knocked on the door, waited patiently until Edison stopped whatever he was tinkering with, and was finally ushered in.

"Hello, Doc," said Edison. "What can I do for you?"

"That depends," answered Holliday. "First, for what it's worth, Geronimo wasn't behind the attack that cost you your arm."

"In retrospect it was the best thing that ever happened to me," said Edison, flexing his metal arm. "The things this appendage can do are just remarkable. Ned's even helped me rig it so that this finger"—he held up part of a pincer that doubled as a forefinger—"acts as an electric drill."

"Probably come in handy if you ever turn to safecracking," commented Holliday.

Edison chuckled. "The US government funds me. I've got all the money I need."

"You should try your luck some night at the Oriental."

Another chuckle. "I'm just smart enough to know not to gamble."

"Which brings us back to my visit," said Holliday. "Are you smart enough to provide me with any electric magic to protect me when I go out to the Clantons'?"

"Who or what are the Clantons?"

"Horse thieves. They've got a spread a couple of miles out of town."

"Why do you need protection?" asked Edison.

"Because there's every chance they were responsible for the attack on you," said Holliday. "And because there are a lot more of them than there are of me."

"You're going out there alone to confront them?"

"Might as well find out for sure. Right now they're the likeliest suspects."

"I think Ned is more able to supply what you need than I am," replied Edison. He went into his office, followed by Holliday, and pulled the switch that summoned Buntline.

"Remarkable stuff, this electricity," said Holliday.

"Someday it will power the whole world," answered Edison.

"For better or worse."

Buntline entered the office. "Hello, Doc," he said. "I assume you're the reason I'm here?"

"Doc is going out to the Clanton ranch—" began Edison.

"Those bastards?" said Buntline, frowning. "Watch yourself, Doc. They're a bad bunch."

"He knows," said Edison. "I told him you might help him even the odds a bit."

Buntline studied Holliday's emaciated figure for a moment, then nodded. "Come on, Doc. Let's see what we can do for you."

He turned on his heel and left the office, with Holliday following him. They traversed the passageway between the two houses, and Holliday found himself inside Buntline's lab for the first time.

It was illuminated by electric lamps, and there was so much brass in so many shapes that the reflected light was almost blinding. There were handguns and rifles, shotguns and hunting knives, armor, prison bars, gates, doors, and mechanical devices that made no sense whatsoever to Holliday. There were heavily notated blueprints for coaches, buildings, for every possible use to which Buntline could put his super-hardened brass.

"What's in there?" asked Holliday, gesturing to a brass door.

"That's where I forge and treat the brass," answered Buntline. "No one's allowed in there, not even Tom." A quick smile. "I don't know why. He could probably suggest half a dozen ways to improve it, but it's mine, and since we're not in the United States, I can't patent the process, so I do the next best thing: I hide it."

"Once all this is over, I wonder if you can make me some dental instruments. It'd be nice not to have to keep replacing broken ones." Holliday suddenly grimaced. "That is, if this cough ever goes away and I can get back to dentisting."

"I'll be happy to, Doc," said Buntline. "Hell, Tom's no doctor, but he *is* a genius. Maybe he can come up with some way to cure your consumption."

"There's only one way," answered Holliday, "and it comes to all of us sooner or later." He looked around the lab. "So what have you got for me today?"

"First of all," said Buntline, producing a shining metal vest, "I've got some lightweight body armor. Won't protect your head, but I guarantee that no bullet can touch you from your neck to your waist."

Holliday looked dubious. "It looks heavy."

"Not as heavy as iron," said Buntline.

"I don't have the strength or endurance of a healthy man," continued Holliday. "They're not going to hold their fire while I get into this out at their ranch, so if I use it I'll have to wear it all the way there." He grimaced again. "I don't know if I can."

"Let's give it a try," suggested Buntline.

Holliday removed his coat and let Buntline help him don the armor.

"Fits like a very stiff vest," commented Holliday. He swung his arms around for a moment, then relaxed them at his sides. Suddenly he drew his gun, twirled it around his index finger, replaced it in its holster, then repeated the process twice more.

"Well?" asked Buntline.

"It feels okay now, but it could take me twenty minutes to ride out to the ranch, and I have a feeling it gets heavier by the minute. Unless . . ." he said thoughtfully.

"Unless?"

"Unless I can take one of your coaches out there, and slip the vest on just as it arrives."

Buntline shook his head. "I'm sorry, Doc. There are four coaches in the Bunt Line, and they're all going about their routes right now. One's free the day after tomorrow, if you're willing to wait."

Holliday shook his head. "No, I want to get this over with. Help me out of this, please."

Buntline helped remove the armor, and put it back where he'd gotten it. "Anything else?"

Holliday shrugged. "What else have you got?"

"I told Wyatt I'd be happy to give you the same kind of gun he has. He said you'd find it too heavy, so I've been working on a light-weight one. Hold on a second."

Buntline opened the brass door, vanished as the door closed behind him, and emerged a moment later with a brass pistol in his hands. Unlike Earp's four-barreled weapon, this one had two barrels, one atop the other.

"I think this may work for you," said Buntline, holding it up for Holliday to see. "Unlike Wyatt's pistol, the barrels don't rotate in Gatling-gun fashion. They're permanently fixed, so for anything but long-distance shooting, for which you'd probably prefer a rifle, it won't affect your aim. It holds twelve bullets, six for each barrel, and you won't have to make any adjustment to switch between barrels. It senses when one barrel is out of bullets and automatically begins firing the second."

"May I?" asked Holliday, reaching his hand out.

"It's for you," said Buntline.

Holliday took it gingerly, studied every inch of it with a practiced eye, hefted it, held it to his eye and sighted along the barrel, and finally handed his own pistol to Buntline and inserted the brass one in his holster.

"It fits," he said, surprised.

"I designed it to fit any holster that can hold a Colt," replied Buntline.

Holliday drew it and replaced it a few times.

"It's comfortable," he said. "I'll take it."

"Good," said Buntline. He walked to a shelf, picked up a small box, and returned with it. "Bullets," he said. "Normal bullets are too big."

Holliday opened the box. "How many have you got here?"

"Sixty. If you survive the afternoon and decide to keep the pistol permanently, I can make up a thousand or more by the day after tomorrow."

"Sounds good to me."

"Can I give you a word of advice?"

"Why not?" responded Holliday.

"None of the Clantons is good news, but watch out for Ike. He's the shiftiest of the lot. Not the best gun, but the one most likely to shoot you in the back."

"I'll take it under advisement."

"I still wish you'd wear the armor."

"It's not comfortable, and I have a feeling it'll get less comfortable with every passing hour."

Buntline lowered his head in thought for a moment, then looked up. "I may have a solution for that."

"You can't change the way it feels before I ride out there," said Holliday.

"I don't have a Bunt Line coach available, but I *do* have something else. Come out back with me."

Holliday followed him through the building to the back door, and then out into the alley behind it.

"There!" said Buntline. "What do you think of it?"

Holliday found himself facing an ornate, baroque brass surrey that was capable of holding two men, a driver and a passenger. The huge wheels looked fragile, but they were made of the same super-hardened brass.

"It's not self-propelled," explained Buntline. "It requires two horses to pull it; it's too heavy for just one. But it offers some protection, and more to the point, you can leave the armor here"—he gestured to the floor—"and put it on just before you get there."

"It sure as hell beats riding out there on horseback," admitted Holliday.

"It's my personal surrey," said Buntline, "so please wear the armor. I'd hate to see Ike Clanton driving it into town tomorrow."

"I'm too mean to die," said Holliday. "I thought everyone knew that. I'll rent the horses from the stable over on Second Street and be back in a few minutes. You've got a harness, I assume?"

"Yes."

"Good. I hope you know how to rig the horses up?"

"Same way as always."

"I've never done it," said Holliday.

"You're kidding, right?"

"I'm a dentist and a gambler, not a stagecoach driver."

"Yes, I know how. Like I said, it's my own surrey."

"All right," said Holliday. "I'm off to get the horses."

"Maybe I'll come along with you," said Buntline.

"Could be some shooting, and you're an inventor, not a shootist."

"I can protect myself from top to bottom," replied Buntline.

"I wouldn't let Morgan come because I didn't want any law around when I ask my questions," said Holliday. "I can't use that reason for you, but I can tell you this: Once we're there, you're on your own. I can't watch out for you."

"You might need someone protecting your back," said Buntline.

"I thought that's what the armor was for."

Buntline smiled. "It doesn't protect your head or your legs. I *have* a pair of brass chaps, but I think you'd find them too heavy."

Holliday pulled his new pistol out of his belt. "See that old poster for Johnny Behan's ladyfriend—the actress?" he said, pointing to a poster on the side of a brick building.

"You mean Josephine Marcus?"

"That's the one."

Buntline smiled. "Word has it she's Wyatt's lady these days."

"Whatever," said Holliday with a shrug. He handed the pistol to Buntline. "Put a bullet through her left eye."

"It's illegal to shoot a gun within the city limits."

"We'll say I did it. If you're going to protect my back, I want to make sure you don't accidentally shoot me in it."

Buntline aimed the pistol and finally pulled the trigger.

"Not bad," said Holliday. "You blew away her left elbow." He took the pistol back. "I thank you for the offer, but you're not coming."

"But—"

Holliday began walking away. "I'll be back in five minutes with the horses. Have the armor in the rig."

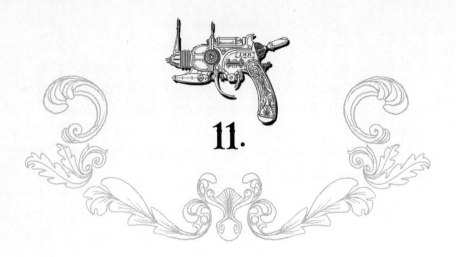

# 11.

HOLLIDAY LET THE HORSES WALK at their own speed while he tried to get used to the slightly different feel and weight of Buntline's pistol. Every now and then he'd shoot at a desert flower to test its accuracy. Finally he put it back in his holster and withdrew a small flask from his coat pocket, uncorking it and taking a swallow. The sun was high in the sky, he was getting sick of the sight of cactus, and he wished he'd brought a hat with a broader brim, then decided that it wouldn't have done much good, since it wouldn't have protected his eyes against the blindingly bright brass of the surrey.

When he was a mile and a half out of town he pulled the horses to a stop, climbed out of the surrey, took off his jacket, and donned the brass vest—and instantly cursed and took it off. The sun had been beating down on it, and it was incredibly hot to the touch.

His hand went down to the butt of his pistol, and he found to his relief that his coat had protected it from the sunlight and it was no warmer than a normal gun. He tossed the armor back into the surrey, climbed back onto the seat, and urged the horses to begin walking again.

In another ten minutes a number of corrals came into view, all of them with wooden rails—that much brass would have been prohibitive—and finally he saw a farmhouse and a number of outbuildings. The house was protected by brass, and so was the barn door; the bunkhouse and outhouse were wood, which was slowly being eaten away by dry rot. There were perhaps a dozen horses in the corrals, which were clearly built to hold a few hundred. He looked around for cattle, but couldn't spot any.

As he approached the farmhouse a pair of men suddenly emerged from it.

"That's far enough," said one of them as he got within thirty yards of the house, and Holliday pulled the horses to a stop. "Who are you and what's your purpose here?"

"I'll be happy to answer your questions," said Holliday, "but do you mind if I get off this rig first? It's damned uncomfortable."

"That's one of Tom Edison's inventions, ain't it?"

"Nope. It's Ned Buntline's."

"Same thing," said the man.

"I wouldn't say that to either of them," said Holliday with a smile, as he clambered down off the surrey. "May I ask which particular Clantons I'm speaking to?"

"I'm Fin Clanton."

"Ah, yes—Phineas." Holliday turned to the other. "And are you Ike or Billy?"

"Name's Bob Passavoy," came the answer.

"Your corrals are pretty empty," noted Holliday.

"They'll be full tomorrow," said Fin Clanton.

"And your father and brothers and the rest of your men are missing."

"They're rounding up strays. They'll be back tomorrow too."

"Yeah," said Holliday. "I must have passed three or four hundred strays on the way out from town. I tried speaking to them, but all they understood was Mexican."

"Okay," said Clanton irritably. "Just who the hell are you?"

"John Henry Holliday, at your service," said Holliday, tipping his hat.

"Doc Holliday," said Clanton. "We'd heard you were coming to town."

"You heard right."

"What's your business here?"

"I just want to ask a few questions," said Holliday.

"We don't feel like answering any," said Clanton.

"You can answer them now," said Holliday. "Or . . ." He let the word hang in the air.

"Or what?" demanded Clanton.

"You can answer them in the next life. It's up to you."

"Do you know who you're talking to? I'm Fin Clanton, by God!"

"The expendable one," said Holliday.

"You're a dead man!" roared Clanton, going for his gun.

Holliday was faster, and pumped one slug into Clanton's knee and another into his shoulder before Clanton could even pull his gun from its holster.

"Don't try to be a hero," said Holliday, turning his gun on Passavoy.

The man held his hands out from his sides where they were in plain view. Holliday walked over and removed his gun. Fin Clanton, sprawled on the ground, finally got his gun out of his holster. Holliday walked over and kicked it out of his hand, and it flew about thirty feet through the air, landing near a water trough.

"Mr. Clanton has made it clear that he has no interest in talking to me," said Holliday, ignoring the groaning man on the ground and walking back to Passavoy. "Are you feeling any more talkative?"

"What gives you the right to come up here and start shooting?" demanded Passavoy.

"I'm holding it in my hand," said Holliday. "Now shall we have a little chat?"

"Wyatt and Virgil sent you, didn't they?"

"What difference does it make? You're going to talk to me no matter who sent me."

"What the hell do you think I know?" said Passavoy.

"I have to admit you're not dazzling me with your intellect," replied Holliday. "But I think you know who shot Tom Edison a while back, and who ordered it."

"I've only been here six weeks."

"Yeah, but people talk," said Holliday. "In fact, most people brag. And shooting Tom Edison is something worth bragging about, wouldn't you think?"

Clanton tried to get to his feet, fell back over, and moaned in pain.

"Fin," said Holliday, "if you interrupt our conversation again, I'm going to be very cross with you."

"You blew my goddamned knee to pieces!" grated Clanton.

"Must hurt like the devil," commented Holliday with no show of concern.

"We'll get you for this!" promised Clanton.

"Sure you will," said Holliday. He turned back to Passavoy. "You were about to tell me who shot Edison."

"I don't know!"

"Take an educated guess," said Holliday. He aimed his pistol at the man's ear. "I'll know if you're right or wrong—and if you're wrong, well, you'll still have one ear left to hear my next question. Let's give it a try. Who shot Tom Edison?"

"I don't know."

Holliday squeezed the trigger. The bullet whizzed past Passavoy's ear. "My hand's not as steady as it used to be," he said apologetically. "I suppose I could take an eye out, instead of an ear. Shall we try again?"

"Brocius!" said Passavoy, his nerve breaking. "It was Curly Bill Brocius!"

"See?" said Holliday, lowering his gun. "That wasn't so difficult, was it?"

"You're a dead man, Passavoy!" grated Clanton from where he lay on the ground. "You're *both* dead men."

"Ah!" said Holliday with a smile. "I see you're up to joining the conversation."

"Fuck you!"

"And romantic as well," said Holliday. He walked over to Clanton and dropped to one knee. "Who told Curly Bill Brocius to shoot Edison? Somehow you don't seem bright enough to have thought of it all by yourself."

"You go to hell!"

"Well, probably I will," said Holliday. "And once I'm there, I'm going to need a guide, someone who got there ahead of me. Perhaps someone like you. Are you going to answer my question?"

"Fuck you!"

"A man of few words," said Holliday. "And most of them the same." He stared at Clanton's mouth for a moment. "What's that I see?" Clanton merely glared at him. "Why, Phineas Clanton, I do believe you have been ignoring your dental hygiene. I think you've got a couple of cavities. Alas, I don't have any alcohol to kill the germs— at least, not any I care to share with you—but I suppose I can just shoot the little bastards." He forced the barrel of his pistol into Clanton's mouth. "Someday you'll thank me for this," he continued. "Not on this plane of existence, of course, but somewhere. Now, would you like to give me the name I need?"

Clanton remained silent, and Holliday turned briefly to Passavoy. "Stand back. This will make quite a mess." He turned back to Clanton and cocked his pistol. "On the other hand, it probably beats the hell out of bleeding slowly to death right in front of your own house. Last chance, Fin. Got a name for me?"

Suddenly all the fight seemed to vanish from Clanton, and he nodded his head.

"See?" said Holliday, removing the barrel from Clanton's mouth. "I knew you were a reasonable man. Now, whose idea was it?"

"Hook Nose."

"This is a little out of his bailiwick," said Holliday.

"He thought Edison was getting too close to a solution," said Clanton.

"A solution?" repeated Holliday.

"To fighting off his magic. So he made a deal with us. If we'd kill Edison, he'd use his powers to protect our operation."

Holliday shook his head. "He can't be too pleased with you, can he?"

"We'll still kill Edison," said Clanton. "And when Ike and the rest of them get back from Mexico tomorrow, we'll kill you and those god-damned Earps, too."

"Like you killed Edison?" said Holliday, getting to his feet. "Well, gentlemen, this has been a most enlightening conversation. Fin, you really ought to tend to those wounds. Lying out here in the dirt can't be doing them any good."

"Give me a hand moving him into the house," said Passavoy, walking over to where Clanton lay on the ground.

"I'm a sick man with consumption," answered Holliday. "Do I look like I can lift a big man like Fin Clanton?"

"We can't just let him lie here."

"He *did* try to kill me," said Holliday.

"Then I'm going into the house to see what I can find to clean his wounds and stop the bleeding."

"He's not bleeding all that much," said Holliday. "He's going to have a permanent limp, but he'll live."

"I'll get a blanket, roll him onto it, and pull him over to the shade beside the house," said Passavoy.

"He wouldn't do it for you," said Holliday. "But you do whatever makes you happy."

Passavoy entered the house, and Holliday looked down at Clanton. "I'm going to make you a deal, Fin Clanton. The last thing I need is for a bunch of your brothers and hirelings to come looking for me. If you tell them that we've come to an understanding and made our peace with each other, I won't tell Curly Bill Brocius who gave me his name. Think about it."

He turned and began walking toward the surrey. As he neared it, he heard a metallic *click!* He whirled and dropped to one knee, pulling his pistol as he did so. Passavoy stood at the open front door, a shotgun in his hands. He fired where Holliday's head and torso had been an instant earlier. He never got another chance, as one of Ned Buntline's bullets thudded home right between his eyes.

"First Curly Bill, now this one," said Holliday to Clanton. "You really ought to hire competent help."

He walked back to the surrey and climbed onto the seat.

"You're not going to leave me lying here in the sun!" shouted Clanton.

"You're home, and you'll be in the bosom of your family as soon as those bastards get back from killing Mexicans and stealing their horses. What more could you want?"

And with that, Holliday clucked to his horses and began the journey back to Tombstone.

## 12.

I T WAS MIDAFTERNOON when Holliday arrived in Tombstone. He returned the surrey to Ned Buntline and the horses to the stable where he had rented them. He then stopped at a restaurant on Allen Street, next to the Bird Cage Theatre, ordered a steak, and had just finished it when Wyatt Earp saw him through the window and entered.

"How'd it go?"

"Curly Bill Brocius did the shooting," answered Holliday.

"Damn!" said Earp. "I had him in jail the night before last on a drunk and disorderly charge, and let him go yesterday."

"Jail's like a second home to him from what I hear. He'll be back."

"Who put him up to it?"

"Believe it or not, Hook Nose," said Holliday.

"Why?" asked Earp, frowning. "He's hundreds of miles from here."

"He thinks our friend Tom may be getting close to being able to counteract his magic, so he made a deal with the Clantons. If they'd kill Edison, he'd protect their operation, which as near as I can tell consists of rustling cattle and horses."

"But they didn't kill Edison."

Holliday smiled. "And Fin Clanton was a little less protected than he might have been."

"You didn't kill him?"

"No," answered Holliday. "But his square-dance days are over." He paused. "I did have to kill one of his hired help, a Cowboy named Passavoy. It was self-defense, though I'm sure Fin will swear that I shot him down in cold blood."

"We'll worry about it if he presses charges," said Earp.

A waiter came by to pick up Holliday's empty plate. "Hi, Wyatt," he said. "She's not due for a couple of more hours."

"I know," said Earp.

"Your ladyfriend?" asked Holliday as the waiter retreated.

Earp nodded. "She performs next door, and takes most of her meals here."

"I seem to remember that Josephine Marcus was going to marry Johnny Behan." Holliday smiled. "I read it in the *Epitaph*, so it must be true."

"You've got it right," answered Earp. "She *was* going to marry him."

"Haven't you already got a wife or two?" continued Holliday.

"Drop it, Doc," said Earp.

"At least she acts on stage. The only time Kate acts is in bed." He paused. "I hear she's Jewish. Is that true? I've only seen three or four Jews in my life."

"I said drop it," said Earp irritably.

"The subject is closed," replied Holliday.

Earp looked out the window. "I'd say we have less than two hours."

"Until what?"

"Sundown."

Holliday shrugged. "I suppose so."

"Then if you're all through eating, we've got work to do."

"I thought the action didn't start until nine o'clock or so," said Holliday.

"I'm less concerned with action than with transformation."

"Transformation?"

"Bat."

"Shit! I'd forgotten all about him."

"We'll lock him in the jail, at least until we see what he's like."

"I told you what he's like," said Holliday. "He's the biggest god-damned bat you ever saw."

"And he killed a cow. I know."

"Well, then?"

"Does he know who he is?" said Earp. "Does he think like a man or like a bat? Can I trust him, or do I have to lock him up every night?"

"Beats me," said Holliday. "He was squeaking, not talking, for the few seconds I was with him before he flew off. And he didn't remember anything from the minute he changed into a bat until the minute he changed back."

"I want Tom Edison to watch what happens and see if he can come up with some way to prevent it, or change him back right away."

"I'm as impressed by what Edison can do as you are," said Holliday. "But I'm even more impressed by what Geronimo can do with one little chant."

Holliday left a dollar on the table, then got up and joined Earp as they walked out the door and headed to the jail. A sheet of brass covered the front door, but the walls were adobe.

"No other brass," noted Holliday as they neared it.

"Don't need it," answered Earp.

"I saw him. You didn't. I don't know if adobe can hold him in."

Earp smiled. "It's adobe on top of brick. You could hitch a team of six plow horses to one of these walls and they couldn't budge it."

Holliday shrugged. "If you say so." He looked around. "Aren't we forgetting something?"

"What?"

"The object of the exercise."

"Virgil's bringing him."

"Alone?"

"If he's still a man, he'll come willingly," said Earp. "And if he's not, nobody on our side can fly."

"Makes sense," Holliday acknowledged. "I hope those brass bars are as strong as you and Buntline think they are."

"They'll hold," said Earp confidently. "He's a bat, not an elephant."

They reached the jail and found Morgan waiting for them in the office.

"How'd it go out there?" he asked Holliday.

"About as expected."

"They're all dead?" said Morgan.

"About as *I* expected," Holliday amended. "Fin Clanton won't be winning any footraces, and one of the hired help did something foolish. Better all the way around that no one with a badge was there."

"Did you learn anything?"

"Brocius did the shooting and Hook Nose is behind it. He thinks Edison might be getting close."

"That's encouraging, at least," said Morgan. "I assume he offered the Clantons protection in exchange for their killing Edison?"

"Yes."

Morgan smiled. "Clearly he knows they failed. He sure as hell didn't protect them from you."

"You can count on Hook Nose or the Clantons or both of them to keep trying," said Wyatt. "They'll figure Tom's got to be closer to an answer now than when he was shot, and Doc just proved that the Clantons can be stopped."

The door to the jailhouse opened and Bat Masterson entered, accompanied by Virgil Earp.

"Hi, Bat," said Morgan. "I fixed your cell to make it as comfortable as I could. Got a real bed, new pillow, couple of blankets, even got a privy in one corner. I'll be here all night. Anything you need, just ask for it."

"He *can't* ask once the sun's down," noted Holliday.

"I'm not sure we weren't both mesmerized," said Masterson. "I don't feel any different."

"We'll know soon enough," said Virgil. He looked around. "Wasn't Edison supposed to be here?"

"We've got another ninety minutes of daylight, Virg," said Morgan. "He'll be along."

"How are we going to do this?" asked Masterson.

"We'll put you in a cell in about an hour," answered Virgil. "If you haven't changed by half an hour after sunset, we'll let you out and assume that whatever happened last night, whether it was magic or hypnotism or something else, isn't going to happen again."

"And if it does?" persisted Masterson.

"Then you'll spend the night in the cell, and we'll let you out when you change back in the morning."

"You know," said Morgan, "I've been thinking, and maybe a cell that's comfortable for a man won't be all that comfortable for a bat. Maybe we should give you something to hang upside down from."

"Bats fly around at night," said Wyatt.

"I wonder what they eat?" mused Virgil. "Besides tearing the throats out of cattle, that is."

"I wish you'd stop talking about me as if I'm already a bat," said Masterson. "It's just too far-fetched to believe."

"I was there," said Holliday. He decided not to mention his morning encounter in the alley with the sometimes-Indian-sometimes-snake.

Masterson had no answer for that, and the five men fell silent for a few minutes. Then Morgan produced a deck of cards.

"Anyone care for a friendly little game of poker while we're waiting?" There was no response.

"Doc?" said Morgan.

"I don't take Earp money," said Holliday. "I'll wait until tonight."

"Maybe you won't win any Earp money," said Morgan with a smile.

"Forget it, Morg," said Holliday. "You're a lawman. I'm a gambler."

Before Morgan could answer, Edison walked into the jailhouse.

"Hi, Tom," said Virgil. "Glad you could make it."

"I wouldn't miss it for the world," replied Edison.

"You don't really believe Geronimo could turn me into a bat just by chanting some prayer or spell, do you?" said Masterson.

"If I didn't, I wouldn't be living in Tombstone," answered Edison.

"Well, I think it's ridiculous," said Masterson.

"You know what's ridiculous?" said Edison. "What's ridiculous is that a nation with twenty times the strength and numbers and firepower of the Indians has been stopped at the Mississippi without a shot being fired. If Hook Nose and the rest of them can do that, and clearly they *have* done it, then turning a man into a bat is schoolboy stuff to them."

"Okay," said Masterson, "let's say for the sake of argument that I turn into a bat in another hour or so. Why should I stay locked up in a cell? Have you ever heard of a bat attacking a man?"

"We don't even want you attacking cattle," said Wyatt. "For one thing, they're not yours. And for another, any rancher would be within his rights to blow you away if you tried to do it."

"Also," added Holliday, "you flew off last night before I could say anything to you, so we don't know how much of you remains in that bat's brain. You and I have been friends for a while, and I'd like to think that you wouldn't attack me if there were no cattle around, but I don't *know* it and neither do you."

"Anyway, Tom's here to see exactly what happens, and maybe come up with a way to stop it," said Morgan. "There's no sense arguing about whether you will or won't become a bat. We'll know soon enough."

"All right," muttered Masterson. "But I feel like the lot of you are pulling some kind of crazy practical joke on me. It's a lot easier to believe I got so drunk when we came back to town that I don't remember anything, including where I left my clothes."

"Too bad Geronimo doesn't put the same curse on Fin Clanton," said Holliday. "He'd be better off flying than trying to walk."

"I heard you went out there today," said Virgil. "What happened?"

Holliday related the story in detail.

"So Ike and Billy and Old Man Clanton are due back tomorrow with a few hundred head of Mexican horseflesh?" said Virgil when Holliday was done.

"So Fin says," replied Holliday. "And if he managed to crawl over to some shade, and his canteen wasn't totally empty, he'll be alive to tell them about my visit."

"You may be facing a murder warrant," said Morgan. "The Clantons own Johnny Behan."

"He's the sheriff, but Virgil's the marshal," said Holliday. "Who's higher up the food chain?"

"The one with the most guns," said Morgan with a smile.

Wyatt looked out the window. "Won't be too much longer," he said. "Bat, let's get you into your cell."

Morgan accompanied Masterson to the cell that had been prepared for him, ushered him into it, then closed and locked the door.

"These are Buntline's brass bars," he announced, "even on the door. There's no way Bat can bust out of here, right, Tom?"

"Theoretically," said Edison, walking over to join them.

Masterson took off his coat and laid it neatly on a chair next to his cot. "Well," he said, feigning a lightness he didn't feel, "now that I'm your responsibility, when do you feed me some dinner?"

"As soon as the sun goes down and I know what you eat," answered Morgan.

"This is silly," said Masterson. "I'm *me*. I feel the way I always do."

"Tell me that in an hour and you're free to go," said Virgil.

"When you find it's all some story Doc made up, I expect you to put *him* in here instead of me," continued Masterson.

"Wouldn't be my first night in a jail," said Holliday. "Probably be my most comfortable, though."

Then, as if by mutual consent, they all fell silent. Five minutes passed, then five more. The sun began sinking in the west, and Virgil flipped a switch that bathed the office and the cells in electric light.

"Should we be doing that?" asked Morgan.

"Why not?" replied Virgil.

"If it's got to be dark for him to change—"

"It doesn't," interjected Holliday. "He changes when the sun sets. Geronimo didn't put any stipulations about how dark his surroundings had to be."

"Maybe Geronimo doesn't know about electric lights," said Morgan.

"He knows," said Holliday, remembering his encounter in the alley and concluding Geronimo could just as easily turn a warrior into a cat or a rat and send him out to observe the enemy.

"And even if he doesn't know anything about electricity, he sure as hell knows how bright a bonfire can be," added Wyatt.

"He's just an old charlatan," said Masterson. "I got drunk and—"

Suddenly he froze.

"What is it?" asked Morgan.

Masterson glared at him and said nothing. Then, as he had done the night before, he began morphing into an enormous bat. His face became elongated, his ears pointed and erect, his canines reflecting the electric light. An arm reached out for Edison, who stepped back . . . and when the arm was withdrawn it had become a wing, its fingers now claws. He opened his mouth to speak, and an earsplitting screech came out. His clothes fell to the ground as the shape of his body changed.

"Fascinating!" said Edison.

Masterson wrapped his claws around the bars of the cell door and pulled.

Nothing happened.

He went to the barred window and pulled at those bars.

"I told you he couldn't make a dent in Buntline's bars," said Virgil.

Masterson, having trouble walking in his new body, shambled to an outside wall and began striking it with his clenched claws.

"He's working off his frustration because he can't bend the bars," said Morgan.

"I don't think so," said Edison as Masterson began pounding the wall rhythmically.

No sooner had the words left his mouth than the wall collapsed, and with a high-pitched shriek of triumph Masterson stepped outside and flew off into the night.

Holliday turned to Edison. "I think you just lost a bodyguard," he said wryly. There was no response from Edison or the Earps, and he added: "Let's hope you haven't gained a predator."

# 13.

THEY FOUND MASTERSON, naked, confused, and very chilly, on a balcony of the Grand Hotel on Fifth Street. The occupant of the room, a middle-aged woman who was visiting relatives, opened the doors to her balcony, took one look at the lawman, and screamed. Virgil Earp showed up a few minutes later, wrapped a blanket around Masterson, and took him back to his own hotel.

Holliday awoke just before noon, had one of the robot whores make his breakfast, and headed over to the Oriental. There were four or five men drinking at the bar, and the faro table was deserted. Wyatt Earp sat alone at a table, sipping a cup of coffee and reading the morning edition of the *Tombstone Epitaph*, and Holliday walked over and joined him.

"You found him, I assume?"

Earp nodded. "Yes."

"I figured. Otherwise you'd be out looking for him. Is he okay?"

"Virg says he's none the worse for wear. We're still waiting for reports of what he was up to during the night."

"Has Edison got any ideas?"

"Not so far."

"One last question: has anyone figured out how to contain him once he becomes a bat?"

"That's what Tom and Ned are working on. I suppose we'll have to construct a freestanding brass building. It's the only thing he can't punch his way through."

"They'd better do it fast."

Earp sighed deeply. "I know."

"It'd be damned ironic if you hired on to keep Edison alive, only to have one of your own men kill him."

"Are you always this cheerful when you wake up?"

"Today's one of my better days," said Holliday, coughing into a handkerchief.

"Maybe Tom can do something about your consumption," suggested Earp.

"The only thing he can do is catch it," replied Holliday. "These are the cards I was dealt."

"Well, it *is* hard to picture you as a genteel Southern gentleman with a dental practice."

"That was me, and not so long ago either."

Henry Wiggins entered the saloon just then. He smiled at Holliday and tipped his hat, and Holliday waved him over.

"Wyatt, say hello to a friend of mine, Henry Wiggins. Henry, this is Wyatt Earp."

"I'm pleased to meet you," said Wiggins, extending his hand. "You're every bit as famous as Doc."

"I'll take that as a compliment," replied Earp, shaking his hand. "Would you care to join us?"

"Thank you," said Wiggins. He turned to Holliday. "I hope the cards are running in your favor."

"I'm sure they will be, once I get rid of the distractions in my life and sit down to play," answered Holliday. "How goes it with you? Did you make your deal with Buntline yet?"

"We're negotiating," said Wiggins. "He's got some stuff that can make us both rich." He frowned. "He's too busy to talk today. He and Mr. Edison are working on some new invention."

"Did they say what it is?" asked Earp.

Wiggins shrugged. "No, just that they wanted to have it done by sunset."

"That's encouraging," remarked Holliday.

"Oh?" said Wiggins. "You know what it is?"

Earp shook his head almost imperceptibly.

"No," answered Holliday. "But it's encouraging that they're so enthused."

"I don't know why he bothers with anything except those metal whores," said Wiggins. "My God, there's a fortune to be made there! They never tire, nothing you can suggest can shock them, your woman can't get jealous of a machine—"

"Speak for yourself," said Holliday with a grim smile. "*My* woman has told me she'll kill me if I so much as touch one of those machines."

"Well, *most* women wouldn't be jealous."

Holliday turned to Earp. "My friend Henry doesn't know a lot about women," he commented.

"Maybe not," said Wiggins. "But I know what I can sell."

"No argument there," said Holliday. "You might combine it, one metal whore and one headstone. It'll save the grieving widow the trouble of having one made up."

"I can't tell if you're kidding or not," said Wiggins.

"Are you married, Henry?"

"Yes. And the proud father of three."

"How would you feel if Buntline made a male lover for your wife?"

"I'd kill them both," said Wiggins promptly.

"Was I kidding?" asked Holliday.

"But men are different," insisted Wiggins.

"We sure are," agreed Holliday. "We're bigger and dumber."

Suddenly a burly man with a mustache and a tiny goatee entered the saloon.

"Vanish, Henry," said Earp in low tones.

Wiggins sensed the sudden tension and didn't need a second invitation. He got to his feet and quickly strode to the far end of the bar.

The man walked over and stood in front of the table where Earp and Holliday were seated.

"I've been looking for you!" he bellowed.

"Doc, say hello to Ike Clanton," said Earp with no show of concern.

Clanton pointed a finger at Holliday. "You're the one who crippled my brother."

"You're looking at it all wrong," said Holliday. "I'm the one who generously let your brother live after he drew on me."

"You'll pay for that!" promised Clanton.

"I already did," answered Holliday easily. "Bullets cost money. I probably wasted a nickel on your brother and his friend, which is certainly more than they're worth."

"You don't know who you're dealing with!" rasped Clanton.

"Sure I do," said Holliday. "I'm dealing with some horse thieves who have to be a great disappointment to Hook Nose." Clanton looked surprised. "Oh?" continued Holliday. "Didn't Fin tell you that we had a little heart-to-heart chat?"

"You're a walking dead man, Holliday!"

"I've been a walking dead man for eight or nine years now," said Holliday. "You're going to need a better threat than that."

"I'm through making threats," said Clanton. "You heard me."

"Well, I'm certainly glad you're through making threats," said Holliday, getting to his feet. "Shall we go out into the street and settle this here and now?"

Clanton opened his coat and spread his arms out. "I'm not carrying a gun."

"That saves you this one time," said Holliday.

"Now get out of here, Ike, before I arrest you for disturbing the peace," said Earp.

"He shot my brother," said Clanton. "Aren't you going to arrest *him*?"

"He says your brother drew first."

"He's lying!"

"I was there," said Holliday. "Were you?"

"If Fin wants to fill out a complaint, I'll be happy to consider it," said Earp.

"The hell you will!" shouted Clanton. "We'll fill one out, but we'll file it with the sheriff."

"That's your right," said Earp. "Now get out of here."

"I'm not breaking any laws," said Clanton.

"You're on private property, which I happen to own, and I want you off of it."

Clanton walked toward the swinging doors. Just before he reached them he turned back to Earp. "This is just the beginning, Wyatt!" he bellowed. "You're not the only one who can import some firepower. I sent for ours as soon as I saw what you did to my brother!"

"Wyatt didn't do it," Holliday corrected him gently. "*I* did."

"We won't forget that," promised Clanton.

"You sure you don't want to settle it right now?" said Holliday.

"I told you: I'm unarmed."

"Except for the pistol peeking out over the top of your left boot, and the little lady's handgun you've got in your breast pocket," said Holliday in amused tones.

"You sound mighty tough now," said Clanton, backing up to the swinging doors. "Let's see how tough you sound when you're facing Johnny Ringo."

And with that he was gone.

"I always wanted to meet Ringo," said Holliday. "From what I hear, we have a lot in common."

"Other than being shootists?" asked Wiggins from his spot at the bar.

"We've both been to college," replied Holliday. "It might be interesting to discuss literature with him. They say he's always got some classics in Greek and Latin in his saddlebags."

"Not anymore, he doesn't," said another of the men at the bar.

"He's given up reading?" asked Holliday.

The man shook his head. "He's given up breathing. He was killed in an ambush down in Waco a few months ago."

"I hadn't heard that," said Holliday.

"Neither had I," said Earp. "Still, it's easy enough to check. I'll wire Waco and ask."

"You don't have to," said the man. "I was there."

"How'd it happen?" asked Holliday.

"Some guy called him out, and while they were facing each other, maybe ten or twelve of the guy's friends shot him in the back. He must have taken thirty, maybe forty bullets, but he still killed three of them on the way down. Fell on his face. It looked for a minute like he had ten or fifteen little fountains on his back. Then he ran out of blood."

"I think I'll check anyway," said Earp.

An hour later it was confirmed: Johnny Ringo had died of multiple bullet wounds in Waco, Texas.

"Well, that's that," said Earp when the message came through.

But of course, it wasn't.

# 14.

HOLLIDAY DECIDED TO GET A LATE LUNCH at the Rose Tree Inn on the corner of Fifth and Toughnut. As he passed the alley between Allen and Toughnut he saw the black snake again. He made sure no one else was watching, then ducked into the alley. The snake instantly became the same warrior he had encountered the day before.

"I have a message from Goyathlay," said the brave.

"I'm listening."

"Ike Clanton has contacted Hook Nose since he spoke to you."

"Hook Nose is here in Tombstone?" asked Holliday, surprised.

"No," came the answer. "But like Goyathlay, he has ways of bridging the distances."

"Okay, Ike Clanton spoke to Hook Nose. So what?"

"Ike Clanton is afraid of you."

"As well he should be," said Holliday.

"He has many men who will fight for him, and there are only three Earps. He knows what Goyathlay has done to Masterson, so he knows that Masterson is no threat if they fight at night."

"Either that, or he's an equal threat to everyone," agreed Holliday.

"But *you*, you are different," continued the brave. "You should have died of your illness many years ago. You should have died in many of your gunfights. Ike Clanton thinks that perhaps you *are* dead, that you have a medicine man keeping you alive."

"Silliest thing I ever heard," commented Holliday.

"A medicine man *could* do that," insisted the brave. "Goyathlay could do that. Hook Nose knows this."

"I assume there's a point to all this?"

The brave nodded. "To use your expression, Hook Nose feels he must fight fire with fire. You might be dead, and animated by a medicine man. Therefore, he has agreed to allow Ike Clanton to recruit a dead man, and in exchange Ike Clanton will continue his efforts to kill the man Edison."

"And the name of the dead man, as if I didn't know?" said Holliday grimly.

"Johnny Ringo."

Holliday nodded. "I don't suppose Geronimo can tell me how to kill a dead man?"

"It is enough that he has warned you."

"Which raises a question," said Holliday. "*Why* has he warned me?"

"The two greatest medicine men are Goyathlay and Hook Nose. One day there will be but one tribe, and there can be but one leader."

"So he's not helping *me*," said Holliday. "He's hindering Hook Nose."

The brave stared at him and said nothing.

"I have a proposition for Geronimo," said Holliday.

"He is listening."

"I'll fight Johnny Ringo if he removes the curse from Bat Masterson."

The brave smiled. "Johnny Ringo is coming to Tombstone to kill you. Goyathlay thinks you will defend yourself whether he lifts the curse or not."

"Tell him I just might leave town instead," said Holliday, but he was talking to empty air. He whirled around, and saw a cat scurrying into the small space between buildings.

He continued walked to the Rose Tree, where he decided he wasn't so much hungry as thirsty, and bought a bottle of whiskey. He nursed it for a few hours, then wandered over to the jail. Morgan Earp was sitting at the desk in the office.

"Hi, Doc," said Morgan. "I hear you met one of our leading horse thieves today."

"I'm still trembling in my boots," said Holliday with a sardonic smile.

"You face him, you're in no danger," continued Morgan. "Just don't turn your back on him."

"I gather I'm more likely to face his surrogate."

"Surrogate?" repeated Morgan.

"Johnny Ringo."

"I thought Wyatt checked and found out that he's dead."

"He is," said Holliday. A grim smile. "You have to admit it makes him a lot harder to kill."

"Maybe Tom can come up with some way."

"Maybe," said Holliday without much conviction. "Where's Wyatt?"

"He's keeping an eye on the Oriental, in case Ike brings some of his men into town. They know we own it, so that figures to be the place they'll try to do the most damage."

Virgil and Masterson arrived a few minutes later, followed by Edison and Buntline. They walked past a cell with a boarded-up outer wall, the one Masterson had broken out of the previous night.

"It'll be a few days before we can get the all-brass jail cell completed," announced Buntline. "So in the meantime you'll have to stay here, Bat."

"This is ridiculous," said Masterson. "I'll break out the same way I did last night."

"Do you remember doing it?" asked Edison.

"Kind of. Like it was a dream, or maybe a nightmare."

"Well, until we build an escape-proof cell, we have some stopgap solutions," said Buntline.

"What are they?" asked Morgan. "And whatever they are, you'd better hurry. The sun will set in another seven or eight minutes."

Buntline pulled a pair of brass handcuffs out of his coat pocket. "Let's put these on you," he said to Masterson. "I guarantee you can't break out of them. If nothing else, it'll stop you from flying off."

Masterson held his hands out, and Buntline locked the cuffs on him.

"Now we'd better put you in a cell," announced Morgan, leading him to a cell at the far end of the cell block.

"You know," said Holliday, "if he pounds the wall down anyway, all this means is he can't fly away, so if he gets hungry—"

"You know," said Buntline, "I should have thought to bring a brass chain, so I could chain the handcuffs to the door."

"Is there time to get it?" asked Virgil.

"I don't know," said Buntline, running to the door. "I'll try."

Edison pulled a small gadget out of his pocket.

"What's that?" asked Morgan.

"Something I cobbled together this afternoon," answered Edison. "I don't know how effective it will be." He paused. "Hopefully we won't have to find out."

Buntline returned a few minutes later with a brass chain, some thirty inches long with a lock at each end.

"Better hurry," said Morgan. "You've got less than a minute."

Buntline went to Masterson's cell and attached one end of the chain to the handcuffs. He was in the process of locking the other end to the brass cell door when the transformation began. Masterson reached out a hand, which was a claw by the time it grabbed Buntline's wrist. The creature he had become uttered an angry shriek and pulled Buntline's arm into the cell. Buntline pulled back, but it was no contest.

Holliday, certain that Buntline's arm would be torn loose from its socket in another few seconds, pulled his pistol and aimed it at the arm/wing that was doing the pulling.

"No!" said Edison, shouldering his way in front of Holliday. He held his device up until it was on a level with the bat's snarling face, and suddenly there was a flash of incredibly bright light. The gigantic bat screamed in pain, released his grip on Buntline's hand, and stumbled blindly back from the door.

"I knew he couldn't handle that kind of light," said Edison as Masterson kept blinking his eyes, trying to focus them. "I created it to briefly illuminate objects in the dark so I could photograph them."

"Now what?" said Virgil, watching Masterson blinking his eyes furiously.

"Unless I miss my guess," said Edison, "now you lose another section of your wall, and hope if he's hungry he prefers cattle to people."

"Won't make any difference," said Holliday as Masterson began pounding down the stone wall as he had done the previous night.

"Why not?" asked Morgan.

"He can't fly out to the ranches," said Holliday. "The handcuffs are still on him."

"Shit!" said Virgil as Masterson tensed and the handcuffs broke apart. "Just how the hell strong *is* he?"

Masterson began pounding on the wall, which collapsed in less than a minute. Then he was gone, soaring ever higher, the moonlight glinting off the handcuffs that were attached to each claw but no longer joined.

"I could use a drink," said Virgil, wiping the sweat from his face.

"I think we could all use one," said Buntline. "I'm buying."

"Thank goodness the Clantons have nothing to match *that*!" said Morgan fervently.

"I wouldn't be too sure of that," said Holliday.

# 15.

KATE ELDER WAS STILL SNORING PEACEFULLY when Holliday awoke just after noon. He dressed quickly and quietly, and tiptoed out of the room. He'd planned to have one of the metal whores fix him breakfast, but for a change they were all with customers despite the early hour, and so he walked out onto the street.

He had heard good things about the bar at the American Hotel just past Fremont Street, and decided to pay it a visit and have a liquid breakfast. It took him a few minutes to get there—he had to stop twice to catch his breath—and he made a mental note to ask Masterson if he had a spare cane, always assuming Masterson had remained in town (or returned to it) and reverted to his human form.

He finally reached the hotel, walked in the front door, saw the bar off to his left, and entered it. It was too early for the girls, who did triple duty as entertainers, whores, and waitresses, to be on call, and the solitary bartender took his order, waited for him to choose a table and sit down at it, and then brought him a bottle and a glass.

"Make that two glasses," said a voice from the doorway.

The bartender practically fell over himself rushing to the bar to get another glass, and Holliday turned to see what had galvanized him into action. One glance was all it took.

Approaching his table was a man of normal height, and that was the only normal thing about him. One ear was attached by a few strips of decaying flesh. His gray eyes were dull and lackluster. A white bone peeked through the flesh of his face. His right hand wore a lightweight glove, the kind favored by so many gunfighters who were always afraid that some sweat on their palms might hinder their ability to draw and shoot with speed. His left hand was missing the index finger; the other three fingers and the thumb were all bone, totally devoid of flesh.

He wore what had once been an expensive shirt and coat, but both had been punctured by a dozen or more bullets. He wore a gun and holster, a pair of pants that looked as old and moldy as the rest of his clothes, and boots that were so mud-caked that his spurs made absolutely no noise as he walked.

As bad as he looked, he smelled worse. He was aware that the bartender was gaping at him, and he flashed him a smile that exposed a mouth full of rotted, discolored teeth.

"Johnny Ringo, I presume?" said Holliday.

The thing that used to be Johnny Ringo nodded. "I've been following you since Toughnut Street," he said. "I'm glad you weren't out for a constitutional. I don't like the sunlight much."

"We have that in common," said Holliday as Ringo sat down opposite him.

"We have a lot more than that in common, Doc Holliday," said Ringo.

"We both read the classics," replied Holliday. "I'd wager we're the only two men within three hundred miles who can make that claim."

"We both kill people."

"That, too," acknowledged Holliday.

"I always knew we'd meet someday," said Ringo.

"I thought so, too," said Holliday. "Until I heard you were killed back in Waco."

"Do I look dead?"

"Absolutely."

Ringo threw back his head and laughed. "Death isn't necessarily a permanent condition these days."

"It's certainly not a sweet-smelling one," said Holliday, wrinkling his nose.

"Now you're going out of your way to offend me," said Ringo.

"*Can* one offend a corpse?"

"You don't want to get me mad, Doc," said Ringo. "If you do, we'll hit leather and it doesn't make any difference who shoots first, because you can't kill a dead man."

"I believe the term is 'zombie,'" said Holliday.

"Whatever." Ringo poured himself a drink. "I've missed this stuff."

"I'm surprised you can taste it," observed Holliday.

"I can't, but I can smell it."

"If your innards aren't working and you're not digesting, it's hard to see how this stuff can get into your bloodstream—if you have one—so it can't be very satisfying."

"Spoken like a man called 'Doc,'" said Ringo, draining his glass and pouring himself another.

Holliday took the bottle back and filled his own glass. "Mind if I ask you a few questions?"

Ringo shrugged. "Why not?"

"Is you name really Ringo?"

"Why do you think it isn't?"

"I heard that it's John Ringgold or Rhinegold, but no one out here could spell it, and you shortened it."

Ringo smiled, exposing his rotting teeth again. "Not so. It's John Ringo on my college diploma. I've got it in my saddlebag if you want to see it."

"You travel with your diploma?" asked Holliday, arching an eyebrow.

"I travel with everything I own."

"Have you met your boss yet?"

"Hook Nose?" said Ringo. "I've never met him . . . but I'm told I *owe* him."

"I meant Ike Clanton."

"Yeah. A real son of a bitch. He'd sooner stab you in the back than look at you."

"That sounds like Ike, all right."

"The others aren't much better," said Ringo. He paused thoughtfully. "The others aren't *any* better," he amended.

"You might consider coming to work for the Earps," suggested Holliday.

"The Clantons are the ones who sent for me."

"You're already dead," noted Holliday. "I don't imagine anyone can make you do something you don't want to do."

"They can bitch to Hook Nose, and he can put me back in the grave."

"Too bad. We could have used you on our side."

Ringo shook his head. "It was never going to happen."

"Never say never."

"You think I give a damn about the Clantons *or* the Earps *or* this Edison? They don't mean shit to me." He paused and stared intently at Holliday with his cold, dead eyes. "But *you* do."

Holliday looked at him questioningly, but made no comment.

"You and I are the two best. It didn't matter when we met, whether I was dead or alive. I relish the highest level of competition, and that means you. Whatever side you were on, I'd be on the other side. If you go to work as the Clantons' enforcer tomorrow, I'll take the same job for the Earps. Twenty years ago, if you'd fought for the Union, I'd have fought for the Confederacy, and vice versa. It was written in the Book of Fate that one day you and I would meet on the field of honor." He raised his glass, almost in a toast. "But in the meantime, we are the two best at our trade, and there is no reason why we shouldn't enjoy each other's company."

"I don't know what your trade is," said Holliday, "but I'm a dentist."

"You're a killer, just like me."

"Take a good look in a mirror and then tell me that again," said Holliday.

"There are only two things that count," said Ringo. He tapped his temple. "This." He flexed his gloved hand. "And this."

"Well, if we're going to visit before we get around to shooting each other, suppose you tell me why you became a shootist in the first place."

"Money," answered Ringo. "My family didn't have any, and I went broke paying for my schooling. So when I found out just how good I was with *this*"—he drew his gun and even Holliday was impressed at the speed with which he did it—"I started making my living with it. How about you?"

"Hard to be a dentist when you keep coughing up blood while you're examining your patients," replied Holliday. "So I became a gambler."

"And a shootist."

"Never for money," answered Holliday.

"Well, I'm not ashamed of being a gunslinger," said Ringo.

"I'm not ashamed," said Holliday. "It just that there's no future in it. Look at the Earps, Bat Masterson, the Clantons, and me. We'll be lucky if any of us lives to thirty-five. You sure as hell didn't."

"But I'm still here."

"Only because Hook Nose made a deal with the Clantons. And when that deal's done, what do you think's going to happen to you?"

"Nothing," said Ringo. "As you said, I'm already dead, so what can he do?"

"He can put you back in the ground."

Ringo smiled a ghastly smile and shook his head. "He'll never run out of jobs for me. Maybe after I kill you he'll bring you back and we'll become a team after all."

"Are you here to kill me or to kill Edison—or just to ride shotgun for the Clantons?"

"I'm here to kill whoever they want me to kill. But even if they don't name you, you'll be my reward to myself."

"I'm flattered."

"You should be," said Ringo. "There's no one else I'd go after just for pride, except maybe John Wesley Hardin, and he's in jail. Last I heard, he was studying to be a lawyer." Another smile. "So maybe there'll be a third shootist with a degree. But no one else interests me. I keep hearing about this kid—"

"Billy the Kid?"

"That's the one. But he's still a teenager, so how the hell many men can he have killed?"

"If you want to ride off to find him and ask him, I'll keep your seat warm," said Holliday.

Ringo laughed. "I *knew* I'd like you, Doc Holliday."

"I always thought you'd be interesting to talk to," acknowledged Holliday. "So why don't we stop threatening each other, and just talk?"

"That suits me fine," said Ringo.

The two most formidable shootists in the West, one alive and one dead, poured themselves another drink and fell to discussing the works of Socrates and Aristotle.

# 16.

I T WAS JUST AFTER MIDNIGHT, and Kate Elder's whorehouse was doing its usual brisk business.

Ned Buntline entered the building, and one of the human whores approached him.

"I never thought I'd see you here as a customer," she said.

"You were right," answered Buntline. "Kate sent for me." He looked around. "I don't see Doc."

"He'll be playing poker or faro over at the Oriental for another few hours. I'll tell Kate you're here."

The girl left, and Buntline walked over to the small bar in the parlor.

"Biggest damned bat I ever saw!" one of the patrons was saying. He downed a drink. "At first I thought I was hallucinating, but Luke saw it too."

"Sure did," said the man named Luke. "Had to be six feet from nose to tail."

"Maybe you two better cut down on the booze," said the girl who was tending the bar.

"Oh, they saw it, all right," said Buntline.

All three turned to him.

"I've seen it too," he added.

"What the hell *is* it?" asked Luke.

"Just what it looks like," replied Buntline. "An enormous bat."

"What does something that big eat?" asked the first man.

There was no answer, and Buntline decided not to enlighten them. *Get enough people knowing that he drinks blood, and pretty soon it'll be human blood, and then they'll start shooting at the poor bastard.*

"Mr. Buntline, she'll see you now," said the whore who had escorted him inside.

"Thank you," said Buntline. "Is she in her office?"

"Yes."

"I know the way," he said, and walked down the hallway. A moment later he opened a door and found himself facing Kate Elder, who was sitting at her desk. Off to her left stood one of the robotic whores.

"We have a problem," said Kate.

"Oh?"

She nodded. "See this metal whore?" Buntline nodded. "You made her too passionate."

"She doesn't have any emotions at all," he replied, "just programmed responses."

"Twice today she's wrapped her legs around a customer so tightly that he couldn't move, could barely breathe—and both times, after he called out for help and we got there, it took three of us just to straighten out her legs and free him."

Buntline frowned. "It must be the relay from the hips."

"It's not her hips," Kate insisted. "It's her legs."

Buntline shook his head. "You don't understand how it works." He looked at the top of her desk. "Can you move these papers and the inkwell?"

She cleared the top of her desk.

"What are you calling this model?"

"Lola," said Kate.

"Lola, lay down on the desk," ordered Buntline.

The robot walked over to the desk and gracefully lay down on it.

Buntline opened a desk drawer, couldn't find what he was looking for, opened another, and withdrew a quill pen.

"Now watch," he said, brushing the pen against the robot's artificial genitals.

"Oh, Baby, you're better than all the others!" crooned the robot. She wrapped her arms and legs around her nonexistent partner.

"You see?" said Buntline. "It starts at the genitals, gets relayed to the hips, and then to the legs. The cost of making every inch of her this sensitive would have been prohibitive. The second she feels something down there, if she's lying on her back as she is now, her programmed response is to wrap her arms and legs around her partner."

He reached a hand between her locked legs and pushed up. Nothing happened.

"There's the problem," continued Buntline. "Any degree of pressure against her legs should cause them to open and extend."

"Okay, you've pinpointed the problem. Can you fix it tonight?"

He shook his head. "I'll have to take her back to my lab and run some tests."

"How long will this take?" asked Kate.

Buntline shrugged. "A few hours at most. I'll get to work on her first thing in the morning." He turned to the robot. "You can get up now, Lola."

"You're the best," crooned the robot. "Do you want to do it again?"

"Not right now," said Buntline. "I'm exhausted."

"Remember to ask for me next time you come by," said the robot.

"I certainly will, Lola. Now go stand by the window until I give you another command."

The robot got off the table, walked to the window, turned to face Buntline and Kate, and froze.

"Do you know how many marriages this invention is going to save?" said Buntline proudly.

"Almost as many as it destroys," replied Kate.

Buntline was about to answer her when they heard a commotion from the parlor. It got louder and more heated, and finally Kate left her office and went to see what was happening.

When she reached the parlor, she found two of her girls—human girls—backed into a corner, and facing them was the thing that used to be Johnny Ringo.

"What's going on here?" she demanded.

"You're open for business," said Ringo, offering her a smile that exposed his rotted, discolored teeth. "Here I am, and I have money to spend."

"Look at him, Kate!" said one of the whores. "He's *dead*!"

"He's not touching *me*!" vowed another.

"It seems to me that there's an easy enough solution," said Kate. "Josie! Get over here!"

A metal whore entered the parlor from an adjacent room.

"*She* won't mind fucking a corpse," announced Elder.

"But *I* mind," replied Ringo. "I have money, and I want service."

"It's my whorehouse," Kate shot back. "You can go with the one I choose, or you can go down the street to some other whorehouse."

"Do you know who I am?" demanded Ringo.

"Yes," said Kate. "You're the man who's about to leave this establishment. We don't want you or your money."

"What you want doesn't interest me," said Ringo.

"I don't even know why you're here," said Kate. "If you're dead you can't get it up anyway."

"There's ways, and then there's ways," said Ringo.

"I'll quit before I let him touch me!" yelled one of the human whores.

*Where the hell is Doc when I need him?* thought Kate. Aloud she said, "You'd better leave now, or I'll send for the marshal."

"Wyatt Earp?" said Ringo with a grin. "That's thoughtful of you, but he's not my type."

"Damn it, I always have to do everything myself!" snapped Kate angrily. She walked over to the bar, leaned down behind it, and pulled out a double-barreled shotgun, which she trained on Ringo.

He laughed, unbuttoned his shirt, and displayed all his bullet holes. "Not only can't you kill me, I don't even feel pain anymore."

"Then you certainly don't feel pleasure either," she said. "I suggest you get out of here while you still have the chance."

He pointed to the shotgun. "Do you really think that's going to stop me?"

"Absolutely," said Kate, lowering the barrel and aiming at his legs. "Maybe I can't kill a man who's already dead, but I can blow his legs off. Think about it, Johnny Ringo: do you really want to spend the rest of eternity being pulled around on a cart?"

Ringo glared at her, a hideous and frightening glare, for a long minute. Finally he turned and walked to the door, where he stopped and turned back to face her.

"You'll be sorry, Kate Elder," he promised, and walked out into the night.

"Too bad he doesn't like metal bedmates," remarked Buntline, who had joined Kate near the bar. "We could have given him Lola and solved all our problems."

# 17.

OLLIDAY KNOCKED ON BUNTLINE'S DOOR. He half expected a robot to answer it, but instead the door bade him "Good morning" and swung inward. He walked through the foyer and turned left into Buntline's combination office and laboratory.

A female robot was laid out on a workbench, and Buntline was making small adjustments with a set of specially made tools.

"Hello, Doc," he said. "Be with you in a minute."

"Take your time," said Holliday.

"I've been working on Lola here for the past hour, and she's still not responding correctly . . . which is to say, she's overresponding."

He touched the genital area with an instrument, and Lola's arms and legs instantly wrapped around a nonexistent partner.

"Oh, Baby, you're the best I've ever had!" she crooned.

"What's the matter with *that*?" asked Holliday curiously.

"Come over here," said Buntline.

Holliday approached the table.

"Okay, you've paid your money and had your way with her. Now you want to get out of bed and climb into your pants."

"Seems reasonable."

"But her legs are wrapped around you. See if you can get them off."

Holliday grasped one leg with both of his arms and pulled. There was no response.

"Oh, Baby, I could do it all over again!" moaned Lola.

"You see?" said Buntline. "If that was you or Wyatt in her arms, she could hold you motionless for an hour, or even a day, while Ike Clanton or Johnny Ringo approached you openly, pulled a gun, and shot you in the back as many times as they wanted."

"It's enough to make you give up sex," said Holliday sardonically. "Well, sex with metal women, anyway."

"It's goddamned frustrating," said Buntline. "All my life I could never get a response like that from a woman. Now I create one that responds like that every time, and I've been ordered to tone it down." He chuckled. "I can't win."

"We all have our crosses to bear."

"By the way," said Buntline, "you weren't surprised when I mentioned Ringo."

"I met him yesterday."

"Your ladyfriend held him off last night," said Buntline. "I was there."

"My ladyfriend's got more courage than brains," said Holliday.

"He's quite something, this Ringo. Dead as a doornail, but animated. Smells like he's been out in the sun for a few days. Starting to grow mold and mildew. But somehow or other, he walks, he talks—"

"And he kills," interjected Holliday.

"I assume so," said Buntline. He turned to the robot. "Lola, he's done now. You've drained him dry. You can uncross your legs."

The robot did as ordered.

"Now get up and stand by the window until I give you another command."

The robot got up and took a step toward the window. Then its glistening prismatic eyes fell on Holliday.

"Hi, there, Big Boy," it whispered. "Got time for a quick one?"

"Some other time," he replied.

The robot continued walking to the window, stopped just short of it, and remained motionless.

"I assume you didn't come to talk about a metal whore," said Buntline.

"No,"

"Ringo, then?"

Holliday nodded. "Like I said, I met him yesterday."

"And you've figured out that since he's already dead you can't kill him with any weapon you own or know about."

"That's right."

"I'll have to talk to Tom about it, to see what we can devise."

"You'd better do it soon," said Holliday. "There's only one reason Ringo was brought back to life, or what passes for life in his case, and that's to kill Edison and probably you as well."

"I wish I knew why. Everything we've done has been to *help* people, not hinder them. They should be building monuments to Tom, not trying to assassinate him."

"Not everyone wants to live in the future," replied Holliday. "Today it's medicine men and horse thieves who want to kill him. Next week it could be blacksmiths and the ships that hunt whales for the oil to light the lamps of Boston. And next month it could be all the whores who are going to starve because your metal whores are cheaper and work longer hours."

Buntline sighed. "When you put it that way—"

"As a matter of fact, I'm surprised Ringo didn't kill you last night when he had the chance."

"He didn't know I was there. I was in Kate's office when the incident started."

"It won't take him long to find out where you live," said Holliday.

"It won't do him much good," answered Buntline. "Tom's got these two houses totally protected. If Geronimo and Hook Nose can't break through and kill us, neither can Ringo."

"The hell you're protected," said Holliday. "I knocked on the door and it practically begged me to enter and make myself comfortable."

"And if you were anyone but yourself, or one of the Earps, or Bat Masterson, you'd have found it easier to enter a heavily armed fortress. Oh, I left out Johnny Behan—"

"He's not on our side, Ned."

"No, but he's the sheriff. The door won't open for him, but a lot of terrible things that will happen to other people won't happen to him."

"What if a normal everyday citizen of Tombstone comes by?" asked Holliday. "Maybe some woman looking for a donation to her church?"

"The door . . . no, the house . . . no, the *mechanism* will ask Tom or me what to do about her."

"And what if Ike Clanton's got a sister who pretends to be looking for a donation to her church?"

"Tom's got a device that will let us know if she's carrying a gun or a bomb. Believe me, if we don't want you in, you could set off twenty bombs around the two houses and they wouldn't leave so much as a scratch or a dent."

"You could sell something like that to every bank on the continent," said Holliday.

"That's exactly what your friend Henry Wiggins said," replied Buntline with a smile. "He seems like an honest man. We may give him the chance to show us what kind of results he can obtain. I assume you vouch for him?"

"Vouch for him?" repeated Holliday, frowning. "I just met him on the way into town a week ago. I've only seen him twice since then, once at the Oriental and once sampling the pleasures of one of your metal whores."

"Well, at least you haven't got anything bad to say about him," said Buntline. "Tom and I are stuck here. We need someone to sell our inventions."

"You'll get rich enough just selling oversexed metal ladies. Not only will whorehouses want them, but there's probably a huge secondary market among ugly-looking foul-mannered bachelors."

"I never thought of that," said Buntline.

"Fine. I'll want ten percent for the suggestion."

"Maybe I'll just give you Lola here when I get her fixed."

"Not interested," said Holliday. "If I even look at her after she's fixed, Kate will have *me* fixed." His index and middle finger made a scissors motion.

"She's quite a woman," said Buntline. "I still can't get over the fact that she stood up to Johnny Ringo."

"Not much bothers Kate, except her name."

"Her name?" asked Buntline, frowning.

"Well, her nickname."

"What is it?"

"Big-Nose Kate."

"Damn!" said Buntline. "I heard of a Big-Nose Kate when I was in Dodge. I never put it together with Kate Elder."

"Don't," said Holliday. "You'll live longer that way."

"Now that you've told me, I'll be concentrating so hard on not saying it that I'll probably blurt it out next time I see her."

"Well, at least you've been warned." Holliday paused. "By the way, did they find Bat again this morning?"

"On the roof of Saint Paul's Church over on Safford Street. Stark naked, as usual."

"Some morning he's going to come to rest on a really steep roof, and roll or fall off it when he changes back into a man," remarked Holliday.

"I know," agreed Buntline. "Tom's working on it, but he's spread awfully thin."

"He'd better come up with something soon. One of these days Bat isn't going to leave the city limits, and then he's going to kill a man or a horse. Either way, I don't think he can do it without getting himself shot."

"He's also becoming a nervous wreck," added Buntline. "He can't remember what he does as a bat, but just the knowledge that he *is* a huge, blood-drinking bat every night and can never recall any details is driving him crazy. And I mean that literally. He couldn't even remember those lights Tom flashed in his eyes."

"How soon before you can put him in an escape-proof cell?"

"A few more days, if it *is* escape-proof," replied Buntline. "I've never seen anything with his strength before."

"It'd be nice if we could just point him at Geronimo."

"The medicine man who cursed him is not going to be in any danger from him."

"I was hoping he'd get scared and just change him back."

"From what I hear, Geronimo's not scared of anything."

"Maybe I'll take Bat out to the Clantons' ranch at sunset, then," suggested Holliday.

"He's as likely to nab you or your horse in the neck as one of the Clantons," said Buntline.

"Are you always this optimistic?" asked Holliday.

"Ever since I moved to Tombstone," was Buntline's answer.

# 18.

HOLLIDAY OPENED THE UNLOCKED DOOR and entered the hotel room. It was newly painted, and held a single bed, a nightstand, a small desk, and a chair. There was no closet, but a wooden armoire served just as well.

Masterson was sitting on the edge of his bed, a frayed Navajo blanket wrapped around his shoulders, a cigarette in his mouth and a dozen more stubbed out in an ashtray. There was an open, half-empty bottle of whiskey on his nightstand.

"How are you holding up?" asked Holliday.

"I'm fine," said Masterson.

"Sure you are," said Holliday. "But you're smoking like a chimney, you're drinking the cheapest rotgut available, and you're shivering so bad you have to wrap yourself in a blanket."

"Damn it, Doc!" snapped Masterson. "*You* turn into some nightmare creature every sunset, and wake up naked in a new place every morning with no memory of what you did, who or what you might have killed, and then tell me about it!"

"Calm down," said Holliday. "I'm not the enemy."

"You're *all* the enemy!" snapped Masterson. "You're a man morning, noon, and night, and I'm only a part-time man." He stubbed out the cigarette, then instantly rolled and lit another. "I'm no use to myself or Wyatt or anyone else. The only reason I don't leave town is that I know one of you will find me every morning and bring me back here. Who the hell knows what a new town will make of a naked stranger cropping up in a new location every morning? If my brain worked at night, I'd kill Geronimo and then myself, but I don't know what I do when I'm a bat, and I can't remember anything in the morning."

"We can piece it together," said Holliday. "There's usually a dead horse or cow with its throat torn out every morning, so we know where you've been."

"How am I ever going to pay for that?"

Holliday smiled. "Only six or seven people know what happens to you at sundown. No one's going to come looking for their money. And besides, John Clum has said if anyone does demand restitution, he'll pay for it."

"Who's John Clum?"

"The editor of the *Epitaph*," answered Holliday. "In case you haven't noticed, this town is split right down the middle. Half of them favor the Earps, and half favor Johnny Behan and the Cowboys."

"Cowboys?" said Masterson, frowning. "There's hundreds of cowboys."

"But these are spelled with a capital C. It's the gang that Curly Bill Brocius and Ike Clanton run, which means it's the gang you and I were imported to fight."

"I thought we were here to protect Tom Edison and Ned Buntline."

"We are," replied Holliday. "But in the end, that means we'll wind up fighting the Cowboys. We already know Brocius is the one who blew away Edison's arm." He took a sip from the bottle and made a face. "And now Johnny Ringo has joined them."

"I thought he was killed down in Waco," said Masterson.

"He was."

Masterson frowned. "Then what . . . ?"

Holliday smiled. "You're not the only one walking around under a spell."

"He's a . . . what's the word? . . . A zombie?"

Holliday nodded.

"Geronimo again?"

"No, Hook Nose." Holliday explained the deal the Cheyenne medicine man had made with the Clantons. "When Brocius didn't kill Edison, I guess Hook Nose figured he needed someone a little deadlier."

"You've actually seen him?" asked Masterson, so interested now that he forgot about his cigarette and let the blanket slide off his shoulders.

"I had a few drinks with him the other night."

"Why didn't you kill him?"

"He's already dead," said Holliday. "Besides, I *like* him."

Masterson blinked his eyes very rapidly. "You like a zombie?"

"Within reason. Sooner or later one of us will have to kill the other, but in the meantime, we had a very interesting discussion about literature and philosophy."

"How can you kill him?" asked Masterson. "Like you said, he's already dead."

"I've got Tom and Ned putting their heads together on that very problem," said Holliday. Suddenly he grinned. "Kate nearly solved it for us."

"Kate Elder?"

"That's the only Kate I know."

"What happened?"

"I gather that Ringo paid her place a visit while I was playing faro at the Oriental. There was some argument or disagreement, and then Kate pulled out a shotgun. Didn't threaten to kill him; she knew better than that. But she threatened to blow his legs away, and he backed off . . . which implies that parts of him *can* be blown away." Holliday smiled again. "I don't think a headless Johnny Ringo will present much of a problem." The smile vanished. "Of course, then I won't have anyone to discuss the classics with, but still—"

"I wish you could aim me at him when I'm busy being a bat," said Masterson.

"I've been there for the change," said Holliday. "You're not real responsive."

The muscles in Masterson's face began twitching, and he clenched and unclenched his hands. "Am I going to live the rest of my life like this, Doc?"

Holliday stared at Masterson for a long minute. "I truly don't know," he said at last. Suddenly he got to his feet. "Come on."

"Come on *where*?" said Masterson.

"Out. You'll drive yourself crazy just sitting here all day and then showing up at the jail or wherever Buntline wants to confine you. Let's grab some breakfast."

"It's early afternoon," noted Masterson.

"What better time for it?" said Holliday. "I'm buying."

"Might as well," said Masterson, standing up and walking to the door. "Thanks for coming by, Doc. I was going a little stir-crazy in here."

"Happy to do it," said Holliday. "Maybe after breakfast I'll take you over to Kate's place. It's got to have been a long time for you."

Masterson shook his head vigorously. "I can't, Doc."

"Why the hell not?"

"What if I changed while we were doing it?"

Holliday looked amused. "They got some unique ladies there who won't bat an eye."

"Bullshit."

"I'm not kidding."

"They really won't care if they start fucking a man and end up fucking a bat?"

"Trust me on this," said Holliday.

# 19.

I T WAS JUST AFTER TEN O'CLOCK AT NIGHT, and Kate Elder was annoyed. Word had gone out that the thing that used to be Johnny Ringo had been there and Kate had run him off, and almost no one believed that he wouldn't be back. As a result, her business was off almost seventy percent tonight.

She was also annoyed that Holliday didn't bear any animosity toward Ringo, despite the fact that he was certain that sooner or later Ringo would try to kill him.

Finally, she was annoyed that Holliday had yet to join her—or take her out—for dinner. She knew he didn't usually start gambling until nine o'clock, but he was always at the jail during dinnertime, and he never confided in her.

Henry Wiggins entered the house while Kate was resupplying the bar, bringing in some bottles from the back room.

"Hi, Henry," she said without much enthusiasm. "How's it going?"

"Can't complain," he said. Then: "Doc won't let me." He laughed at his own joke.

"Hilarious," said Kate without cracking a smile.

"I stopped at the Oriental a few minutes ago. He's on a hot streak."

"Good," said Kate. "He can start paying for his room and board."

Wiggins chuckled.

"What's so funny?" asked Kate.

"He told me you'd say that."

"He's just a bundle of laughs, that Doc," she said grimly. "Can I sell you a drink?"

"Yeah, I suppose so," said Wiggins. "I was looking for Lola, but I guess she's with a customer."

"She's with Ned Buntline," replied Kate.

"That's surprising," said Wiggins. "You'd figure Ned would build and keep a metal lady at his house, rather than pay to use one he made for you."

Kate shook her head. "You misunderstand. She's in Ned's laboratory being fixed."

"Ah," said Wiggins. "Any chance she'll be back tonight?"

"No."

"Well, maybe I'll just have my drink and wander on back to the Oriental."

"Henry, I have four other metal whores. What's so special about Lola?"

"She *cares*," he replied.

"Lola is a machine," said Kate. "She *can't* care."

"But she does," Wiggins persisted doggedly.

"Rubbish."

"She *does*. She never wants it to end, never wants to let me go. None of the other metal whores act like that."

Kate sighed. "That's why she's being repaired and they're still here."

"*Repaired?*" said Wiggins. "You mean she won't be like *that* any longer?"

"I sure as hell hope not," replied Kate.

"You're making a huge mistake," continued Wiggins. "She was special."

"She was dangerous," said Kate. "What if she hadn't let you go for an hour rather than five minutes? Or three hours?"

"I'd have been flattered."

"You'd have been uncomfortable and panic-stricken."

"You just don't understand," said Wiggins bitterly.

"Tell you what," said Kate. "If Ned can't fix her, I'll sell her to you at cost."

"Deal!" cried Wiggins. Then his face fell. "Oh, wait. I can't."

"She's not that expensive."

"It's not that," said Wiggins miserably. "My wife would never understand."

Kate shrugged. "We specialize in serving men whose wives don't understand."

"And I couldn't take her traveling from town to town with me," he continued. "Sooner or later someone would take her away from me. I'm no gunslinger, and just about anyone can beat me in a fistfight."

"Then I guess you're doomed to keep patronizing my place," said Kate.

One of the half-girl half-machines walked by, the light reflecting off her brass arms, and Wiggins turned to study her with open admiration.

"I suppose there are worse things," he said as a robot whore returned from an assignation and seated herself upon a plush divan.

Suddenly the front door opened and three men entered. Their clothes were covered with dust, as if they'd been riding out in the desert, and each wore a holster with a Colt .45 in it.

"Good evening, gentlemen," said Kate. "It's against the law to go armed in Tombstone, so I'll have to ask you to check your guns with me. I'll put them in my office until you're ready to leave."

"You're Big-Nose Kate, ain't you?" said one of the men.

"Yes I am," she replied as the smile vanished from her face, "and the price for you just doubled."

"We're more than a little bit mad at you, Kate," said a second man.

"What are you talking about?" demanded Kate. "I've never even seen you before."

"Yeah, but you've seen our friend."

"What friend?"

"Johnny Ringo," said the third man. "We all work for Ike Clanton, and Ike doesn't like the way you treated Johnny."

"Tough shit for Ike," said Kate. "Johnny Ringo made threats and wouldn't behave himself."

"Maybe we'll make some threats ourselves," said the first man, pulling his gun.

"And if you call for the lunger, so much the better," said the second. "We're going to have to face him sooner or later."

"This has all been a misunderstanding," said Kate nervously. "We can iron out any problems."

"Suddenly she's the voice of reason," said the third man.

"I'll tell you what," said Kate. "Each of you can have a free one, compliments of the house. We'll talk later."

"This won't get you off the hook," said the third man.

"It'll put us all in a better bargaining mood," said Kate. "Have any of you ever been with a metal whore?"

They all indicated that they hadn't.

"Then let me introduce you," said Kate. "Mimi! Doris! Belle! Come over and say hello to these gentlemen."

The metal whore who'd been sitting on the divan got up and approached them, and two other shapely robots entered the room.

"Ladies," said Kate, "these gentlemen will be your partners for the evening. I want you to do everything they ask, no matter how bizarre. Do you understand?"

All three robots signaled their agreement.

"I don't know," said one of the men. "I like my women soft."

"I can be soft for you," crooned the robot named Mimi.

"You'll really do *everything* I ask?" said another of the men.

"Everything," said Doris.

"And some things you never thought of asking," added Belle.

"Now why don't you give each of them a hug before you go off to your rooms," said Kate.

Each robot put her arms around one of the men.

"You don't have to be so gentle," said Kate. "These men are *tough*."

The whores hugged them more tightly.

"Tighter!" cried Kate. "And don't let go! That's an order!"

The men began cursing and trying to break free, but the robots held them as easily as if they were rag dolls.

Kate walked behind the bar, reached down, and came away with a small pistol in her hand. She walked over to where the robots were holding the men and put a bullet into each man's head.

"Nobody threatens me in my own whorehouse!" she snapped. "Henry, you were a witness. They drew their guns and threatened me."

"I'll testify to it."

"And you two?" she said to a fully human whore and one with prosthetic arms and a brass jaw.

They echoed Wiggins.

"The Clantons are not going to be happy about this," said Wiggins.

"Neither am I," complained Kate. "Look at the carpet. Do you know how much scrubbing it will take to get the blood out of it?"

The three robots, under Kate's supervision, carried the dead men out back, left them there for the Earps to collect in the morning, and a few minutes later were on their metal hands and knees, cleaning the bloodstains out of the carpet.

"And that son of a bitch is playing cards and drinking whiskey," muttered Kate, "while a poor, defenseless woman like me has to protect house and home as best she can."

Wiggins was almost surprised that the robots didn't laugh at that.

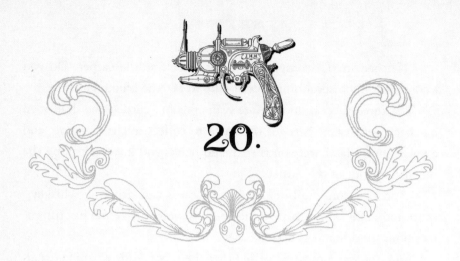

# 20.

OLLIDAY AWOKE TO A HAND grabbing his shoulder and shaking him. It took him a moment to remember where he was, and to realize that the hand belonged to Kate Elder.

"What is it?" he asked groggily.

"Wyatt wants you. He's waiting in the parlor."

"He doesn't want me," mumbled Holliday. "He's here to arrest you for killing those men. The whores told me all about it when I got back from the Oriental."

"That's all over and done with," said Kate. "Wiggins and the girls told him what happened. Now get up."

"What time is it?" asked Holliday, swinging his skinny legs to the floor.

"Not quite seven."

"In the evening? I don't feel that well rested."

"In the morning."

"The morning?" he bellowed. "I only got back here at four o'clock!"

"He's *your* friend," said Kate with a shrug.

Holliday spent the next few minutes muttering to himself and getting dressed. When he was done he made his way to the parlor, where Wyatt Earp was waiting for him.

"Sorry to bother you this early—" began Earp.

"What's up?"

"We can't find Bat. Every morning he's shown up somewhere near the Oriental or his hotel, but today there's no sign of him." Earp paused. "There a chance some rancher took a shot at him while he was feeding off some livestock, or that he just didn't remember where to go before he changed back."

"All right," said Holliday. "I assume you and your brothers have divided the area up."

"Yes. And John Clum has volunteered about half his staff to help."

"Do they know what he's become?"

"No. Only you, my brothers, and Clum."

"And the Apaches," added Holliday. "Well, where do I go?"

"Anywhere but the Clantons'," answered Earp. "They're not thrilled with you *or* Kate."

"Yeah, I heard about that." A self-deprecating smile crossed Holliday's gaunt face. "Now you know why I never win an argument with her. Put *her* in charge of protecting Edison and we can all go on vacation."

Suddenly Morgan Earp burst into the building, breathless from running.

"We found him!" he gasped.

"Where was he this time?" asked Wyatt.

"Jebediah Cray's livery stable. The horses were spooking, so Virg went into that little corral out back, and he found Bat sitting kind of dazed in a corner, stark naked as usual—and a dead horse about twenty feet away."

"Throat torn out?" asked Holliday.

"Yeah." Morgan made a face. "It was a real mess. Both of them are covered with blood—Bat and the horse."

"Take him to his hotel, clean him up, and get him dressed—" began Wyatt.

"Virg is already doing that," said Morgan.

"And then bring him to Edison's. We've got to find some way, if not to stop him from changing, then to know where he is and what he's doing when he's a bat."

"Give me a second to catch my breath," said Morgan.

"Tell you what," said Wyatt, "I'll go get him. Doc, as long as you're up, you go to Edison's and wait for him."

"What about me?" asked Morgan.

"You and Virg and I are going to have to patrol the streets. There's three dead Cowboys out back of this building, waiting for the undertaker to collect them."

Morgan turned to Doc. "You took out three of them by yourself?"

Holliday smiled. "No, I deferred to an even greater killer."

Morgan looked puzzled.

"I'll tell you all about it later," said Holliday. "Right now I've got to get over to Edison's." He took a few steps toward the door. "Damn! A crippled old man like me really needs a cane. I must remember to get one today."

Morgan held the door open for him, and Holliday began walking toward Edison's house. A Bunt Line coach was just arriving in town, with a number of bullets flattened out against its doors but none of the passengers any the worse for wear. Holliday flagged it down and cadged a ride for the final three blocks. It let him off in front of Edison's house, and a moment later he was inside it, sipping from a cup of coffee that Edison gave him and pretending that he liked it.

A few minutes later Wyatt arrived with Masterson.

"I can't stay," he said. "A bunch of Cowboys just rode into town. They're peaceful so far, and the more badges they see, the more likely they are to *stay* peaceful. Doc, stay here with him until Tom's done. Then, depending on the time, get him back to his hotel or to the jail."

"How are you feeling?" asked Edison as Earp left, closing the door behind him.

"Same as always," replied Masterson. "I don't know where I've been or what I've done."

"We know what you did," said Holliday. "There's one fewer horse in Jebediah Cray's stable."

"If you and Wyatt say it, it must be true—but I'll be damned if I can remember it."

"We're still a few days away from having a totally escape-proof facility for you," said Edison, "so we're going to attack the problem in a different way."

"Can you stop me from changing?" asked Masterson, without much hope.

Edison shook his head. "No." Then: "Not yet, anyway."

"Then if you can't confine me and you can't stop me changing, what are you talking about?"

"Keeping an eye on you."

"I don't understand."

"One of these days you're going to wake up out in the desert and die of heatstroke before anyone can find you," said Edison. "Or you might change back in a location where even if you yell at the top of your lungs, we won't hear you." Edison paused. "And there's always a chance that some morning we might find some man or woman with their throat ripped out. You'd be the likeliest suspect, but that doesn't mean someone who knows about your problem—and more will every day—hasn't arranged it to throw the blame on you."

"So what are you going to do?" asked Masterson.

"My job is done," answered Edison. "Now it's up to Ned to see if he can build what I designed."

"*Build?*" repeated Masterson. "You make it sound like I'm going to carry something around with me."

"In a way," said Edison.

"How heavy is it? And how can you *make* me carry it when I'm a bat?"

"It's not much heavier than a silver dollar," answered Edison with a smile. "As for how we make you carry it, that's another problem. We'll see if Ned has any answers."

"Where is he?"

"Working on this project. Would you like some breakfast while you're waiting?"

Masterson frowned. "I feel full."

"You *are* full," said Holliday. "All thanks to one of Cray's horses."

Masterson closed his eyes. "I don't want to know the details."

"Not a problem," replied Holliday with a smile. "I don't *know* the details."

They waited for another ten minutes, and then Ned Buntline joined them with a small device in his hand.

"Hello, Bat," he said. "Good morning, Doc. Early for you, isn't it?"

"Don't ask," said Holliday.

"Were you able to build it?" asked Edison.

"It works in theory," replied Buntline. "We'll have to give it a field test."

"What the hell is it?" asked Masterson.

"It's half of Tom's latest invention," said Buntline.

"Where's the other half?"

"In my pocket." Buntline reached into his pants pocket and withdrew a small bracelet.

"Is that some kind of stone in it?" asked Holliday. "A sapphire, perhaps?"

"Not quite," answered Edison. "It's a tiny battery that's good for maybe fourteen hours."

"And *this*," added Buntline, holding up the metal device, "can locate that battery from as much as two miles away. As long as the battery's working, we can find it."

"How are you going to keep the bracelet on Bat?" asked Holliday. "You've seen the way his clothes fall off him when he changes."

Buntline smiled. "It's not a bracelet, it's a necklace. It locks in the back, and I've seen those claws that pass for hands when he's a bat. If we put it on him while he's a man, he'll never be able to detach it once he's changed."

"You sure it won't choke the life out of me?" asked Masterson, frowning.

"I can't say I've actually measured your neck, but I've seen it close up when you're a bat, and I promise this won't choke you. But I also promise you won't be able to slip it off or open the lock."

"And it's good for two miles, you say?" asked Holliday.

"Two for sure. Possibly as much as three."

"You know he flew something like twenty miles the night Geronimo cursed him," said Holliday.

"I also know that since then, every sighting and every dead animal has been within two miles of the jail," said Buntline.

"If this works," said Edison, "and we'll know by tomorrow morning, there are endless adjustments I can make. I think, given a few days to tinker with it, I can even find a way to give him a mild shock every time he approaches a herd of cattle or horses—always providing I *know* he's approaching them. I'll probably need a map with every ranch and stable indicated on it."

"I don't know that I'm thrilled with being shocked," said Masterson dubiously.

"It would just be a correction, not an execution," explained Edison.

"Even so," said Masterson.

"What else can this thing do?" asked Holliday.

"If I can make enough of them, and make them even smaller, we could try to hide them in the Cowboys' saddlebags when they come to town. That way we'd be able to keep track of them. I'd especially like to put one on Curly Bill Brocius and another on this creature that Johnny Ringo has become."

"Won't work," said Holliday.

"Why should you say that?" asked Edison.

"You said they're only good for fourteen hours. You might sneak them into saddlebags or the like once, but you sure as hell aren't going to manage it twice a day."

"A point well taken," admitted Edison. "I've been concentrating on too damned many things at once this week."

"Well, there's always the flying thing," said Buntline.

"*What* flying thing?" asked Holliday. "You're not talking about Bat, are you?"

"No," said Edison.

"Well, then?"

"I've been experimenting—"

"With flying?"

Edison shook his head. "No. If something the size of a man is going to fly, it's got to be shaped differently, and of course it has to have hollow bones—which Bat has from dusk to dawn."

"Then what are you talking about?" persisted Holliday.

"How can I explain it?" said Edison. "This is going to sound silly, but have you ever blown up a balloon? Or seen one blown up?"

"Didn't have any when I was a kid," said Holliday. "Or at least I never saw one. But my niece used to play with them from time to time."

"What happens when you let the air out?" asked Edison.

"It explodes."

"No, you're talking about puncturing it. What happens if you blow it up and then let go of it?"

Holliday shrugged. "I don't know."

Edison smiled. "For every action there is an equal but opposite reaction. The force of the air rushing out through that little hole at one end of it forces the balloon to fly in the opposite direction."

"But the balloon goes off in crazy directions," added Masterson.

"True," agreed Edison. "But what if you could control the flow of air? Do you see that you could make the balloon fly wherever you wanted it to go?"

"I suppose you could at that," said Holliday.

"The possibilities are endless. You could theoretically patrol the whole town with a fleet of balloons, each hovering above a section of the street, each with a small camera equipped with that flashing light that blinded Bat the other day. But that's in the future, once we figure out how to keep one afloat all night and also how to manipulate the camera from the ground." Edison paused. "But for the current circumstance, consider a big enough balloon, tied to that necklace by an unbreakable brass chain. All we'd have to do is spot the balloon—an easy enough task since Bat's never inside at night—to know where he is at any moment during the night, and to find him in the morning."

"Can you really do that?"

"Not today or tomorrow," admitted Edison. "I still need to know how to keep the balloon afloat for eight or ten hours. I have a feeling that the answer lies with hydrogen or helium. But what Ned has here will prove an effective stopgap."

"You're sure I won't be able to take it off once I change?" asked Masterson.

"Pretty sure," said Edison.

"Positive," chimed in Buntline.

"Seems a shame, though," said Holliday.

"What are you talking about?" asked Buntline.

"A creature such as Bat becomes ought to be just the thing to go up against Johnny Ringo."

"An interesting thought, but Bat doesn't have any weapons once he changes."

"He's got enough to kill a twelve-hundred-pound horse that probably didn't want to die," answered Holliday. He turned to Masterson. "You got any marks on your body, any wounds from all these animals you're killing at night?"

"If I have, no one's told me about it," said Masterson.

"Even Ringo is sporting a set of bullet holes," said Holliday. "Maybe you were meant to take him on."

"Forget it, Doc," said Buntline. "He'd be just as likely to kill you as Ringo—assuming he could kill either one of you."

"I don't want to kill anyone," said Masterson miserably. "I just want to stop turning into this . . . this *thing* every night." He turned to Edison. "You've *got* to cure me."

Edison and Buntline exchanged looks that said, *Cure him? Hell, we can't even communicate with him or control him.*

"I'm working on it," said Edison, without much hope.

## 21.

I T WAS JUST AFTER ELEVEN O'CLOCK AT NIGHT. Masterson had been transformed at sunset, as usual, and this time Edison and Buntline were able to track him . . . until he flew beyond the range of the device, at which point Edison went to bed, determined to wake up just before sunrise and find Masterson as soon as he became a man again.

At the Oriental, something that would never become a man again had entered, ordered a bottle of whiskey, and walked over to the table where Doc Holliday was playing poker.

"I'm sitting in," announced Ringo. The three other card players took one look at him and all left the table.

"I should charge you for that," said Holliday. "They were lousy card players."

"Yeah, but you'd rather talk to me."

"I don't know that I'd rather smell you, though," said Holliday, wrinkling his nose. He stared across the table at Ringo. "How do you manage to talk? I mean, you need to exhale for the sound to come out, and dead men don't breathe."

"Beats me," said Ringo with a shrug. "I open my mouth and out come the words."

"And I'm still trying to figure out how you metabolize whiskey when you don't have any metabolism at all."

"Magic."

"Hook Nose knows his stuff," acknowledged Holliday. "I don't know if Geronimo could have done that."

"I heard he did a job on Masterson."

"Half a job," said Holliday, shuffling the cards.

"I used to be pretty good at poker," said Ringo. "I think."

"Got a memory problem?" asked Holliday curiously.

"It's selective," said Ringo, frowning. "Some things I remember clear as day." He paused, staring off into space. "I remember every detail about the day I was killed."

"How did it happen?"

"I'd just come out of a bar in Waco, and I was looking for a fight. I get pretty mean when I'm drunk. And I saw Malcolm Adams walking down the street and called him out. So we face off in the middle of the street, and while I'm waiting for him to go for his gun, half a dozen men fill me with lead from behind. The shots spin me around, and I catch another ten shots in the chest and belly. Never even got my gun out of its holster 'til I was nine-tenths dead." He paused, reliving the moment. "Gonna happen to you too, Doc, and to your pal Wyatt. Sooner or later it happens to all of us, one way or another." Suddenly he grinned, exposing his rotted, discolored teeth. "Only difference is, it didn't stop me."

"Well, if a bullet doesn't nail me pretty soon, the consumption will," replied Holliday. "That's probably why I'm still alive."

"I don't follow you," said Ringo.

"I don't care if I live or die—so I never hesitate, never flinch, never worry about losing. Having one foot in the grave—or one lung, as the case may be—is what's kept me alive."

"Until you go up against me," said Ringo. "I don't even care if you get the first five shots in."

"Oh, you'll care, all right," said Holliday.

"What makes you think so?"

"Because I won't go for your heart or your head. After all, you're already dead, so what harm can that do?"

"What *will* you go for?" asked Ringo.

"Your eyes."

"Couldn't let you do that, Doc. I'm halfway through Pericles on the Peloponnesian War in the original Greek."

Holliday smiled. "Want me to tell you who won?"

"It's been my understanding of history that God always favors the side with the best weapons."

Virgil Earp entered the saloon at that moment. He looked around, spotted Holliday and Ringo, and walked over.

"I heard you were back," he said to Ringo.

"Ah, but back from where? That is the question," said Holliday.

"Nope," said Virgil. "My question is: back for *what*? Why are you here, Ringo?"

"I'm here to drink and discuss literature with my dentist," answered Ringo. "There's no law against that."

"No," said Virgil. "But starting tomorrow, there'll be a law against dead men entering the Oriental."

"What are you gonna do," laughed Ringo. "Hang me?"

"It's possible."

"You can't kill me."

"No, but think about how you'd like hanging by your neck, with your hands tied behind your back, for the next twenty years."

Virgil walked off to the back room before Ringo could answer.

"I don't like *any* of those fucking Earps!" muttered Ringo. "I think I'm going to have to kill them, just as soon as I finish the job I came here to do."

"I can't let you do that," said Holliday.

"Which—kill Edison or kill the Earps?"

"Either."

"You really think you could take my eyes out from, say, thirty feet away?"

"There's only one way to find out," said Holliday.

"Can you even lift that fancy-dancy gun you're wearing?" asked Ringo. "You look like a strong wind could blow you away."

"A strong wind might," acknowledged Holliday. "But a dead gunslinger won't."

"Our day will come," promised Ringo. "But in the meantime, what did you think of *De re publica*?"

"By Cicero?"

"Who else?"

"Doesn't quite measure up to *De Legibus*."

"Now why would you say that?"

They spent the next hour arguing the merit of Cicero's works, and another hour discussing whether Plutarch had done him justice. Finally Holliday got to his feet.

"Where are you going?" said Ringo.

"I got up very early today. It's time I went to bed."

"I never sleep."

"I envy you," said Holliday. "If you never sleep, no one can ever wake you up when you've had half the sleep you need."

Ringo threw back his head and laughed. "I *like* you, John Henry Holliday. It's going to be a real shame to kill you."

"Then don't," said Holliday as he began walking to the door.

"Can't help it," said Ringo. "The grave's cold and narrow and tight, and while I don't remember much about it I know I didn't like it. I was the best damned gunslinger you ever saw when I was alive, and if killing's what I have to do to stay here, then killing it'll be."

Holliday turned as he reached the swinging doors. "You remember what it was like when you were dead and buried?"

"Yeah," said Ringo with a grin. "And trust me, you ain't gonna like it at all."

Holliday walked out into the street just before his body was seized by a coughing fit. He put a white handkerchief to his mouth. When he pulled it away a minute later it was covered with blood.

*Maybe I won't like it*, he thought as another spasm of coughing racked his body, *but how much worse can it be than right here, right now?*

## 22.

ANOTHER DAY AND NIGHT HAD PASSED, and this time, a few minutes after sunrise, Edison and Buntline went unerringly to the
alley behind Sixth Street where they found Masterson, naked and disoriented as usual. They'd brought his clothes with them, and after they helped
him into his pants, shirt, and boots they escorted him back to his hotel.

Holliday had risen early (for him), stopped at Edison's a few minutes before noon to see how the device worked, and suggested they'd
attract less attention by carting Masterson off to Kate Elder's when
they found him each morning. He'd be exhausted, having been flying
all night, and there was, Holliday noted with a smile, no shortage of
beds there.

"I've dealt with the lady," said Buntline. "She's not inclined to give
anything away for free—even a bed."

"Make it part of your fee for keeping her metal whores in working
order," answered Holliday.

"You mean *I* have to tell her we're using one of her rooms?" said
Buntline nervously.

"Don't worry about it," said Holliday.

"Don't worry about it?" repeated Buntline. "She'll kill me!"

"I doubt it—and if she does, you can always keep Johnny Ringo company."

"Damn it, Doc! I saw her run Ringo right out of her house! Nobody else has ever made him back down."

"All right," said Holliday with a sigh. "I'll take care of it."

"No hard feelings," said Buntline. "Care for some lunch?"

"It's too early in the day for lunch—but I'll take a late breakfast."

"Maybe I'll join you," said Edison.

"There's supposed to be a nice restaurant in the American Hotel," suggested Buntline.

"Over on Fremont Street?" said Doc. "They're supposed to make a fine omelet."

"Sounds good to me," said Edison. "I need some coffee. I've been up most the night."

"What are you working on today?" asked Holliday as the three of them began walking toward the hotel.

"Magic."

"You can do magic too?" asked Holliday, surprised.

Edison shook his head. "I'm trying to learn how it's done, so I can counteract it. I've been doing that, on and off, for the better part of a year." He paused. "I have a feeling I'm getting close."

"So does Hook Nose. That's why he had you shot."

"I don't think so," replied Edison. "That was a year ago. I think he was aware of my reputation and just didn't want me looking into the subject."

"What have you discovered so far?" asked Holliday.

"Nothing definite. I can't *prevent* the magic. What I'm trying to do is find ways to negate it. It's a combination of chemistry and physics and electricity . . . and luck. *Especially* luck."

"I hope you can find some way to make Bat normal again," said Holliday. "He's half crazy during the daytime."

"So would you be if you turned into a gigantic bat that killed things during the night and you couldn't remember any of it in the morning."

"I've been to Europe," said Buntline, "and they have legends about men turning into bats too . . . but they retain their identities. Wampyres, they call them—for vampire bats, of course."

"Those are legends," said Holliday. "Bat is real, and when he's a bat he no more remembers what it's like to be a man than he remembers about being a bat when he's Masterson."

"I know," said Buntline. "But you don't get a legend without a grain of truth in it. I was just wondering what the legends say about how you combat the spell."

"I'm ahead of you, Ned," said Edison.

"You've read up on it?" said Buntline.

"For the past few days, since Geronimo cast his spell," replied Edison. "And the problem is that the legends offer ways to *kill* a vampire, but nothing about how to *change* him, temporarily or permanently, back into a man."

"How *do* you kill one?" asked Holliday.

"You drive a wooden stake through its heart," answered Edison. "Or you make him stand in direct sunlight."

"But he's never a bat when the sun's out," said Holliday.

"Doc, these are *legends*, not facts," said Edison.

Holliday sighed deeply. "I know," he said. "I keep forgetting, but deep down I know. You're not going to be able to help him, are you?"

"I don't know. I haven't yet, but it's still early days. I know he's your friend—"

"We're not exactly friends," said Holliday. "We just tend to find ourselves on the same side most of the time."

"Wyatt Earp's side, from what I've seen," offered Buntline.

"That pretty much defines it," agreed Holliday.

"Wyatt has some formidable friends," remarked Buntline.

"He's only got four or five in the whole world," replied Holliday, "so it's just as well that the ones he has are able to take care of themselves."

They reached the American Hotel, walked through the lobby, and entered the dining room. Edison ordered coffee, Buntline requested a steak, and Holliday, after looking at the menu, decided it was too early in the day to chew anything, even an omelet, and ordered a glass of whiskey.

"You keep drinking that stuff for breakfast and it'll kill you, sure as shooting," said Buntline.

"How soon?" asked Holliday.

"I don't know," admitted Buntline. "But you can't live to an old age on a diet like that."

"Well, you could be right," said Holliday, lifting the glass and draining its contents. "Personally, my money's on the consumption, or maybe a bullet from Johnny Ringo or Curly Bill Brocius."

"A telling point," replied Buntline. "Forget I said anything."

The steak arrived, and the coffee cup and whiskey glass were refilled. Edison quizzed Holliday on exactly what Geronimo had done the night he cast his spell on Masterson.

"Same as I told you last time you asked," said Holliday. "He sang a chant, and that was it."

Edison shook his head. "There had to be something more to it. Otherwise any Apache who heard the words and saw the steps could do the same thing and produce the same result, yet we know Geronimo is the only Apache medicine man with this power."

"Maybe they can do it, but they don't," suggested Holliday. "After all, how the hell many men do they want to turn into bats? Besides, he only chose a bat because it's Bat's nickname. If he was Bull Masterson, my guess is that Geronimo would have turned him into a bull."

"True enough," admitted Edison.

"There's something I haven't mentioned," continued Holliday. "I wasn't hiding it. It just never came up."

"What is it?"

"A couple of days ago, I had a chat with one of his braves. Except that when I first saw him he was a snake, about the size of three men laid end to end. He became a warrior when we were alone, but when anyone else approached he turned into a mouse or a cat, something perfectly normal."

"What did he want?"

"That's a matter of some debate," said Holliday. "But I *think* he wanted me to know that Geronimo hadn't resurrected Johnny Ringo, that it was Hook Nose, and he's only partially here to kill you."

"What else?"

"To kill me, too. Hook Nose thinks I might be dead already, only I just don't know it. You know the expression about fighting fire with fire? Well, he believes in fighting the dead with the dead." He coughed into a handkerchief and smiled ruefully. "If I was dead, I wouldn't be doing *that*."

"Where is this warrior now?" asked Edison.

Holliday shrugged. "Wherever Geronimo wants him to be. He could be back at the camp, or be that dog I see through the window, or maybe a roach sitting on the floor and listening intently to us."

"If I could just observe Geronimo or Hook Nose while they're doing their magic!" said Edison, his face a mask of frustration. "There have to be rules and procedures. If I knew what they were, I could duplicate them or negate them. It's very frustrating, working in a vacuum! I was happy to move out here when my government asked me to, but I haven't accomplished anything in Tombstone that I couldn't have done in Chicago or Boston."

"Perhaps," said Buntline with a smile. "But you wouldn't be living next door to a genius who could put all your theories into practice."

"I meant no insult, Ned."

"I know, Tom. Sometimes it just gets—"

"Frustrating," concluded Holliday.

"Precisely," said Edison.

Buntline was about halfway through with his steak and Holliday and Edison were on their second refills when Wyatt Earp entered and walked up to their table.

"Hello, Wyatt," said Edison. "Won't you join us?"

"No, thanks. I came looking for Doc."

"What's up?" asked Holliday.

"I want you to come out to Ben Castleman's ranch with me."

"Now?"

"Right now."

"What happened?" asked Holliday, getting to his feet.

"Ben and his son run the place," said Earp. "They've got a crew of five men helping them."

"And?"

"We just got a report that Johnny Ringo went out there and killed all seven of them. Morg's in court with a couple of drunks we rounded up last night, and there's half a dozen Cowboys in the Oriental, so Virg has to stay there and keep an eye on them. And," concluded Earp grimly, "if I'm going to have to arrest whatever it is that Ringo has become, I want at least one man I trust backing me up."

# 23.

OLLIDAY HATED BEING ON HORSEBACK, but once again the four Bunt Line coaches were all on their routes, and Earp didn't want to waste time rigging a pair of horses up to the brass surrey.

The Castleman ranch was about three miles north of town. Holliday stared at every prairie dog, every lizard, every snake, every buzzard, wondering if they were what they appeared to be, or if Geronimo was keeping an eye on him (and if so, why?).

"You given any thought to what you're going to do if the reports are true?" he asked Earp as they crossed a dry streambed.

"I don't know," admitted Earp. "I don't suppose he'll be amenable to being arrested, and I haven't yet figured out how to kill a dead man."

"You'd better be clear on all your options," said Holliday. "Because if he really killed all of them, he obviously stuck around for someone to see him, and if he didn't vamoose before there were any witnesses, I don't suppose he's inclined to do so now. He might even have done it just to draw you out to the farm."

"The thought has crossed my mind," said Earp.

"You know," said Holliday, "maybe you ought to go back to town right now and let me talk to him."

"I'm the marshal."

"Wyatt, you couldn't beat him when he was alive, and you sure as hell can't beat him now."

"Can you?" Earp shot back.

"I think I can," said Holliday. "But more to the point, we've talked a couple of times. We're almost friends. I can approach him."

"I can't let you take my risks for me, Doc."

"Let's be honest, just the two of us," said Holliday. "The whole reason you called me out to Tombstone was to take some of your risks for you. I'm your enforcer, just the way Ringo is the Clantons'."

"Is that what you believe?" asked Earp sullenly.

"It's the truth. None of you Earps can go up against Curly Bill when he's sober. You couldn't go up against Ringo when he was alive. That's just the way it is, Wyatt."

"I can fight my own battles."

"Then what are Bat Masterson and I doing in Tombstone?" said Holliday.

"Let's stop talking, and maybe we won't wind up fighting each other," said Earp.

"Whatever you say," answered Holliday with a shrug.

They rode the next mile in silence. Holliday became increasingly uncomfortable, not only from being atop the horse, but also because he had disdained a Stetson in favor of his derby, and the Arizona sun was beating down on his forehead and eyes.

Finally they sighted the barn, then a pair of corrals filled with horses, and finally the farmhouse, one of the few that boasted no brass anywhere on it.

"Not much moving," remarked Holliday. "Looks like the report was true."

As they rode closer they saw movement on the house's veranda. Holliday squinted, holding up a hand to shade his eyes.

"Is that who I think it is?" he said.

"Looks like," said Earp grimly.

Johnny Ringo sat on a rocking chair, rocking gently back and forth, watching Earp and Holliday approach. He made no effort to hide, or to get up and greet them.

As they came closer still, Earp said softly, "Off to the left."

Holliday looked. Four bodies lay dead in the dirt.

"Another one by the barn," said Earp.

"Two more just off to the side of the house," said Holliday.

"That's all seven," said Earp.

"Well, look who's here," said Ringo. "I was wondering how long it would take the law to arrive."

"It's here now," said Earp, "and you're under arrest."

"What for?" asked Ringo pleasantly.

"Seven murders, unless there's another body or two that we don't know about."

"Seven's the right number," said Ringo. "But murder's the wrong word."

"Oh?" said Earp.

"Try executions," said Ringo.

"You want to explain the difference?"

"See those two strawberry roans in the corral on the left?" said Ringo.

"What about them?" said Earp.

"Go take a look at the brands on them." Earp stared sharply at him. "Go ahead. I'll still be sitting here when you get back."

Earp turned his horse and approached the corral. When he got there he tied his reins to the top rail, then entered on foot and walked over to the two roans.

"What brands do they carry?" asked Holliday.

"The Running C," answered Earp.

"The Clantons' brand," said Ringo. "And you'll find it on five or six more horses here." He smiled at Earp. "Like I say, it wasn't murder. I'm told you execute horse thieves in Cochise County."

"Not without a trial, we don't," said Earp.

"Ah, but they confessed their crime to me," said Ringo.

"Just how did you get them to do that?" asked Holliday.

Ringo smiled and got to his feet. He climbed down the broad veranda steps to the ground, picked up three small rocks with his left hand, and threw them into the air. He drew his gun and blew all three rocks apart before they'd reached the apex of their ascent.

"I just showed them that little trick, and asked if they'd rather fight or talk. They talked."

"And then you killed them."

"Well, I did give them a chance to draw on me."

"Why bother?" said Holliday. "They couldn't have done you any harm even if they'd hit you."

"I gave them a better chance to live than a hangman would have," replied Ringo.

Holliday glanced at the bodies. "Not really," he said. "None of them had a shotgun, so they couldn't do what Kate threatened to do."

"They might have blown my eyes out," said Ringo.

"There's only one shootist good enough to do that from more than ten or twelve feet away," said Holliday.

"You?" asked Ringo with a smile.

"I suppose someday I'll have to prove it to you."

"Maybe you and I should go for our guns right now."

Holliday smiled. "If you win, you won't find anyone else within a thousand miles who can discuss Kant's categorical imperative with you."

Ringo threw back his head and laughed. "By God, I *like* you, Doc. I'll have to kill you one of these days, but not before we have a few more conversations."

"I guess you get to keep your eyes for another day," responded Holliday.

Earp rejoined them. "Are there any witnesses to back up your story?" he asked.

"Tom and Frank McLaury were here when it happened," answered Ringo. "You find 'em, and they'll corroborate my version. Except they shouldn't have to. You saw the brands."

"For all I know, you brought the horses over yourself," said Earp.

"Now why would I do something like that?" asked Ringo.

"Because half these horses *are* from Mexico," answered Earp. "That means Castleman was in competition with the Clantons. Now he's not."

"Maybe I'll have to kill everyone at the Clantons' ranch to prove I'm just a public-minded citizen who has no use for horse thieves," said Ringo. He turned to Holliday. "Although you made a nice start of it. No one cares about the Cowboy, but all Fin talks about is killing you, and the slower the better. You should really have put him out of his misery. Don't pretend you couldn't have."

"I like the thought of keeping him *in* his misery," replied Holliday.

"I *knew* we were soulmates!" said Ringo with another laugh.

"I doubt it," said Holliday. "Mine's destined for a very unpleasant climate zone, and yours, if you ever had one, has already departed."

"You sure know how to hurt a man's feelings," said Ringo with mock emotion.

"Dead men don't have any feelings," said Earp.

"They also don't do jail time for killing horse thieves," said Ringo. "I'm not ready to kill Doc yet, but I have no problem trying my luck with *you*."

"What'll happen to you if I put three slugs into your heart before you get a shot off?" replied Earp.

"It wouldn't happen if I was alive, and it's not going to happen now," said Ringo.

Holliday stared at Ringo for a long moment, then turned to Earp. "Let it be, Wyatt. He killed a bunch of horse thieves. Let's go back to town."

"What are you talking about?" demanded Earp.

"Either draw on him or let's go," said Holliday.

"Damn it, Doc—you *know* he killed them in cold blood," said Earp. "Look at them. Five of them never got their guns out of their holsters."

"They'd be just as dead if he'd given them a half-minute head start before he drew," said Holliday. "Let's go."

Earp glared furiously at Holliday, then at Ringo. Finally he turned his horse and began heading back to Tombstone. Holliday followed some fifty yards behind him for the first mile, then urged his horse into a trot until he caught up with Earp.

"You made me back down in front of that *thing*," said Earp angrily.

"If I did, then you should thank me for saving your life," replied Holliday. "You couldn't blow away his legs with that little brass pistol, and you're not a good enough shot to take out both his eyes before he could plant a bullet in you."

"I wasn't going to draw on him," said Earp. "But you made me— *us*—look weak."

"Not to worry," said Holliday. "You'll have a lot more chances. That's why I called you off."

Earp frowned. "What the hell are you talking about?"

"It suddenly occurred to me that Johnny Ringo's going to be with us for a while."

Earp simply stared at him, unable to see where Holliday was going with this.

"Think about it, Wyatt," said Holliday. "Why is Johnny Ringo here?"

"What do you mean?"

"Why is he here?" Holliday waited a few seconds, then answered his own question. "To kill Tom Edison."

"So?"

"He's been here three days already," said Holliday. "He's been to Kate's whorehouse. He's bought me a drink. He's killed seven men for the Clantons. But he hasn't even approached Edison's place, let alone tried to kill him. What does that imply to you?"

"What *should* it imply?"

"That at some level he knows he was resurrected by Hook Nose for one thing and one thing only—to kill Edison. And the second he does it, he's back in the grave. So he's going to drag it out as long as he can, or as long as Hook Nose will let him."

Earp's eyes widened with comprehension. "Son of a bitch!"

"And that's why I called you off. We're not ready to confront him yet. But we'll have time to *get* ready." Holliday grimaced as he stated the obvious conclusion. "He's not going anywhere."

# 24.

THERE WAS A POUNDING AT THE DOOR.

"Get up and see who's there," muttered Kate, putting a pillow over her head.

"It's *your* whorehouse. It's got to be for you," said Holliday, keeping his eyes closed.

"I'm not wearing anything," said Kate.

"And if it's a man, he'll only be the two thousandth to see you with your clothes off."

The pounding continued, and Holliday grunted as her foot jammed into the small of his back.

"Open the door, damn it!" snapped Kate.

"All right, all right," growled Holliday, getting to his feet and pulling his pants on. "And if it's the Clantons here to exact their revenge on you, I promise to invite them in and go down to the bar while the bunch of you talk business."

She muttered an obscenity, but it was muffled by the pillow.

Holliday walked over to the door, opened it, and found himself facing Thomas Edison.

"What's up?"

"I think we need your help, Doc."

"Aren't you supposed to go to the Earps for help?" complained Holliday grouchily, as he put on his shirt and began buttoning it. "What the hell time is it, anyway?"

"About six fifteen."

"In the *morning?*" demanded Holliday.

"Yes."

"Do you know what time I got to bed?"

"I'm sorry, Doc, but I really think we need you *and* the Earps."

Holliday strapped on his holster, walked to the nightstand where he'd placed his gun, and brought it back to the door with him.

"What's happening, who's causing the trouble, how many are they, and where are they?"

"It's not like that, Doc," said Edison.

"You'd better tell me what it *is* like before I put my boots on," grumbled Holliday.

"It's Bat."

"If he's naked in a tree somewhere, get the volunteer fire department to help him down."

"He's still a bat. It won't be daylight for another twenty minutes."

"Then what the hell's the problem?"

"He's spent all night at the Clantons' ranch."

"You're guessing," said Holliday. "It's still dark and you're in town. How could you know?"

Edison held up the device he'd displayed the previous day. "We can track him. Don't you remember?"

"All right, he's at the Clantons'. So what? He can always fly back to town. He does it every night."

"He's been perfectly still for about twenty minutes," said Edison. "Dead?"

"I don't know. He could be dead. He could be wounded. He could just be dining on the blood of one of their horses. But I think no matter what, you and the Earps should get out there. I'm told that Johnny Ringo's living out there in a bunkhouse. You've already seen what he does to horse thieves; think of what he'll do to a horse eater."

"He does it very selectively," remarked Holliday, looking around for his hat and jacket, and finally retrieving them from a closet.

"If he's dead, we have to know," said Edison. "And if he's alive, we have to bring him back."

"It's almost daylight. He's probably flying back right now."

Edison pulled the device out of his pocket and studied it. "No, he hasn't moved."

"I assume you've already awakened Wyatt, Morgan, and Virgil."

"I got Morgan and Virgil. I went to Wyatt's house, but Mattie says he hasn't been home all night." Edison frowned. "She was all grogged-up on laudanum. I don't know if I can believe her."

"In this case you can," said Holliday. "You'll find Wyatt at the Grand Hotel."

"He has a room there?"

"So to speak," said Holliday with an amused grin. "Go to the desk and get the room number for Josephine Marcus."

Suddenly Edison looked very nervous. "Um . . . you're his closest friend," he began hesitantly. "I don't suppose you . . . ?"

"Oh, so you think he'll be happier to see me than to see you?" asked Holliday.

**170**

"I can't just walk in on him when he's . . . well . . ." Edison let the words dangle in the air.

"Right," said Holliday. "You can only bother dentists who are in bed with their women, not lawmen."

"Damn it, Doc, I hope you're amusing yourself."

"Enormously," said Holliday. He paused. "I don't suppose it ever occurred to you to have one of his brothers fetch him?"

"I just found out where he was half a minute ago!" snapped Edison.

"*Shut the fuck up!*" bellowed Kate from beneath her pillow.

"Let's go," said Holliday, walking out into the corridor. "You don't know it, but she can be a hell of a lot more formidable than Wyatt."

They walked to the main parlor, where three whores—one human, one robotic, and one a combination—were relaxing.

"Good morning, ladies," said Holliday, tipping his hat.

"You're up early," noted the cyborg.

"Kate throw you out?" asked the human whore.

"Sorry to disappoint you, but I'll be back," said Holliday.

"Makes no difference. Hell, Kate would shoot both of us if she found us together."

"You underestimate her business acumen, my dear," said Holliday.

"Oh?"

"She'd only shoot *me*. *You're* still capable of earning money for her."

"Yeah, when you get right down to it, that sounds like Kate," said the whore.

"I hate to interrupt, but we're in a hurry," said Edison.

"Bet you make love the same way," said the cyborg. Edison looked at her questioningly. "In a hurry."

The human whore laughed, and the robot made a sound that might have been laughter, or merely unoiled gears grinding against each other.

"Come on, Doc," said Edison uncomfortably, heading out the door.

Holliday followed him, and was surprised to see the brass surrey sitting right outside.

"I know you don't like riding horses," explained Edison as he and Holliday climbed onto the broad driver's seat. He clucked to the horses, and another moment found them in front of the Grand Hotel.

"I'll take care of it," said Holliday, clambering down to the street and entering the hotel.

"Can I help you?" asked the night clerk.

"Tell Wyatt Earp he's needed."

"We don't have a Mr. Earp staying here," said the clerk.

"Yes you do. He's in Josie Marcus's room."

The clerk looked at the registration book. "I'm sorry, sir, but—"

There was an ominous *click!* and the clerk found himself staring down the twin barrels of Holliday's brass pistol.

"Let's try once more. Tell Wyatt Earp to get his ass down here."

"But—"

"I am not a patient man," said Holliday. "Especially at six in the morning. Now *move!*"

The clerk practically ran to the staircase, and didn't slow down until he was out of sight. About five minutes later Wyatt Earp walked down the stairs, looking almost as sleepy as Holliday. The clerk trailed him at what he clearly felt was a safe distance.

"What the hell's going on, Doc?"

"Ask *him*," said Holliday, jerking a thumb in Edison's direction.

"Hi, Tom. I didn't see you there."

"Good morning, Wyatt," said Edison. "I hate to bother you at this ungodly hour, but we may have a problem."

"*May* have?" said Earp.

"Bat's been out at the Clantons' ranch all night. I have a feeling he may have killed one of their horses. If he doesn't fly to town in the next three or four minutes, he's not going to make it before sunrise. They'd have no problem killing him as a bat, and they'd be even happier killing a man who's working for the Earps—especially a man with his reputation."

"Where are Morg and Virg?"

"Waiting at the edge of town," answered Edison. "I gave them the tracking device. They should be able to spot him as he comes back, and pinpoint him when he finally comes to rest."

"We'd better get moving," said Earp. "I don't suppose any of Ned's coaches are available?"

Edison shook his head. "No. But I have a surrey with a team of horses right here. Where's your own horse?"

"In the stable. I haven't needed him."

"He's a quarter horse," noted Holliday, "and the Clantons are two miles out of town. The horses pulling the surrey will hold up longer."

"Makes sense," agreed Earp. "Let's go, Doc."

"I'm coming too," said Edison.

"No you're not," replied Earp. "It's my job to protect you. You can't handle a gun, and any time any of the Earps meets any of the Clantons, there's likely to be gunfire."

"Damn it, Wyatt! I have to be there to see if this tracking device is working. I *say* he's at the Clantons' ranch, and I believe it . . . but what if I'm wrong? I've never tried this mechanism out before. What if he's on his way to Mexico?"

Earp turned to Holliday. "What do you think?"

"He's all grown up," said Holliday. "He can make his own decisions."

"Damn it!" yelled Edison, opening his jacket. "I'm wearing Ned's body armor! Now let's stop talking and go!"

They stopped talking and went.

## 25.

**T**HEY'D TRAVELED ABOUT HALF THE DISTANCE when they heard the sound of large, leathery wings flapping overhead. All three men searched the sky, and finally Holliday pointed off to the south.

"There he is!"

"Well, it looks like your device works, Tom," said Earp. "He was clearly at the Clanton ranch."

"It's a relief to know it works," said Edison, "and even more of one to know that Bat's still alive after spending the night there."

"I haven't heard any shooting, and no one's reported any," said Earp. "Probably they're all still asleep."

"All but one, anyway," added Holliday. Earp looked at him curiously. "I don't think Ringo *can* sleep."

"Then why didn't he shoot the gigantic bat when it killed one of the Clantons' horses?"

"First, we don't know he *did* kill one, though I agree it seems likely," answered Holliday. "Second, those horses are the Clantons' property, not his; I'd be surprised if he gives a damn about them.

**174**

Third, the fact that he doesn't sleep doesn't mean that he's hired on as a night watchman. I would imagine he spends all of his spare time reading. Well, the part he doesn't spend drinking, anyway."

Earp brought the horses to a halt and then turned them back to town. "No sense going out there now—Bat's safe, and if they lost a horse, let them prove it was Bat's doing."

"Suits me fine," said Holliday.

"And me," added Edison.

They returned to Tombstone in relative silence, and Earp drove immediately to Edison's house, where he dropped the inventor off.

"Where'll it be, Doc—Kate's place, or the Oriental?"

"Why don't you go back to your ladyfriend at the Grand Hotel?" said Holliday. "I'm going to need the surrey."

"What for?"

"I'll tell you later," said Holliday. "You know, you really ought to marry that actress."

"I've already got a wife."

"Not for long," said Holliday. "She's going to kill herself with laudanum inside of six months."

"She didn't used to take it," said Earp unhappily.

"She didn't used to be married to every outlaw's number one target."

The surrey stopped in front of the Grand Hotel just as the sun was rising.

"We'll let Morg and Virg get Bat and take him to his room," said Earp.

"Sounds good to me," said Holliday as Earp climbed down from the surrey and entered the hotel.

Holliday turned the team and began retracing his route. In another five minutes he was on the outskirts of town, and twenty minutes after that he was within sight of the Clanton ranch.

There was a group of men in one of the corrals, a group that included Ike and Billy Clanton. They were gathered around a dead horse, and as Holliday got closer he saw that its throat had been torn out.

"What the hell are *you* doing here?" demanded Ike.

"Just paying a friendly social call," replied Holliday.

"Bullshit! You're the man who crippled my brother."

"Your brother ought to thank his lucky stars he's still alive. I didn't *have* to shoot him in the knee and the shoulder, you know."

"*I* don't know that," said a familiar voice off to his left. Holliday turned and found himself facing Johnny Ringo, who had attracted about half the flies that had been congregating on the dead horse. "Maybe that's the straightest you can shoot."

"Maybe it is," answered Holliday with a shrug.

"Hey, Ike," said Ringo. "You want me to kill him?"

"No," replied Clanton. "You kill him now, the Earps will come out here with a posse of thirty or forty men. We'll have our shot at them, the Earps and the lunger, but it'll be a time and place of our choosing."

"You're a lucky man," said Ringo to Holliday. "You get to live another day."

"My gratitude is boundless," replied Holliday sardonically.

"You still haven't answered my question," said Clanton. "What the hell are you doing here?"

"I thought I might buy a horse, but I see the one I wanted is dead."

"We've heard about your pal Masterson, and the curse Geronimo put on him. He killed the damned horse."

"He's Wyatt's friend, not mine," said Holliday. "And for all you know it was a wolf that did it."

"There hasn't been a wolf in these parts in thirty years," said Clanton. "It was Masterson, and he was doing the Earps' bidding."

"You're misjudging both of them, Ike," said Holliday.

"Sure I am."

"I'll tell you what," said Holliday. "Let me examine the dead horse, and if I agree that it's the work of a bat, giant or otherwise, I'll make restitution right here and now. Fair enough?"

Clanton stared at him suspiciously. "What are you up to?"

"Try not to be so distrustful. You all just heard me: if I agree that it was killed by a bat, I'll pay for it before I leave. Even Johnny Ringo will tell you that's a pretty good deal."

Ike conferred in whispers with his brother Billy, and then with a young Cowboy named Billy Claiborne. Finally he turned back to Holliday.

"You got a deal," he said.

Holliday climbed down off the driver's seat, entered the corral, and walked over to the dead horse. He squatted down, gave the carcass a perfunctory examination, then straightened up.

"Well?" demanded Clanton.

"Looks like the work of a bat to me," said Holliday. "Must have been one hell of a big one."

"Then you'll pay for the horse?"

"I said I would." He paused thoughtfully. "Tell you what. I really did come out here to buy a horse. Let me look at a few of these other horses in the corral, and maybe we'll make a second deal."

"Take your time," said Ringo, twirling his gun on his index finger. "You're not going anywhere 'til you pay for the dead one."

Holliday spent the next five minutes examining a dozen horses. Finally he stood back, hands on hips, and took a last look.

"I'll take the chestnut gelding with the white blaze," he said.

"Fine," said Clanton.

"Now, how much do I owe you?"

"Three hundred dollars."

Holliday frowned. "I can get a nice healthy one from Finnegan's livery stable for seventy-five dollars. Let's see if we can't negotiate a more reasonable price."

"That's the price, take it or leave it," said Clanton.

"I'll leave it." Holliday pulled out his billfold, counted off one hundred and fifty dollars, and handed it to Clanton.

"Fifty more," said Clanton.

"What are you talking about?" demanded Holliday.

"Two hundred for the dead one. He was a much better animal than the chestnut."

"How the hell would you know?" said Holliday. "He probably never had a saddle on him."

"Hey, we all heard you, Doc," said Ringo with a smile.

Holliday muttered a curse, but he pulled a final fifty dollars out of his billfold and handed it to Clanton.

"It's a pleasure to do business with you, Doc," said Clanton. "Send the bat by any time."

Everybody laughed at that, and Holliday, fuming, climbed onto the surrey, turned it toward Tombstone, and cracked the whip. The team broke into a canter, and he kept them running until they were long out of sight of the ranch. Then he slowed them down to a walk, pulled out a flask, smiled happily, and took a victory drink.

# 26.

OLLIDAY ENTERED THE ORIENTAL, nodded to the bartender, stopped by to greet Henry Wiggins who was becoming a regular customer of both the Oriental and Kate Elder's, and went to the back room, where he found Morgan and Wyatt Earp sitting at a table, drinking coffee.

"Where were you?" asked Wyatt.

"Socializing with the Clantons and Johnny Ringo." Holliday turned to Morgan. "I assume you found Bat?"

"Yeah," said Morgan. "There's a shaded area out back of the *Epitaph*'s offices. That's where he came to rest. The device led us right to him."

"Forget about that!" said Wyatt. "What the hell were you doing at the Clantons'?"

"Paying them for the horse that Bat killed."

"*What?*" yelled both Earps in unison.

"And if the marshal's office has any discretionary funds, it owes me two hundred dollars. Otherwise I suppose I'll have to collect it from Bat. After all, he *did* kill the horse."

"You don't *look* like a crazy man," said Morgan. "Why the hell would you pay two hundred dollars for a dead horse?"

"It was the only way I could examine it, and about a dozen others," answered Holliday.

"Doc, you don't know one end of a horse from the other," said Wyatt. "You want us to play stupid guessing games, or are you ready to tell us what you really did there?"

"Have you got a piece of paper and a pen?" asked Holliday.

Wyatt walked to a small desk in the corner, opened a drawer, pulled out a pen, ink, and paper, and brought them back to Holliday, who immediately began drawing a number of symbols on the paper.

"What's this?" he asked.

"The Running C," said Morgan. "That's the Clantons' brand."

"And this?"

"That's the McLaurys'."

Holliday drew three more, all local.

Then he drew a twisted spear with a blade at each end.

Wyatt and Morgan exchanged looks. "Are you *sure* you saw that, Doc?"

"I'm sure. And I'm pretty sure it doesn't belong to any white man."

"It's the mark of the Hualopai tribe," Wyatt confirmed.

"That's what I was hoping for," said Holliday. "Not that I've ever heard of the Hualopai before, but I was counting on finding at least one horse that had been stolen from the Indians."

"Okay, you found one," said Wyatt. "So what?"

"So if they've got a medicine man," replied Holliday, "we've got a card to play." Suddenly he smiled. "I'm sure you've never heard the term, but I'm going to show you how a *quid pro quo* works."

## 27.

OLLIDAY HATED RIDING ON HORSEBACK, but Wyatt convinced him that driving Buntline's surrey might appear to be an act of aggression, since none of the Hualopais could see what was inside it.

The land was flat and barren, sparsely dotted with cactus and sagebrush. They stopped frequently along the way. Twice the horses needed water, once Holliday had a coughing fit that took almost half an hour to pass, and once they stopped by a small stream to light a fire and cook a meal.

"You know," said Holliday, his back propped against a tree as he took a sip from his flask and watched Earp wolfing down his steak, "there was a time when, if I saw a coyote like that one"—he pointed to a coyote that was watching them from fifty yards away, prepared to race in and grab any scraps they left—"I'd have figured it was just what it looked like." He smiled. "Now I keep wondering if it's Cole Younger or Clay Allison, or maybe this Billy the Kid we keep hearing about."

"If there's any justice, the Kid'll be a loon, not a coyote," replied Earp. "He's crazy enough. What is he—eighteen or nineteen years old? And he's killed a man for every year he's been alive."

"So they say."

"There's got to be a hell of a reward for him," continued Earp. "Maybe when we're through here, you ought to go hunting for him."

"The only way we'll be through here is if someone kills Edison," answered Holliday. "Unless you figure there'll come a day when he decides not to invent anything else."

"Him? He can't stop inventing any more than he can stop breathing. If we keep him breathing, he'll keep inventing."

"It'd be nice if he could invent a way to make Johnny Ringo stay dead," said Holliday.

"I think he's trying, though in a roundabout way," replied Earp.

"How do you figure that?"

"He's trying to find a way to combat the medicine men's magic. Once he does that, it should be the end of Ringo. After all, it's their magic that's keeping him alive."

"That's one way of looking at it," admitted Holliday.

"You look doubtful."

"Ringo doesn't want to die, or go back to whatever Hook Nose pulled him out of," said Holliday. "Like I said, if he didn't care, he'd have gone after Edison already."

"Maybe," said Earp with a shrug. He picked up a stone and threw it at the coyote, which ducked but stood its ground.

"Maybe that coyote isn't a killer at all," said Holliday with a smile. "Maybe it's a refugee from that newfangled sport they're all playing back East."

"You mean baseball?"

"Yes."

"Ever see a game?" asked Earp.

"No."

"I have. And they try to hit the ball with a special stick, not side-step or duck it."

"Think it'll catch on?"

"It already has," said Earp. "Almost every city back East has got a team, and they actually pay people to play for them." He chuckled. "Stupid way to make a living."

"Right," said Holliday with a smile. "Not smart like going up against Ringo and the Clantons for free."

Earp lit a cigar. "You are the most complaining man I know."

"I take that as a high compliment."

Earp held out a cigar to Holliday. "Want one?"

"I better not. I don't need another coughing fit."

"Why don't you see if Tom can cure it?"

"By shooting electricity through my lungs?" responded Holliday with a grimace. "I don't think so."

Earp tore off a small portion of his steak and threw it at the coyote. It ducked, then cautiously sniffed at it where it landed, and incautiously pounced on it and gobbled it up.

"Just in case it's some lawman instead of some outlaw," explained Earp.

"And if it's just some coyote, he's going to trail us all the way to your medicine man's camp now that you've fed him."

Earp sighed. "It must have been nice to live back before there was all this goddamned magic."

"There was always magic. *It's* not new to the West—*we* are." Holliday paused. "Hell, it's not new to anywhere. Haven't you ever heard of Merlin?"

"Merlin who?" asked Earp.

"Forget it," said Holliday, getting slowly to his feet. "Shall we go?"

Earp nodded. "Might as well." He got up, mounted his horse, waited for Holliday to do the same, and began riding north.

"About how much farther?" asked Holliday.

"Maybe twenty miles, maybe thirty. They move around a lot."

"You've met them before?"

"A couple of times. The one we want is the chief, Que-Su-La."

"I thought we wanted the medicine man," said Holliday.

"He's both," answered Earp.

"Probably a good thing he doesn't have to run for election."

"He'd win in a landslide," said Earp. "They're not a big tribe, the Hualopai. He's kept them independent when the Apaches wanted to assimilate them, and he's made his peace with the few white settlements he's come in contact with."

"Good," said Holliday. "I hate dealing with a stupid man. He never knows what he wants, and then when he asks for something, he changes his mind the next day."

"I don't think anyone's ever called Que-Su-La stupid."

"If he's lived long and fended off the Apaches and the Cheyenne, he must be pretty smart. How old is he?"

Earp shrugged. "Beats me."

"Gray hair? Still got his teeth?"

"Doc, he looked like he's in his early twenties," said Earp. "And I've been told by a couple of graybeards that he looked that way sixty or seventy years ago."

"I didn't think Indians could grow beards."

"It's just a way of saying they were ancient," replied Earp. "Truth to tell, I can't remember if they had beards or not. But their hair was white, and they were wrinkled top to bottom."

"Either this Que-Su-La knows his magic, or he's the vainest Indian I ever heard of, or both," said Holliday.

"Whatever he is, he's done a pretty good job of staying neutral in a land that doesn't much favor neutrality."

Earp's cigar went out, and he tossed it to the ground. A prairie dog ran up to it, sniffed it a couple of times, and scampered away.

"Well, *he's* never going to cough his guts out," remarked Holliday.

Earp watched the prairie dog retreating. "Damn," he said at last. "It sure as hell reminds me of Urilla."

"Urilla?" repeated Holliday.

"My first wife. Used to wiggle just like that when she walked."

"You never mentioned her."

"She died just a few months after we were married."

"Sorry to hear it," said Holliday. "When did you marry Mattie?"

Earp shifted uncomfortably on his saddle. "We were never officially married."

"But she calls herself Mattie Earp."

"She can call herself anything she wants," replied Earp. "She told me once that Mattie's not her real name either." He paused. "She was a whore back in Kansas. We hooked up together, and she came out to Tombstone with me—her and a couple of cases of laudanum."

"All the more reason you should marry Josie Marcus, now that there's no law stopping you."

"I don't know if I'm the marrying kind, Doc. So calling Mattie Mrs. Earp means I don't have to rush into anything." He paused again. "It took me a long time to get over losing Urilla."

"So we're each living with whores," said Holliday. He shrugged. "Well, what the hell—who else are you going to find to live with out here?"

"Maybe just an actress."

"She's too classy for you, Wyatt," said Holliday with a smile. "You'd better marry her while you can."

"I'm thinking about it," answered Earp. "But first things first—and the first thing is to keep Edison and Buntline alive long enough to find some way to fight the Indians' magic."

"Speaking of magical Indians, there's a brave on horseback about half a mile off to the left," noted Holliday.

"Watching us. Yeah, I see him. Que-Su-La will have braves watching us all the way to his lodge."

It was as Earp predicted. Every mile Holliday spotted a new warrior, always watching from a distance, never approaching, never acknowledging them, never trying to communicate. He was sure that, medicine man or not, Que-Su-La knew exactly where they were at any given minute, and knew when they'd be arriving.

When they were about half a mile from the lodge, six warriors rode up and joined them—two in front, one on each side, two in back. They didn't say a word, didn't ask for Earp and Holliday's weapons, merely rode along with them as they passed some smaller lodges, and finally reached the medicine man's impressive lodge. There were two women out front, one weaving a rug, the other repairing some buckskins. Then, as if at a signal, they stood up, gathered their materials, and walked around to the back of the lodge as Earp and Holliday dismounted.

Que-Su-La emerged a moment later. He was tall and lean, and his face was totally unlined. He stared at Earp for a moment.

"You I know," he said in reasonably unaccented English. He turned to Holliday. "You I have never met, but I have heard many tales of the merciless killer Holliday."

Holliday tipped his hat. "And I have heard much about Que-Su-La," he answered.

Que-Su-La gave him an expression that could almost be translated as *Cut the crap or we're never going to get anywhere.* Then he looked at Earp again.

"Why have you come to the land of the Hualopai?" he asked.

"I'd rather let my friend explain it," said Earp.

"Please explain, Holliday," said the medicine man.

"Just outside Tombstone there is a ranch owned by a family named Clanton."

"I know of them," said Que-Su-La. "Bad men."

"Very," agreed Holliday. He pulled a piece of paper out of his vest pocket and handed it to Que-Su-La. It displayed the Hualopai brand. "Does this look familiar?"

"It is our brand. You know that."

"I found it on a horse in the Clantons' corral."

"Now I know why you are here," said Que-Su-La. "But I cannot help you. The Clantons are the enemy of my blood, but they are protected from me."

Holliday frowned. "Can you explain that, please?"

"Last year they stole my village's horses, and when my son tried to stop them they killed him. I wanted to take my revenge, but Woo-Ka-Nay has protected them from my magic. So I cannot help you."

"Woo-Ka-Nay?" repeated Holliday.

"The white men know him as Hook Nose."

"Well, maybe *we* can help *you*," said Holliday.

"Explain," said Que-Su-La.

"The Clantons are protected, but only against magic. I shot one of them the other day, and I am perfectly willing, with the help of the Earp brothers, to shoot the rest."

"Truly?" asked Que-Su-La, his eyes widening.

"Truly."

The medicine man turned to Earp. "And you will help him?"

"You have my word," said Earp.

"How can I repay you?" asked Que-Su-La.

"I was hoping you'd ask," said Holliday.

"I have no daughters."

"That's no problem. The woman I've got is more than I can handle anyway."

"Then I repeat: how can I repay you?"

"With your magic," said Holliday. "Geronimo has put a spell on a friend of ours, a man named Bat Masterson."

"I have heard of him," said Que-Su-La.

"Every time the sun goes down, he turns into a real bat," continued Holliday. "And when the sun comes up, he is a man again. Can you remove the spell?"

Que-Su-La closed his eyes and stood motionless for a moment. "Yes," he said at last.

"Then I believe we have a deal," said Holliday, extending his hand.

Que-Su-La stared at the hand. "You will carry my vengeance to the Clantons first. I will know when it has been accomplished, and on that day I shall lift the spell from your friend."

"Are you sure you can't change him right now?"

"I can, but I will not. I have been waiting to avenge my son longer than your friend has been living with his curse."

"That looks like the best bargain we're going to get," said Holliday to Earp. To Que-Su-La he said, "I agree."

The Indian finally took his hand.

"It is done," said the medicine man. "We have a pact."

"Good," said Holliday with a smile. "I was afraid for a minute there that I was going to have to throw in a lifetime of free dental service."

"It would be meaningless," said Que-Su-La.

"Why?" asked Holliday curiously. "You've still got all your teeth."

"It would be meaningless," said Que-Su-La seriously, "because you will die as a relatively young man."

## 28.

THEY RODE INTO TOMBSTONE just after the sun had set. Bat had already undergone his nightly transformation, and in fact they spotted him flying south out of town as they arrived.

"You know," said Holliday, as they watched the huge winged creature making its way across the sky, "if it takes another couple of weeks he won't be worth saving. He's half crazy right now."

"We've got to wait for the right moment, Doc," said Earp. "I'm a law officer. I can't just call the Clantons out and have a shoot-out in the street."

"I know."

"Well, then?"

"*I'm* not a law officer," said Holliday, "and I don't have any problem having a shoot-out in the street."

Earp shook his head. "There are a *lot* of them, Doc. Not just the ones you saw at their ranch the other day."

"Who else?"

"Word has it they're doing a lot of business with Tom and Frank McLaury."

"Good," said Holliday. "I played poker with them the other night. I didn't like them much."

"Damn it, Doc!" complained Earp. "I sent for you and Bat because I needed you both! Bat's lost to us. I don't need you going out and getting shot full of holes."

"Is that what you think will happen, Wyatt?" asked Holliday. "I don't want to seem churlish, but how many times have I saved your ass in Dodge and elsewhere? And have you *ever* had to come to *my* aid?"

Earp made no answer.

"I can take Ike Clanton as easily as I took Fin," continued Holliday. "And if he brings baby brother along, so much the better." He patted his brass pistol. "I've got twelve rounds in this baby. I figure I can kill both Clantons and have ten left."

"And if Johnny Ringo's with them?" asked Earp.

"Then he and I will go off to discuss Descartes and Spinoza, and I'll call them out the next time they're alone."

"Descartes and Spinoza? I don't know what the hell you're talking about."

"But *he* will," said Holliday.

"Doc, if you do have it out with them, make sure you've got witnesses who'll swear they started it, or at least drew first. Otherwise I'll either have to arrest you or quit my job, and in either case it'd be tantamount to signing Tom Edison's death warrant—and probably Ned Buntline's as well."

Holliday stared at his friend for a long moment, and finally spoke. "I've never asked before, but just what the hell do you get out of this, Wyatt? Do you really give a damn whether the United States stops at a river instead of an ocean?"

Earp looked around to make sure no one but Holliday could hear his answer. "Doc, maybe you don't know it, but when I was starting out I was arrested for horse stealing. It was a legitimate arrest. I was a lousy horse thief. I played poker with you just one time, because I knew in ten minutes that I was overmatched. I'm not much of a gambler. I was a part owner of the whorehouse where Mattie worked back in Kansas. It went broke." He paused. "The only thing I'm good at is being a lawman. If I'm ever going to make a mark, if people twenty years from now are ever going to know that I was here, it's only going to happen if I'm the best lawman I can be. So to answer your question, no, I don't give a flying fuck if the country ends at the Mississippi or the Pacific—but I care if I'm the one who makes a difference."

Holliday continued staring at Earp and made no reply.

"What is it?" asked Earp irritably.

"Wyatt, I do believe that was the longest speech I ever heard you make. And it was a good one. Okay, I'll go this far: I won't call Ike Clanton out." A grim smile crossed his face. "But if *he* calls *me* out . . ." He let the sentence hang in the air.

Earp urged his horse forward again. "Let's go," he said, closing the subject. "We've got time for dinner before the big spenders show up."

Suddenly Holliday had another coughing seizure. When it was finally over and he'd finished gasping for air, he turned to Earp. "You go ahead and eat. I'm not up to it."

"I can wait if you'd like."

Holliday shook his head. "It's not necessary. I think I'll be drinking my dinner tonight." A quick forced smile. "But since you're so concerned, I'll tell the bartender that it's your treat."

"You're sure?"

"That you're paying? Absolutely."

"Damn it, Doc!"

"Yes, I'm sure. I'll be okay. I do this all the time. You know that."

Earp studied him in the moonlight, then shrugged and turned his horse, riding off toward the American Hotel. "I'll see you later."

"I certainly hope so," said Holliday softly. He steered his horse back to the livery stable, paid the dollar rental fee, tipped the groom a dime, and walked over to the Oriental. He went directly to the back room, where he found Virgil Earp sipping a cup of black coffee.

"How'd it go?" asked Virgil.

"Pretty good, actually," answered Holliday. "Que-Su-La can take the curse off him."

"Thank goodness for that!" said Virgil. "Bat's been getting more and more squirrelly every day. At least that's over!"

"Not quite yet," said Holliday.

"Oh?"

"We made a trade. First I kill the Clantons, and *then* he lifts the spell."

"Oh, shit, Doc—you can't just walk up to them and blow them away!"

"You sound remarkably like your brother," said Holliday with an amused smile.

"Isn't there anything else you can do for the Indian instead?"

Holliday shook his head. "They stole his tribe's horses and killed his son." He took a bottle off the desk and poured himself a drink. "I suppose you could arrest the Clantons and hang them for murder."

Virgil shook his head. "I don't have any jurisdiction for a murder that was committed forty or fifty miles from here on Hualopai land." He grimaced. "Hell, I don't have all that much jurisdiction in Tombstone beyond keeping order in the streets and saloons at this end of town."

"Well, it looks like the day is coming when you can't avoid a fight with the Clantons," said Holliday. "Just make sure I'm there."

"If I can," said Virgil. "It's not the kind of thing you can plan."

"Actually, it's the kind I'd be more than happy to plan, if it wasn't for you damned Earps," said Holliday, only half in jest.

"I'll just bet you would," said Virgil, with no show of amusement.

"You're depressing the hell out of me," announced Holliday, getting to his feet. "I think I'll go mingle with the citizenry, or at least that portion of it that's frequenting the saloon."

He got up, took his half-full glass with him, and went back into the main room. He took one look at the bar and smiled. "Thank you, God," he said in a very soft voice.

Then he walked over to the bar and stood next to Ike Clanton.

"Hi, Ike," said Holliday. "I missed you when I came in."

"I was with some of my Cowboys at a table over in the corner," replied Clanton, slurring his words slightly. "Now I'm here—closer to the booze."

"Better go easy on that stuff," said Holliday. "It'll rot your teeth, turn your brain to putty, and ruin your beautiful complexion. In fact, it already has."

"I thought I'd heard that you left town, lunger," said Clanton. "I knew it was too good to be true."

"I went to visit an old friend. Now I'm back."

"You got a friend?" said Clanton. "I'm amazed."

"An Indian known as Que-Su-La," said Holliday. "He doesn't like you very much, Ike."

"Don't know the name."

"Probably not," agreed Holliday. "But I'll bet you know the tribe. He's a Hualopai."

"Never met one."

"Well, I can see where you probably didn't meet a whole lot of them, since you stole their horses. But Que-Su-La's pretty adamant that you met one of them: his son."

"Why would I remember that?"

"Don't you remember the men you've killed?" asked Holliday pleasantly. "I always do."

"Are you calling me a killer?"

"No, I'm calling you Ike. It's Que-Su-La who calls you a killer."

"So that's why you came out to the ranch yesterday," said Clanton. "You just wanted to see if I had one of this tribe's horses. Whose money did you pay me with?"

"That's a matter of some debate," answered Holliday. "But if I were you, I think I'd take up a new profession. The Mexicans may not be able to go to court and prove that you've stolen their horses, but my friend can."

"It'll just be his word against a white man's word," said Clanton.

"His and mine," Holliday corrected him.

"I've about had it with you and your accusations, lunger!" snapped Clanton. "You want to step outside and settle this here and now?"

"If you insist," said Holliday, unable to suppress a smile.

"Just a minute," said a familiar voice.

Holliday turned and saw Johnny Ringo, as foul-smelling and hideous in appearance as ever, approaching them.

"Ike, you don't want to go up against him," said Ringo.

"I'm not afraid," insisted Clanton.

"That's because you've been drinking for the past two hours," said Ringo. "There's only one man who can take him."

"Well, that's stretching the definition of 'man' a bit," said Holliday.

"Ike, go home and sleep it off," continued Ringo.

Clanton finished the drink that was before him, then turned to Holliday. "This isn't done, lunger," he said, slurring his words. "If I were you, I'd be real careful before I walked down any empty streets or alleys."

"Obviously you haven't read Bishop Berkeley," replied Holliday, and Ringo laughed.

"Who's this bishop, and what's he doing in Tombstone?" demanded Clanton drunkenly.

"He's the man who formulated the argument for the Unseen Observer," said Ringo.

"What the hell are you talking about?"

"It's a proof for the existence of God," answered Ringo. "It holds up a hell of a lot better than Thomas Aquinas's First Cause argument."

"It means we're never alone," added Holliday, "especially when you're trying to back-shoot me in the dead of night."

Clanton tried to focus his eyes and concentrate, found he couldn't do either, and staggered toward the swinging doors. He'd made it halfway there when he reeled against a table and collapsed. Ringo gave him a moment to get up on his own, then ordered the Cowboys to pick him up and take him home. When they were gone he turned to Holliday.

"Looks like you get to live another day."

"Me?" said Doc with an amused chuckle. "He couldn't take me if he was sober. He sure as hell can't do it falling-down drunk."

"I agree," said Ringo.

"Well, then?"

"I'd have taken his place."

"Before or after I shot him?" asked Holliday.

Ringo laughed. "You'd be just as dead either way."

"Could be an interesting experience, being dead," remarked Holliday.

"An understatement."

"Do you remember anything about it?"

"I told you: it was cold and cramped."

Holliday shook his head. "I don't mean in the grave. I mean the afterlife, if there is one."

"I remember being very unhappy, because of the one thing that was missing."

"What was that?"

"There was no Doc Holliday to test myself against," said Ringo. "I truly believe I'd have come back for you, even without Hook Nose's help."

"Won't be much of a fight," replied Holliday. "I think we both agree that a bullet can't hurt you or even slow you down."

"I'll know if you beat me," said Ringo. "And if you do, I'll acknowledge it—right before I shoot you down."

"That's a cold comfort."

"I can promise that in your case it's going to get a lot hotter very soon," said Ringo with a laugh.

# 29.

HOLLIDAY AWOKE A LITTLE AFTER NOON. Kate was already up and around, and he slowly got dressed, considered shaving, decided to have it done at the barbershop instead, took a quick swallow from the bottle he kept on the nightstand, pulled on his boots, and walked down the hallway to the kitchen, where Kate and two of the cyborgs—women with brass appendages—were having coffee.

"Well, look who's up," said Kate sarcastically. "And it's not even one o'clock."

Holliday grunted and sat down at the table. "Coffee, please."

"I hear you had another run-in with the zombie last night," said Kate, pouring him a cup.

"He probably saved Ike Clanton's life," said Holliday.

"The word I get is that he's here to end some lives—Tom Edison's and yours."

Holliday sighed deeply. "We'll have it out one of these days. It's a pity, too. We could have been friends."

"Come on, Doc—you've only got one friend. Everyone knows that."

"I didn't say we *were* friends," answered Holliday. "I said we could have been."

"A killer like that?"

"Oh, we'd have faced off in the end, but sometimes it gets a little lonely being the only man within a hundred miles who's ever read a book."

"Don't you go putting on airs with me!" snapped Kate. "I've read my share of books."

"You've read your share of dime novels," Holliday corrected her. "I saw one on your nightstand. It's some cock-and-bull story about how Wild Bill Hickok took on twenty outlaws at once."

"It's not a novel," she said defensively. "It's true."

"I'm looking at the only person who ever took on twenty outlaws at once, and not the way that writer suggested," said Holliday, staring at her.

Kate turned to the two cyborgs. "You'll have to forgive him. He's always this unpleasant before he's had his first gallon of cheap whiskey."

"I think next time Johnny Ringo comes by, I'll let him have his way with you," said Holliday.

"You weren't around to save me the last time," retorted Kate.

"I wonder if he can?" mused one of the cyborgs.

"Can what?" asked Holliday.

"Can . . . you know," she said awkwardly.

"A historic first," said Holliday with a smile. "I've never seen a whore blush before."

"That's because their blood runs cold whenever they look at you," interjected Kate.

"Do you two really hate each other as much as you seem to?" asked the other cyborg.

Kate looked surprised. "I don't hate him at all." She paused thoughtfully. "He's kind of comfortable to have around, like an old, well-worn piece of furniture."

"She makes a good cup of coffee and she doesn't hog the bed," said Holliday.

"Not exactly the stuff of romantic stories," said the cyborg.

"Never confuse romantic stories with real relationships," said Holliday. "I'm an alcoholic gunfighter with consumption. She's a whore who's been run out of half a dozen towns." He forced a smile to his lips. "Who else would have us?"

"That's not much to build on," remarked the cyborg.

"Your brass leg and jaw are going to last forever," said Holliday. "How long do you think either Kate or I figure to be around?"

"Well, *I'm* going to marry for love," said the cyborg. "I'm just doing this to pay Ned Buntline for my various body parts and to get a nest egg."

"Every forty-year-old whore I ever met got into the business as a teenager and was just going to work two or three years to get a grubstake or a dowry," replied Holliday.

"Stop picking on her," said Kate irritably.

"I'm not picking on her," answered Holliday. "We're just having a conversation."

"You've had more conversations end in bloodshed than anyone I know," said Kate. "Leave her alone."

Holliday turned to the cyborg. "I apologize if I've offended you, my dear," he said.

"You haven't," she assured him.

"Really?"

"Really."

"Perhaps you'd like to cement our friendship later?" he suggested.

"You do," said Kate ominously, "and you can face Johnny Ringo on equal terms."

Holliday shrugged and smiled apologetically at the cyborg. "The fates are against it." He finished his coffee and got to his feet. "Perhaps next week. She could be dead of old age by then."

He made it out of the kitchen just before Kate's coffee cup crashed against the wall where his head had been a second earlier. He walked through the parlor and out into the street.

A Bunt Line coach was just rolling past. He stood back, watching it as it went down the street. He considered having some breakfast, decided he wasn't hungry, and just began wandering aimlessly. In a few minutes he heard the sound of hammers banging against metal and, curious, he followed the sound until he came to the jail, where Ned Buntline was supervising the construction of a special cell in place of one of the stone ones Bat Masterson had demolished a few nights ago. Sheets of brass were being affixed, and Holliday could see that in perhaps two more hours the entire cell—floor, walls, ceiling, door, and bars—would be made of Buntline's impenetrable and unbreakable brass.

"Hi, Doc," said Buntline. "Lovely day, isn't it?"

"I prefer the nights," replied Holliday. "Geronimo turned the wrong one of us into a bat."

"Well, our Bat is going to spend the whole night here," said Buntline. "That much I guarantee."

"I saw him break out of your special handcuffs," noted Holliday. "What makes you think your walls or bars are any stronger?"

"New formula," said Buntline. "That's why I didn't do this two or three days ago. Tom worked out a way to reinforce this brass, and now *nothing* can break through it."

"You better hope you're right."

Buntline smiled. "The government's paying for it."

"What I mean is, if it was me, and *I* got loose, I know the first man I'd be looking for."

"He doesn't remember a thing once the change hits him," replied Buntline.

"Are you sure?"

"Yes. Why do you ask?"

"Because Johnny Ringo remembers everything, including what it felt like to be in the grave," said Holliday. "And dead is a more permanent condition than transformed."

"I don't know why it works the way it does," answered Buntline. "But I do know that Bat doesn't remember anything that happens to him in his other form. When he's a man, he can't remember being a bat, and vice versa."

"So far."

"So far," agreed Buntline. "Wyatt was by this morning. He tells me that Bat may not be a nocturnal flying machine too much longer."

"That depends," said Holliday.

"Yeah, he told me the conditions for lifting the curse."

"He's a good lawman and a staunch friend," said Holliday, "but he's just not bright enough to see all the ramifications."

Buntline frowned. "Such as?"

"Ringo's biding his time, because he knows his job is done when he puts Tom Edison in the grave."

"We've noticed that."

"Well, as soon as he finds out we've got a medicine man on our side, what do you think he's going to do?"

Buntline looked puzzled and remained silent.

"He's going to go after Edison, because if he kills him, there's always a chance Hook Nose will call him forth again—but if we can talk Que-Su-La into putting Ringo back in the grave *without* killing

Edison, he has to figure Hook Nose will think he was a washout and won't bring him back anymore."

"That's a very tenuous chain of reasoning, Doc," said Buntline.

"You want to bet that I'm wrong?" asked Holliday. "Because what you'll be betting is Tom Edison's life."

Buntline turned to one of the laborers. "You guys will be okay without me for an hour, won't you?" The man nodded. "Come on, Doc."

"Where are we going?"

"Tom's house. It's better protected than you think."

"Why show it to me?" asked Holliday. "I'm no inventor."

"You just tell me if you can find a weakness. Tom and I can address it once we know it's there."

"You've got more than one weakness," said Holliday. "Hell, I've walked right up to the door and knocked on it. You can't let Ringo get that close."

"We'll be there in a couple of minutes," said Buntline. "Then you can point out everything that needs fixing."

Holliday shrugged and kept silent. As they walked, he again made a mental note to buy a cane. Simple physical actions, like walking and breathing, seemed to be getting more difficult almost daily, and he found himself wondering if he could make a trade with Que-Su-La: some service, maybe killing some enemy of the medicine man, in exchange for curing the consumption that was robbing him of oxygen every time he took more than ten steps.

"Here we are," said Buntline as they finally reached the side-by-side houses. "Just wait here a minute."

Holliday was happy to stop and stand still as Buntline walked up to Edison's door and knocked on it. The inventor opened the door, the two men spoke in low tones, and then the door closed and Buntline returned to Holliday.

"All right, Doc," said Buntline. "There's the house. You're Johnny Ringo. Go to work."

Holliday reasoned that Ringo would approach the house directly. He couldn't be hurt, so why be circumspect and approach it covertly, or look for an open window or an unwatched back door? He had gone halfway to the door when he felt a sharp pain in his foot and jumped back.

"What the hell was that?" he said, looking down at the ground but finding nothing.

"That was an electric charge," explained Buntline. "It circles the house at a distance of twenty feet, and is there as a warning."

"It won't stop Ringo."

"It doesn't have to," said Buntline. He walked back to the street, picked up a stone, and brought it back to Holliday. "I can't ask you to take the next few steps. It would kill you." Holliday looked his disbelief. "Here," continued Buntline, handing him the stone. "Throw it at any part of the house, but try not to do it at a height of more than six feet."

Holliday took the stone and hurled it at the middle of the front window. There was a crackling, sizzling sound, and the rock disappeared when it was within ten feet of the house.

"What the hell happened?" demanded Holliday.

"Tom has erected an electric barrier—he calls it a force field— around his house. Around mine, too. Ringo may not feel any pain, but this stuff will turn him to ashes anyway."

"And if it doesn't?" asked Holliday, still dubious.

"Then there are more protections inside the house," said Buntline. "Trust me, Tom is safer there than if you and the Earps were surrounding him with guns drawn. That's why he usually keeps the external field turned off—otherwise you couldn't approach the house, let alone knock on the door." He waved once at the house, and Edison waved back through a window. "All right, the field is down now."

Edison walked out to join them. "What's up?" he asked. "Are we expecting an attack today?"

"Not today, but soon, perhaps," answered Holliday.

"Brocius, Clanton, or Ringo?"

"If it's Brocius or Ike Clanton, you don't have to worry," said Holliday. "Ned was just showing me what you've got rigged to protect you from Ringo."

"It *should* work," replied Edison. "And I'm improving it all the time."

"I wonder . . ." began Holliday.

"What?"

"Sooner or later I'm going to have to face Ringo. Can you make me a gun that will do what your barrier does?"

"I don't know, Doc," said Edison dubiously. "That's a defensive field. You need something that will destroy Ringo, not just protect you."

"I don't even know if something as small as a gun could generate a protective field," added Buntline.

"Ah, well, it was just an idea," said Holliday.

"We can discuss it some, Tom and I," said Buntline. "But I wouldn't get your hopes up."

"I suppose if he kills me I can track him down in hell and call for a rematch."

"Are you always this optimistic?" asked Edison with a smile.

"Only on days that have a 'y' in them," answered Holliday.

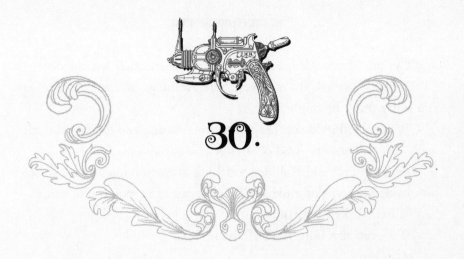

## 30.

"I T LOOKS FLIMSY," said Masterson as he was led into his new cell. "The stone walls looked much more solid."

"You tore those walls apart in less than a minute," said Buntline. "I guarantee you won't do that to *these* walls."

"So I'm going to spend my whole life showing up here just before sunset," said Masterson. "Maybe you should just shoot me now."

"You won't be doing this much longer," said Holliday, who was standing next to Buntline.

"Geronimo's changed his mind?" asked Masterson hopefully.

"No. But we've got our own medicine man. We're trading him a favor for a favor. Lifting the curse is his favor to us."

"And what did you have to pay for that?"

"Nothing much," said Holliday. "Something we were probably going to do anyway."

"What is it?" insisted Masterson.

Holliday was about to answer when Masterson's body went rigid and the transformation began.

"Get out of the cell quick!" said Buntline, rushing out the door.

"He hasn't attacked a man yet," said Holliday, following him. "Do you really think he might?"

"Why take the chance?" said Buntline, closing and locking the cell door. "You've seen the kind of strength he has as a bat."

"I wonder . . ." said Holliday, watching Masterson intently as his face became darker and elongated and his arms began to morph into wings.

"What?" asked Buntline.

"If we can aim him," said Holliday.

"Aim him?"

"Point him at Ike Clanton and say, '*Kill!*'"

"He doesn't understand, and he also doesn't remember who his friends are," said Buntline. "He'd be just as likely to kill you."

"Can he be hurt?"

"He always comes back with a few cuts and scratches."

"Too bad," said Holliday. "It might have been interesting to lure Johnny Ringo here and lock the two of them up together."

"It's my considered opinion that Ringo would blow him away in two seconds. And even if he *wanted* to kill Ringo and could get to him before Ringo was able to draw his gun, how do you hurt a man who's already dead?"

"All right," said Holliday, as Masterson's transformation was completed. "It was just a thought."

Masterson shuffled to the outside wall and began pounding on it, as he had on the stone wall.

"Hah!" said Buntline triumphantly after a minute had passed. "Not even dented."

"Then I think I'll take my leave of you," said Holliday.

"Off to the Oriental?"

"Eventually," replied Holliday, walking back through the office and out the front door of the jail. It was too early for the bigger money games to have started, and he briefly considered stopping at the whorehouse and asking Kate to cook his dinner, but she'd been in a foul mood when he'd left, so he stopped by the Grand Hotel instead. Wyatt wasn't around, so he ate in isolation in the farthest corner of the room. The light could have been better, but experience had taught him always to sit with his back to a wall.

As he was having a cup of coffee after his meal, Josephine Marcus entered the restaurant, spotted him, and walked over to his table.

"Hello, Doc," she said. "Do you mind if I join you?"

"I'm just finishing, but sure, sit down, Josie."

"Do you know where Wyatt is?"

"Riding herd on the Cowboys, I assume," said Holliday.

She frowned. "Or with Mattie."

"If he's with Mattie, it's just to pick her up from wherever she's fallen and toss her onto a couch or a bed."

She toyed aimlessly with an empty ashtray, and finally spoke. "I have a question, Doc."

"I'll answer it if I can," replied Holliday.

"Why do men like you and Wyatt always wind up with whores?"

"Take a look around, Josie," said Holliday. "Tombstone's not exactly overrun by virgin schoolmarms."

"That's no answer. There are more than just whores living here."

"Not for men like us. You know when you take up our profession that the odds are against you living long enough to have any permanent relationships, so you form the ones you can."

"Well, I'm going to have a permanent one with Wyatt, once I get him out of this terrible business."

"This terrible business is the one thing he's good at, Josie," said Holliday. "I'd think twice before I took him away from it."

"He's a bright man and a hard worker," she said. "He can learn another trade. After all, if he survives Tombstone he's going to be around for a good long time."

"Well, that's where he and I differ," said Holliday wryly.

"Oh, I'm sorry, Doc! I didn't mean—"

"It's all right, Josie. If I didn't know I was dying, I'd be long dead."

She frowned. "I don't follow you, Doc."

"A bullet will just put me out of my suffering a little sooner," he said. "So I never duck, I never flinch, I never worry about losing." A sardonic smile. "And so I never lose."

She stared at him for a long moment. "I don't know what to say."

"Say, 'Good luck, Doc,'" he replied, getting to his feet. "I'm off to try my luck at the Oriental."

"Good luck, Doc."

"Why, thank you, Josie," he said, bowing deeply. As he walked to the door he passed the waiter, and slipped him two dollars. "For me and the lady," he said softly.

Then he was out the door, and a few minutes later he arrived at the Oriental. He entered through the swinging doors, saw that none of the high-stakes games had started yet, spotted Henry Wiggins at the bar, and walked over to join him.

"Hi, Doc," said Henry. "Have a drink. I'm treating."

"That's a quick way to go broke," said a man standing a few feet away.

"Good evening to you too, Frank," said Holliday. "Henry, say hello to Frank McLaury, but keep your hands in your pockets." Wiggins looked at him curiously. "When you deal with the McLaurys, *someone's* hands are going to be in your pockets. They might as well be your own."

"And when you deal with Doc Holliday," replied McLaury, "you don't even have to ask whose bullet is going to wind up in your back. You *know*."

"Who *is* he?" asked Wiggins uncomfortably.

"A friend of the Clantons'," answered Holliday. "That's all you have to know." A pause. "Well, of course, you know one other thing as well."

"What?"

"You know he's not here alone, or he'd never have the guts to talk to me." Holliday looked around the room. "See that ugly-looking Cowboy in the blue shirt at that table by the window? That's his brother Tom. It's difficult to say which one's dumber, but I think Frank's got my vote. At least Tom has enough brains to pretend I'm not here—either that, or else he's so stupid he can't remember how to walk over to the bar."

"Just keep talking," said Frank McLaury. "Your time is coming."

"How would you like to go out in the street, and we'll see whose time comes first?" said Holliday.

McLaury opened his coat and spread his arms. "I'm not wearing a gun."

"I hope you don't think that bothers me in the least," replied Holliday.

Suddenly McLaury looked very nervous. "Fuck you, Holliday!"

Holliday smiled. "You see how changeable he is, Henry? First he wants to kill me and now he wants to fuck me."

"I don't have to listen to this shit!" snapped McLaury, walking off to join his brother.

Wiggins watched them in rapt fascination, ready to duck if guns appeared—but none did, and he finally turned back to Holliday. "I thought I was going to see you in action for a minute there," he said.

"Maybe we ought to rent out a stadium and sell tickets," said Holliday. "The winner could get rich."

"I thought your fight was with the Clantons and maybe Johnny Ringo," said Wiggins. "Tell me about these McLaurys."

"Ever heard of Fred White?" asked Holliday.

"No."

"He was the first marshal of Tombstone. Curly Bill Brocius and the McLaury brothers killed him."

"Then why aren't they in jail?"

Holliday smiled. "It's one thing to know they did it. It's another to get any witnesses to testify when the Cowboys threaten to kill anyone who talks."

"I had no idea this town was so dangerous!" exclaimed Wiggins.

"Most of the folks are law-abiding citizens who just want to get rich from silver mines—or off the people who *are* getting rich from them. There are only about forty or fifty Cowboys."

"And Ringo," said Wiggins.

Holliday nodded. "And Ringo."

"What are you going to do about him?"

"Ringo?" asked Holliday. "Have a drink or three, and introduce him to the works of Chaucer."

"I'm being serious, Doc."

"So am I, Henry."

Wiggins studied him for a long moment. "You like him, don't you?"

"Not very much," answered Holliday.

"Then why spend so much time talking to him?"

"If I want to talk about literature, there isn't anyone else, except maybe John Clum, and John's too busy putting out the *Epitaph* to have any spare time."

"So you *do* like talking to him."

"It's a hell of a lot easier than fighting him."

"You could talk to Bat Masterson," said Wiggins. "I'm told he used to be a writer."

"He used to be a man," responded Holliday. He shrugged. "We never talked much anyway."

"I get the feeling that you live a very lonely life."

Holliday remembered his morning with Kate, then looked around the saloon, at the McLaurys sitting at their table, and at Ike Clanton just entering with Johnny Ringo.

"Really?" said Holliday. "There are times when it feels positively crowded."

# 31.

I T WAS EARLY AFTERNOON of the next day. Holliday had elected to eat at the American Hotel, and found Buntline already there.

"Good morning," he said, sitting down opposite the older man.

"Good afternoon," Buntline corrected him.

"One or the other," said Holliday with a shrug. "How's Bat?"

"He spent the entire night in the cell. He's in his hotel now."

"Poor son of a bitch," said Holliday. "Well, it shouldn't be much longer. All I need is an excuse."

"By the way, I spent about an hour talking with Tom about the gun you want," said Buntline. "He's been thinking about how to do it."

"Good. I don't know how long Johnny Ringo will wait." Holliday shook his head. "I'd have loved to have faced him when he was alive."

"Good God, why?"

"To see who was the best, of course."

"Well, whoever was second best wouldn't have much time to sulk, I'll admit that," said Buntline with a smile.

A waiter came over and Holliday ordered a muffin and a coffee.

"You're never going to put on any muscle eating like that," observed Buntline.

"I'm not trying to," answered Holliday, suppressing a cough. "I'll settle for not losing any more weight."

"Your friend Henry Wiggins was telling me what a wonderful cook his wife is. Maybe you should spend some time with them when you're done here."

"Let's see if I'm still alive then," said Holliday. "As for Henry, I'm sure he loves his wife, but I can't remember a night I didn't see him at Kate's place. His wife'll never buy his explanation."

"What is it?" asked Buntline curiously.

"He only beds the all-metal ones, so he can't form an emotional attachment. Think she'll go for it?"

Buntline smiled. "Not a chance."

"Then I probably shouldn't visit. You never know what might slip out."

"Matter of fact, he's going to be home even less than usual," said Buntline. "Tom and I are probably going to grant him the right to sell some of our inventions."

"Hell, just sell electric streetlights to Chicago and New York, and you can retire," said Holliday. "And if you need more money, run the Bunt Line up and down the Atlantic seaboard."

"That's why his territory will be west of the Mississippi," answered Buntline with a grin. "I'm not without my contacts back East."

Holliday put his muffin down on a plate. "You want the rest of this?"

"No, thanks."

"I guarantee there are no germs on it. I gargled with whiskey not twenty minutes before I got here."

"Some other time."

The two men chatted for a few more minutes, then left the restaurant and began walking back toward Buntline's house. Along the way they became aware of a commotion just outside the Oriental, and they walked over to see what was happening.

When they arrived they found Wyatt and Morgan Earp with their guns drawn, and a tall, curly-headed man with his hands in the air. The three of them were surrounded by a crowd of perhaps thirty men and women.

"Take his gun, Morg," said Wyatt.

Morgan did so, then stepped back.

"You made a big mistake coming back to town," said Wyatt.

"Not as big a mistake as you're making now," said the man.

"We'll see about that."

"Is that who I think it is?" whispered Buntline.

"Curly Bill Brocius," replied Holliday.

"I'm arresting you for the shooting and attempted murder of Tom Edison," said Wyatt.

"I've got ten witnesses who will swear I wasn't even in town that day," said Brocius. "I was riding shotgun for Ike Clanton while he was buying horses and cattle down south."

"You shot Edison, and you're going to jail for it."

"Excuse me, Wyatt," said Buntline, stepping forward, "but may I make a suggestion?"

Wyatt turned to him. "What is it?"

"Before you lock him away, Tom's got an invention I think might interest you."

"Oh?"

Buntline nodded his head. "It can tell if a man is lying or not."

"No machine can do that," said Wyatt.

"This one can. He finished work on it last month, but hasn't had a reason to test it out."

"I don't know—"

"I'm all for it," said Brocius. "And when it says that I'm telling the truth, do you agree to let me go?"

"Hell, no!" snapped Wyatt.

"Then I don't agree to take the test," said Brocius.

"Just a minute, Wyatt," said Morgan. "You know Ike will produce twenty men who'll swear he was in China, if that's his story. We don't have any eyewitnesses, we're never going to depose Geronimo, so why not try the machine and agree to his terms? If it can't prove he's lying, what's the point of feeding him for days or weeks if the court will just turn him loose?"

Wyatt considered it for a moment, then shrugged. "What the hell. Where's this contraption at, Ned?"

"In Tom's lab."

"Is it bulky?"

"No, why?"

"Because I'd rather administer the test at the jail, in front of witnesses. I don't want Curly Bill claiming we beat a confession out of him."

"I'd like to see you try," said Brocius pugnaciously.

"That's a pretty daring challenge," commented Holliday with a smile.

"Go get the machine," said Wyatt to Buntline. "Bring it to the jail. And bring Tom, too. It's his invention; I want him to be the one to work it."

"I'm on my way," said Buntline, heading off.

Wyatt turned to Holliday. "You want to come along?"

"Wouldn't miss it for the world," replied Holliday.

"Okay, Morg. March him to the jailhouse."

Brocius, Holliday, and the Earps led a parade of perhaps twenty people to the jail, where they found Buntline and Edison waiting for them.

"Where's your contraption, and how does it work?" asked Wyatt.

"It's on the desk in the office," said Edison. "But I can administer it out here if you'd rather."

"It'll be a lot more comfortable out here on the street than with twenty people crammed into the office."

Edison disappeared inside the jailhouse and emerged a moment later with a small box that had a number of switches and levers, and a pair of electrical cords. Buntline carried a chair out, then entered the jail again and soon brought out a small table.

"Okay, how does this thing work?" asked Wyatt.

"I attach one wire to his head, and one to his wrist," explained Edison, setting the box on the table.

"Is this gonna hurt?" asked Brocius, sitting on the chair as Buntline indicated.

"Not at all," answered Edison. He turned back to Wyatt. "The brain undergoes electrical activity whenever it functions, but depending on what it's thinking, it doesn't display the same type of activity. If the subject is telling the truth, we'll get one kind of response from the machine; if he's lying, the brain's activity will be different, and his pulse will increase abnormally."

"What if he's just a natural-born liar, like, say, Curly Bill?" asked Holliday.

Edison smiled. "We'll ask him to lie at the start, so we can see if there's a difference."

Edison reached out to attach a wire to Brocius's head.

"You're *sure* this won't hurt?" demanded Brocius.

"Shut up, tough guy," said Morgan, holding his gun a few inches from Brocius's nose.

Edison finished attaching the two wires.

"Now," he said, "I'm going to ask you two questions, and I want honest answers. First, what is your name?"

"Curly Bill Brocius."

"And how old are you?"

"Thirty-six."

Edison studied the tiny dials on his machine. "All right," he said. "I'm going to ask you the same two questions, and this time I want you to lie."

"What name do you want me to give?" asked Brocius.

"If I tell you, then you won't have to think up a lie, and that could affect the machine. Now, who are you?"

"Abraham Lincoln."

"And how old are you?"

"Eleven."

Edison looked at the machine again. "All right," he said. "There's a clearly discernable difference. I guess we can get down to business. Wyatt, do you want to ask the questions?"

"Why not?" said Wyatt. He walked closer to Brocius. "Did you shoot Tom Edison?"

"No."

"Are you lying to me?"

"No."

"Do you have witnesses who can testify to the fact that you were nowhere near Edison on the day he was shot?"

"Dozens of them."

Wyatt turned to Edison. "Well?"

"His first two answers were lies," said Edison.

"And his third?"

"His third was the truth, but you worded the question badly. He *does* have witnesses who will swear he was elsewhere. May I ask it differently?"

"Go ahead."

"Mr. Brocius, these witnesses you refer to," said Edison. "If they swear you were elsewhere on the day I was shot, will they be telling the truth?"

"Yes."

Edison smiled. "This time it was a lie."

"The hell it was!" yelled Brocius. "Who are you going to believe— me or that dumb machine?"

"I'm glad you asked," said Wyatt. He turned to the crowd. "You all saw and heard it." Then: "Morg, lock him up."

"Right," said Morgan, gesturing to Brocius to stand up.

"This is crazy!" complained Brocius. "You don't even know if that little box works! All you have is Edison's word for it."

"Which is a damned sight more believable than yours," said Morgan. "Let's go."

"And Morg," said Wyatt. "Don't put him anywhere near the all-brass cell."

"Yeah, I know," said Morgan, and he and Brocius entered the jail.

"That's some contraption," said Earp. "It's going to make judges' and lawyers' jobs a lot easier."

"It's going to need much more experimentation before I'd feel safe condemning a man to death because of its conclusions," said Edison.

"Fortunately I don't share your trepidations," replied Earp.

"You know," said Holliday, "I think that machine could be even more effective if it could deliver a hell of a shock every time the subject lies."

"It *would* encourage people to tell the truth," said Earp.

Edison shook his head. "One thing I didn't tell you, because I didn't think it would apply to Brocius . . . but if the subject is extremely nervous, either about the questions, or the potential consequences of his answers, or even about the machine, a true answer might read as a lie."

"You're not going to tell that to the judge, I hope," said Earp.

"Only if asked," answered Edison.

"Do you suppose the day will ever come when that can work without wires?" asked Holliday.

"Someday, I suppose. Why?"

"I'd love to play poker with someone who's rigged with it. It'd tell me when he was bluffing."

"Well, I'll be damned!" said Earp, looking up the street.

Holliday and Edison followed his gaze, and saw Masterson approaching them.

"How are you feeling, Bat?" asked Earp.

"Like shit," said Masterson. "But I couldn't stay in that room all day. My life has got to be more than a hotel room by day and a metal cell by night."

"We're on our way to the Oriental," said Earp. He looked at the sky. "You're good for maybe three or four more hours. Why not join us?"

"I'd rather meet this Indian who can change me back."

"Can't be done," said Holliday.

"Why the hell not?" demanded Masterson.

"You can't get there before dark, and once the sun sets, you know you're going to lose your clothes and weapons, and you're probably going to kill your horse as well. Come morning you'll be alone and naked in Indian territory. Trust us: we have a deal with Que-Su-La. We do our part and the spell is lifted."

Masterson sighed heavily. "You're right. I know that. But I just can't take much more of this."

"I know," said Holliday more gently. "Maybe you could do with a visit to Kate's place."

Masterson shook his head. "I'd look at all those lovely throats and wonder which one I'd rip out first when I get tired of horses and cattle." He grimaced at the thought. "Let's go to the Oriental. I just need to be with people."

"Well, I wouldn't go so far as to call the Clantons and McLaurys *people*," said Holliday. "But what the hell, they're probably still sleeping."

"Does Johnny Ringo ever sleep?" asked Edison.

Suddenly they became aware of a presence down the street in the opposite direction. They turned, and found themselves facing the thing that used to be Johnny Ringo. He grinned at them, pointed his finger at Edison as if it was a gun, and pretended to pull the trigger, then did the same to Holliday.

"I guess not," said Masterson.

# 32.

I T WAS EVENING, and the Oriental was doing a brisk business. Holliday hadn't had much luck at the faro table, and he'd moved over to a poker game. Wyatt and Virgil Earp sat at a small table in a corner, not socializing, not drinking, just making sure that nothing got out of hand. Morgan was patrolling Third Street and Allen Street, keeping a watchful eye on the other drinking and gambling establishments.

Suddenly John Behan burst into the Oriental, looked around, and walked over to the two Earp brothers.

"What's the meaning of it?" he demanded.

"Of what?" asked Wyatt.

"You arrested Bill Brocius!"

"That's our job, arresting lawbreakers," said Virgil. "I thought you knew that."

"Besides," added Wyatt, "*someone's* got to do it."

"He hasn't done anything!" shouted Behan.

"Not today," agreed Wyatt. "But he blew Tom Edison's arm off a few months ago."

"Says who?"

"Well, now, Johnny," said Wyatt with a smile, "that's the interesting part: says Brocius."

"What are you talking about?" yelled Behan.

"In fact," continued Wyatt, "he said it in front of twenty witnesses." He stood up and raised his voice. "Is there anyone here tonight who was at the jail when Bill Brocius confessed to shooting Tom Edison?"

Three men stood up.

"Well, there you have it," said Wyatt.

Behan stalked off to question each of the three men. He was back in front of the Earps a couple of minutes later.

"You put him in jail because some cockeyed *machine* told you to?" he demanded.

"Calm down, Johnny," said Virgil. "You're going to have a stroke."

"And why is he in *your* jail and not mine?" continued Behan. "After all, I'm the sheriff!"

"He's there because we don't want him escaping," answered Wyatt.

"You can't lock him up just because the victim invents something that says he did it when he denies it."

"Sure we can," said Virgil with a smile. "In fact, we did."

"I'll be in court first thing in the morning, and I'll have the judge release him before noon," promised Behan.

"If that's the same judge who found Ike Clanton innocent of stealing horses, I don't think I'm inclined to pay much attention to him," replied Virgil.

"You're a representative of the people and their government," snapped Behan. "You can't flaunt their laws."

"I'm a representative of the mine and business owners who weren't getting any satisfaction from their elected sheriff," answered Virgil.

"Now why don't you have a drink and calm down? Everyone knows you're just doing this because Josie left you for Wyatt."

"People get hanged for horse stealing," said Behan. "What do you think they should do to a man who steals another man's woman?"

"I didn't steal anyone," said Wyatt. "She came to me of her own free will, which makes a lot of sense when you consider what she was leaving."

"You'll turn her into a laudanum addict, just like the one you came here with," said Behan. "That's the only way a woman can live with you."

"That's enough," said Wyatt, so softly that no one but Virgil and Behan could hear him. "Not another word."

Behan looked into Wyatt's eyes and didn't like what he saw there. He began backing away, and his courage returned as the distance between them increased.

"I'll be in court tomorrow morning," he promised. As he reached the swinging doors he raised his voice. "You want her? You can have her! Even if she keeps off the laudanum, she's going to wind up working at Kate Elder's!"

Then he was gone.

"It's comforting to know that Johnny Behan is watching out for all the citizens of Tombstone," said Holliday in the silence that followed, and most of the patrons laughed.

Wyatt got up from his chair and turned to Virgil. "I'll be back in an hour or so. You can handle things alone."

"Where are you going?"

"I'm buying Mattie a train ticket to her parents' town. I'll wire them in the morning and let them know she's coming."

"That won't take but ten minutes," noted Virgil.

"I know. Then I'm going over to the Grand, and I'm going to ask Josie to marry me."

"If she says yes, I'm buying the next couple of rounds," said Virgil.

"Fair enough," said Wyatt. He walked to the swinging doors, made sure Behan wasn't lingering just beyond them, and finally went out into the street.

"This place is getting more interesting by the minute," remarked Holliday to the other men at his table, pushing a stack of chips into the center.

"Too rich for my blood," said one of the players, tossing in his cards.

"And mine," said another, doing the same.

"In fact," said the first one, "I think I'll call it a night."

"Me, too," said the second. "I'd like to have enough money left to buy breakfast tomorrow."

They got up and left, and Holliday raised his voice. "Two open seats over here."

Frank and Tom McLaury, who had just entered, walked over and sat down at the table.

"Well, look who's here," said Holliday.

"It's a small world," said Frank McLaury.

"Crowded, I'd say," replied Holliday. "Still, I'm flattered that with twelve gambling joints up and down the street, you've decided to lose your money to me."

"I don't like you much, Holliday," said Frank.

"Well, you have that in common with a lot of other men," said Holliday easily.

"Oh? Sounds like they'd be interesting men to know." He looked around the saloon. "Where are they?"

"Buried in graveyards from here to Texas," said Holliday. "And a few in Colorado, just for good measure."

"You don't make friends real easy, do you?" said Tom.

"Let's just say that I'm choosy," answered Holliday. He shuffled the cards. "The game is five-card stud, and the ante is fifty dollars."

"That's a pretty high ante," noted Frank.

"You'll just have to start stealing a better breed of horse," said Holliday.

"We didn't come here to be insulted," said Frank heatedly.

"If you'd like to step out in the street, I'd be happy to insult you there," said Holliday.

The two brothers exchanged looks.

"The time's not right," said Tom.

"I could ask you again in half an hour," said Holliday.

"Just deal."

Holliday shuffled the cards, then offered the deck to Tom to cut, after which he began dealing, one down and one up. Frank had a queen showing, Tom a king, the other two men a nine and a three, and Holliday himself had an eight.

On the next round, Frank got an ace, Tom a deuce, the other two men a jack and a four, and Holliday a five.

"Looks like they're not running your way," commented Tom, putting another fifty into the pot.

"You never know," replied Holliday, matching it, as did the other three players.

Holliday dealt again. This time Frank got another queen, giving him a pair. Tom got a deuce, also giving him a pair. One of the other two got a five and immediately folded, the other got a ten, and Holliday himself got a six.

Frank bet two hundred dollars, Tom and the other man folded, and Holliday matched it.

Then came the final card. Frank got an ace, giving him two pair face-up on the table, and Holliday got a seven.

"You're high," said Holliday, staring at Frank McLaury.

"I know," said Frank. "Don't rush me."

"You've got aces and queens, and he's got garbage," said Tom. "Put your money in. He'll fold."

"He should have folded already," said Frank, frowning. "But he didn't. Would he have stuck around if his hole card was an eight or a five? I mean, hell, I had that beat on the table. But he's got a five, six, seven, and eight showing." Finally he pushed four hundred dollars to the center of the table.

"I'll see that, and raise you a thousand," said Holliday, counting out his money and putting it on the pile.

"Damn!" said Frank. "I *knew* he had a straight!" He looked at Holliday's expressionless face. "Which is it, a nine or a four?"

"It'll cost you a thousand dollars to find out," answered Holliday.

Frank agonized over his cards for another minute, then folded. "I *know* he's got it!"

As Holliday was pulling in his money, Tom said "Let's see whether he did or not."

He reached a hand out to turn over Holliday's hole card, but before he could reach it Holliday grabbed the knife he wore around his neck, breaking the thin thread that held it, and buried the point in the table between two of Tom's fingers.

"Turn that card over and it'll cost you a thousand dollars or four fingers," he said without raising his voice.

"Are you crazy!" snapped Tom, jerking his hand back.

"You know the rules," said Holliday.

"I know more than that," said Tom, getting to his feet. "I know your days are numbered!"

"Since I doubt that either you or your brother can count past one, we can settle matters right now," replied Holliday.

Tom looked like he was about to agree, but Frank got to his feet and began ushering his brother to the doorway. "We'll take you up on your offer," he said, "but at a time and place of our own choosing."

Then they were gone. Virgil walked over to the table and sat down opposite Holliday.

"You okay, Doc?" he asked, as Holliday pulled his knife out of the wood and laid it on the table.

"Couldn't be better," said Holliday. "I wish those assholes came by more often. That was the easiest money I ever made."

"You've got a strange smile on your face," said Virgil

"I can't imagine why," replied Holliday, turning over his hole card.

It was the jack of diamonds.

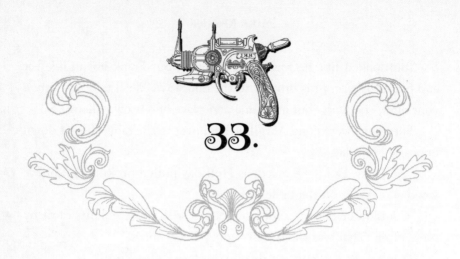

# 33.

WYATT EARP PUT MATTIE ON A TRAIN back to Kansas in the morning. Masterson had developed serious gashes in both his hands trying to pound down the brass walls of his cell, and Earp and Holliday took him to a local doctor to get him patched up.

When it was done, Earp offered to buy both his companions breakfast.

"Sounds good to me," said Masterson. "And the farther we are from Brocius, the better."

"Did he threaten you?" asked Earp.

"When did the threats of a drunken Cowboy ever bother any of us?" replied Masterson.

"Then what—?"

"He sang dirty songs all night long," said Masterson. "As loud as he could."

"I thought you couldn't remember what happens when you're a bat," said Holliday.

"He was singing them when I changed, and he was still singing them when I changed back."

"Well, you'd better get used to it," said Earp. "We're pressing charges this afternoon, and I don't care how low his bail is set, he hasn't got two cents to his name."

"Will Ike make bail for him?"

"I sure as hell doubt it. He was supposed to kill Edison. If he doesn't fuck it up, you and Doc don't come to Tombstone."

"I'm tired of eating at the American and the Grand," said Holliday. "Let's try a new restaurant."

"There's one over on Sixth Street that's supposed to be okay," replied Earp.

"Has it got a name?"

"Delmonico's."

"Why do I think it's not the real McCoy?" said Holliday.

"It's named after a restaurant in New York," said Earp. "The owner ate there when he was visiting some family, liked it, and decided to open his own Delmonico's."

"I guarantee it won't cost as much," said Masterson. "You could pay as much as four dollars for a meal at one of those top New York restaurants. And that's not even including a bottle of wine."

They arrived at Delmonico's and entered. There were only four tables in the restaurant. Three were occupied by diners, and a large tawny cat lay sleeping atop the fourth. Earp brushed him away, he yowled and hit the floor running, and Holliday, Masterson, and Earp seated themselves.

"What do you think of it?" asked Earp.

"I think we're in Tombstone," said Masterson with a smile. "Hardly any of those fancy New York restaurants have cats on the tables."

A bearded waiter—they suspected that he was also the chef, and possibly the owner as well—brought out well-worn menus and handed one to each of them.

"Well," said Holliday, perusing the single sheet, "it appears that we can have beef steak or horse steak. He probably also serves cat steak when he runs low on supplies."

"You can have a steak sandwich, too," noted Masterson.

"With or without the bread," added Holliday.

"I suppose you can have Maine lobster, too," said Masterson, "as long as you don't mind if it looks and tastes like steak."

They ordered and a few minutes later the waiter brought their steaks out to them.

"I hear you had a little run-in with the McLaury brothers last night," said Wyatt.

"A minor one," said Holliday. "They're not half as tough as this steak is."

"Watch out for them," cautioned Earp. "They carry grudges."

"I relieved them of their money," replied Holliday. "That should make their grudges much easier to carry."

"Just be careful anyway." Earp turned to Masterson. "I didn't even look. Did you do any damage to Ned's brass walls? Put a dent or two in them?"

Masterson shook his head. "Maybe you could do it with a sledge-hammer or a pickax, but not with flesh and blood—and especially not with those claws I develop when I change."

"Do you think that other version of you is smart enough not to injure himself again tonight?"

"I don't know, Wyatt. I don't remember doing it in the first place."

"I was afraid of that," said Earp with a sigh. "That's why I asked the doctor to coat your hands and forearms with a medicine like sheep sorrel rather than bandages. The bandages would probably come right off during the transformation. Hopefully the medication can keep working."

"How much longer before it ends?" asked Masterson.

Earp shrugged. "I don't know. A few days, a week. Almost certainly less than a month."

"I can't take much more of it, Wyatt."

"Just try to stick it out."

"I don't know if the bat minds it," continued Masterson. "I can't remember his thoughts. But lately I've been thinking more and more of putting a gun to my head and ending it all."

"Why?" asked Holliday.

Masterson stared at him incredulously. "Have you heard a word I've said all week?"

"I've heard it. And what registers most is that you can't remember a damned thing about being a bat. So if you can't remember it, if you're not haunted by terrible things you may have done, why should that make you suicidal?"

"Because half my life is missing!" snapped Masterson. "If I want a woman, I can only have her in the daytime. If I want a card game, I have to find people who'll play before sunset. Wherever I am, I have to report to that tiny brass cell while I can still see the sun. *That's* why."

"It's temporary," noted Holliday.

"Yeah—and what if you can't deliver your half of the bargain to this Indian?"

"Then we'll be dead and you'll still be better off than we are."

"You don't understand, Doc."

"I never did understand whining," said Holliday. "I've been dying a slow, painful death for close to ten years now. I have to adjust to it, but on days I feel cheated or morbid, I do my best to keep it to myself."

Masterson stared at him for a long moment, and then his expression softened. "I'm sorry, Doc. It's all new to me. If I have to adjust to it, I will."

Holliday pulled his flask out of a coat pocket and offered it to Masterson.

"Have a drink, and we'll all be friends again."

Masterson took a swallow, passed it to Earp, who sipped it, and then it came back to Holliday, who drained it.

"I think I'll just stretch my legs a bit and take a walk through town," announced Masterson, getting to his feet.

"Makes sense," said Holliday. "You've been stretching your wings enough every night."

"I don't remember any details," said Masterson, "but somehow, I remember the feel of the wind in my face, and a sense of total, absolute freedom." He shrugged. "Or maybe I'm just imagining it."

"What the hell," said Earp. "I'll walk with you."

"Loan me your cane, and so will I," added Holliday.

Masterson handed his cane to Holliday. "Let's go."

The three men walked out into the street, and in about ten minutes found themselves in front of the jail, where Curly Bill Brocius was there to meet them.

"What are you doing loose?" demanded Earp.

"The judge threw the case out of court," laughed Brocius. "I knew *someone* in this town would take a human's word over a little electric gadget. And the fact that the guy reading the gadget's dials was the man I was supposed to have shot prejudiced the case anyway."

"You were lucky," said Earp.

"I don't hold it against you, Wyatt," said Brocius. "Hell, if truth be known, those were the first decent meals I've had in a month. I could do with a few more arrests."

"Don't tempt me," said Earp.

"See you tonight," promised Brocius, heading off.

"Shit!" muttered Earp. "He was the most dangerous of the Cowboys, at least until Ringo showed up. Now we're going to have to wait for him to maybe shoot somebody, and then arrest him all over again."

"Don't blame the judge, Wyatt," said Holliday. "He's never seen Tom's invention before."

"He's seen the electric streetlamps, and the horseless coaches, and—"

"It makes no difference," persisted Holliday. "Until they write a law making Tom's evidence acceptable, it's always going to be disallowed."

"But you know he was lying!" said Earp.

"I've heard it from two sources," said Holliday. "Fin Clanton, who'll deny he said it, and Tom Edison, who was the victim. That kind of testimony was never going to keep him in jail."

"Maybe not," said Earp. "But damn it, it *should* have!"

"I should have no trouble breathing, and Bat should spend twenty-four hours a day looking like he looks now. The world is full of should-haves."

"All right," said Earp. "We might as well head over to the Oriental until it's time to put Bat in his cell again."

"I've *seen* the Oriental," said Masterson. "I want to see the parts of town I haven't been to yet."

"Whatever you say," replied Earp with a sigh.

"That's too much walking for me," said Holliday. He handed the cane back to Masterson. "I think I'll take a nap over at Kate's place. I'll see you tonight, Wyatt. Take care of yourself."

"Not to worry," said Earp. "Nothing exciting ever happens in Tombstone."

# 34.

OLLIDAY SHOWED UP AT THE ORIENTAL just after eight o'clock. Most of the games hadn't started yet. Henry Wiggins was sitting alone at a table and waved him over.

"Hi, Doc," he said. "I hear they let that guy out of jail—Curly somebody-or-other."

"He'll be back in before too long," replied Holliday, sitting down opposite Wiggins.

"Could be," agreed Wiggins.

"*Will* be," said Holliday firmly. "He's a Cowboy."

"You say it like that's something rare. There are cowboys everywhere."

"Around here you spell it with a capital C," said Holliday, "and Cowboys work for the Clantons or the McLaurys."

"That does explain it," said Wiggins.

"And here comes another Cowboy," announced Holliday, making no attempt to lower his voice. "You can tell by the incredibly stupid look, the misplaced arrogance, the inability to use words of more than two syllables, the fact that women shrink from his touch. Hi, Tom."

Tom McLaury glowered at him.

"You feel pretty safe when you've got all these damned Earps protecting you," he growled.

"I feel pretty safe just being around you, Tom," said Holliday. "I know you want to kill me, so I figure I'm the safest guy in the room when you start firing your pistol."

"I wouldn't bet on it!" snapped McLaury.

"Oh, you can afford the table stakes, Tom," said Holliday easily. "Just put up your life and we have a wager."

"You keep riding me, and—"

Holliday's gun was in his hand, aimed right between McLaury's eyes. "Or what, Tom?"

"Your time is coming," promised McLaury, heading off to the bar.

"My heart is racing a mile a minute!" exclaimed Wiggins, holding his hand to his chest. "Weren't you frightened?"

"Of what?" asked Holliday.

"Of dying, of course," said Wiggins.

"I'm already dying, Henry. Speeding up the process is hardly a cause for concern."

"Damn, I'm glad you're my friend!"

"Am I?" asked Holliday with open curiosity.

"Of course you are."

"I'm very pleased, Henry. I don't have a lot of friends." A pause. "Alive."

"Given the life you lead, I can't say I'm surprised," replied Wiggins.

"Well, as long as we're friends," said Holliday, "let me buy the next round."

"If you insist," said Wiggins. "It's very unwise to say No to Doc Holliday."

"You'd be surprised how many women have done just that," replied Holliday with a sardonic smile.

"I'm even more surprised you didn't shoot McLaury where he stood."

"This is Wyatt's town, and killing McLaury in the Oriental would just make trouble for him." Holliday paused. "I think the only one I'd be willing to kill in here is Johnny Ringo—and of course, he can't *be* killed."

"I have to ask: Why Ringo, who you seem to like? Why not Ike or one of the McLaurys—or that man they released this afternoon?"

"A lot of people think Ringo's the best," said Holliday. "And if you're going to be the best, you have to beat the best."

"Think of the damage you two could do to the Cowboys if you were on the same side."

Holliday smiled and shook his head. "We would never be on the same side. Sooner or later we'd have to meet out in the street."

"Even though he's a zombie?"

"Even so."

"I don't understand you."

"It's not the glory," said Holliday. "There isn't any. It's not the reward. There's never been one for either of us." He paused again. "It's the competition."

"I don't know how the hell you plan to beat a dead man," said Wiggins.

"Neither do I."

"Even if you beat him to the draw, even if you plant a slug in his head or his heart before he can fire, it won't stop him. He'll still kill you."

"But I'll have had the satisfaction of knowing I beat him," said Holliday.

"For maybe half a second," noted Wiggins.

Holliday smiled again. "That's better than never knowing at all."

"Damn!" said Wiggins. "Every time I think I understand you, I find out that I don't."

"Try not to worry about it, Henry. Have another drink."

"Thanks," said Wiggins, reaching for the bottle. "I think I will."

Earp approached the table just then. "Good evening, Doc. Hello, Mr. Wiggins."

"Henry," Wiggins corrected him.

"Care for a drink, Wyatt?" asked Holliday.

"Maybe in a few minutes," answered Earp. "I've got to go to work."

Holliday looked around. "There aren't any disturbances that I can see."

"I just got a report that Ike Clanton got dead drunk over at the Cactus Flower, and he's been walking up and down the street, shooting out windows. Want to come along?"

"Ike Clanton? Sure, why not?"

"May I come too?" asked Wiggins.

"I think not, Henry," said Earp. "I can't be worrying about you while I'm arresting Ike."

"Tell you what, Henry," said Holliday. "You can come if you stand behind me once we spot him."

"All right," said Wiggins.

"And remember, I'm not as noble as Wyatt. If you show yourself, you're on your own."

"I won't. Hell, I don't even own a gun."

"All right," said Earp. "Let's go."

The three of them walked out of the Oriental and into the street.

"The Cactus Flower is over on Fremont Street," said Earp, turning to his left.

As they approached Fremont, a crowd was hurriedly leaving it.

"Clanton?" asked Earp.

One of the men pointed behind him.

"Now would be a good time not to stick your head out, Henry," said Holliday.

They turned onto Fremont Street and suddenly saw Ike Clanton standing in the middle of the street, a rifle in his hand, swaying drunkenly.

Earp walked up to him. "I'll take that rifle, Ike."

"I haven't killed anyone," said Clanton. "Yet."

"Let's keep it that way," said Earp, grabbing the rifle and pulling it out of Clanton's hands.

"That's *my* rifle!" bellowed Clanton. "You can't do that."

"It's done."

Clanton reached for his pistol, but his movements were slow and uncertain. Earp had his gun out of the holster before Clanton's fingers could even find his own, and he cracked Clanton across the head with it. The Cowboy fell to the ground in a senseless heap.

"Henry," said Earp, "you want to make yourself useful?"

"Sure," said Wiggins. "What do you want me to do?"

"Take his feet," said Earp, lifting Clanton by the arms. "We're going to carry him to the jailhouse. He can spend the night there. Doc, can you take his gun and his rifle?"

"Yeah, I need a cane anyway," said Holliday. He pocketed the pistol, then ejected a bullet from the rifle and began walking with it, muzzle down in the dirt.

"He's going to have to take that thing apart and clean it before he can use it," said Earp.

"Poor fellow," replied Holliday with a smile.

It took them five minutes to reach the jail. Earp unlocked the building, opened an empty cell, and left Clanton lying on the floor, still unconscious.

"He's going to have one hell of a headache when he wakes up," noted Holliday.

"Well, hopefully he'll think a little more carefully before he goes looking for trouble again," said Earp.

"Well, you can hope," said Holliday.

## 35.

**"D**OC!"

Holliday groaned and covered his head with a pillow.

"Doc, damn it!"

"Go away," mumbled Holliday.

"Get up!"

Holliday opened one eye and found himself staring at Kate Elder. "What time is it?"

"Two o'clock."

"All right. I'll get up in a few minutes."

"Now!"

Holliday sat up on the side of the bed and blinked his eyes rapidly. "What the hell's the matter?"

"Something's up."

Holliday looked down at his lap. "The hell it is."

"Goddamn it, Doc!" She took a glass of water and threw it in his face.

"All right, I'm awake," he said bitterly. "What's going on?"

"I don't know," she said. "But we've been getting reports in for the last hour. The Earps are holed up at the Oriental."

"Kate, they *own* the Oriental. Of course they'd be there."

"And Ike Clanton and a bunch of Cowboys are down by Fly's Photo Studio, near the O.K. Corral."

"All right, so there are some Cowboys in town. There usually are."

"Some of our customers say each side has been threatening the other for the past few hours. Johnny Behan is with the Cowboys right now."

"You're making too much out of this, Kate," said Holliday. He got to his feet. "What the hell. I'm awake, I might as well get dressed." He was suddenly overcome by a paroxysm of coughing, and sat down again. She brought him a handkerchief, and he handed it back to her a few minutes later when he was done.

"That's more blood than usual," she noted, staring at it.

"I don't know what you expect me to do about it. Cough out the window, maybe."

She stared at him for a long moment. "I don't know which to do," she said at last, "nurse you or kick you in the balls."

"Do I get a vote?" he asked.

She smiled. "You are the most infuriating man." She walked to the door. "Get dressed. I'll have some breakfast ready for you."

She left the room, and Holliday began getting into his clothes. When he was through, he buckled his holster and tied it around his right thigh.

Kate had scrambled some eggs and made him a pot of coffee. He sat down at the table, prepared to eat, when he suddenly frowned.

"What is it?" asked Kate.

"The windows are open."

"So?"

"It's too quiet. I can't even hear a bird."

"It's the middle of the day on a quiet street," she said.

"It's too quiet anyway."

He heard the front door open, and assumed it was another customer. Instead Ned Buntline, a package under his arm, was ushered into the kitchen.

"What are you doing here?" asked Holliday. "Did you build another whore?"

"No," said Buntline.

"Well, then?"

"There's going to be trouble. I thought you could use this."

He unwrapped the package to reveal a set of brass body armor.

"That's thoughtful of you, Ned," said Holliday, "but I can't even lift it, let alone fight in it."

"You've got to take *some* of it," urged Buntline.

"Maybe the vest."

"And something for your knees. You don't want to spend the rest of your life on a cart."

"The rest of my life isn't going to last long enough for it to make much difference," said Holliday.

"Doc!" said Kate harshly.

"Okay, okay, the knee things too."

"And a Gatling pistol."

"I can't hold it up long enough to aim it," protested Holliday.

"Just think about it," said Buntline, laying the pistol on a table next to the vest and the knee guards.

"I hope to hell you're making the Earps suffer with this stuff too."

"They asked for it."

"I guess they mean business," said Holliday. "I haven't noticed them wearing body armor before—or at least, not all three of them at once. Give me a hand with this damned stuff." As Buntline was adjusting the vest, Holliday suddenly frowned. "Kate says Ike is waiting by the photo studio. I thought he was in jail."

"They had to let him go this morning. The sentence for blowing out a couple of windows is one night in jail."

"I'll bet he's got one hell of a headache."

"I wouldn't know. I haven't seen him all day."

"Is Johnny Ringo with him?" asked Holliday suddenly.

"I don't know. Like I say, I've only seen our side, not the other one."

Holliday looked at the Gatling pistol. "This won't stop him," he announced. He pulled his own gun and looked at it. "Neither will this." He shrugged. "I'll just have to improvise."

"Let me help you with the leg guards," said Buntline, kneeling down and beginning to attach them.

"I thought these were *knee* guards," complained Holliday. "They go all the way down to my feet."

"Just shut up and wear them," said Kate.

"I'm going to be so tired from lugging this stuff to Fly's that I won't have the energy to pull my gun."

"It's lighter than it looks," said Buntline, affixing the other leg guard.

"Damned well better be," muttered Holliday.

Finally Buntline stood up. "There!" he said. "You're as ready as I can make you."

"Nobody's asked me to join in," said Holliday. "Maybe I'll just sit out front, with my chest and my legs protected from mosquitoes."

"Shut up, Doc!" said Kate. She turned to Buntline. "He thanks you, Ned. He's like this when he's just out of bed."

"It's all right," said Buntline. "He's my friend."

He left the kitchen, walked through the parlor, and exited the house.

"We have to move to another town," said Holliday. "I've got too many friends in this one. They're starting to become a pain in the ass."

"You can go anywhere you want," said Kate. "Me, I like it here."

"Oh, well," said Holliday, "as long as I'm wearing this junk, I might as well see if I can walk all the way to the corner in it."

"Don't forget the gun."

"My own gun is fine," he replied. "And I can lift it. Now where the hell's my cane?"

He left the house, walked out onto the street, and turned to his right. When he reached Fremont Street he paused for a moment, and was about to keep going when a movement off to his left caught his attention. It was the three Earp brothers, all wearing brass vests and leg guards. Wyatt and Morgan also wore protective goggles.

Holliday stepped forward, meeting them at the corner.

"Go home, Doc," said Wyatt. "This is *our* fight, not yours."

"That's a hell of a thing for you to say to me," replied Holliday, falling into step. They walked another thirty yards down Fremont, and Holliday asked: "Does anyone know if Ringo's there?"

"We don't know who's there, except for Ike," answered Wyatt.

"If he *is* there, he's mine. Not that this peashooter will do any good."

Virgil handed him a shotgun. "Take this, and give me your cane."

"That's a fair enough trade," said Holliday. "What's this all about?"

"We got word that Ike's been talking about how he's going to kill us," said Virgil. "He's holed up in an empty lot next to the O.K. Corral, between Fly's and the assay store. We know Billy's with him, and I think maybe one of the McLaurys, and someone else, maybe two others. I gave him an hour to get out of town. That was at noon. As far as we know, he's still there, so we're going to disarm him and put him back in jail for disturbing the peace."

"Except that we're not," said Morgan. "He'll never hand over his gun and go meekly, not when he's got a bunch of Cowboys with him."

Holliday nodded his head. "Sounds about right. You worry about the Cowboys. I'll take care of Ringo." He paused. "Where's Bat?"

"He's too jumpy," said Wyatt. "You've seen him."

"Many times," said Holliday. "He's good in a situation like this."

"He *was*," said Wyatt. "And hopefully he will be again. But not now, not while he's still under Geronimo's spell."

When they were a block from their destination, Johnny Behan came running up to them from the alleyway between Fly's studio and the MacDonald assay office.

"It's all right," he said. "I've disarmed them. There won't be any trouble."

"That's up to them," said Wyatt, without slowing his pace.

"But they're disarmed!" repeated Behan.

"Then you're right and there won't be any trouble," repeated Wyatt.

In another minute they came to the alleyway between Fly's and the assay office, which backed up to the O.K. Corral. Ike Clanton, his head swathed in bandages, was there, as was his brother Billy, and a hired gunman, young Billy Claiborne. And rounding out his group were Frank and Tom McLaury.

"Where the hell is Ringo?" muttered Holliday as the Earps came to a halt about twenty feet away from Clanton and the others.

"You sons of bitches been spoiling for a fight, and now you've got one," said Wyatt.

"Just drop your weapons to the ground and there won't be any trouble," said Virgil.

Billy Clanton's hand dropped to the handle of his pistol. He mouthed the word "Never!"

"Hold on!" said Virgil. "I don't want that! I—"

Whatever he said next was lost beneath the sound of gunfire.

All three Earps drew the guns that Buntline had designed for them. Billy Clanton, Frank McLaury, and Billy Claiborne drew their own and began firing. Tom McLaury ducked behind his horse, pulling his rifle from where it was tucked, and putting a bullet through Morgan's shoulder, just outside his armored vest.

"Where's Ringo?" roared Holliday. He fired one barrel of the shotgun in the air, and as Tom McLaury's horse shied from the sound and exposed McLaury, Holliday emptied the second barrel into him, killing him instantly, then threw the empty shotgun away and pulled his pistol.

Ike raced up to Wyatt, claiming he was unarmed. Wyatt shoved him away with a terse, "Get to fighting or get to running." Ike got to running.

Billy Claiborne decided he wasn't getting paid enough for this, threw his gun to the ground after getting off three shots, and raced into Fly's Photo Studio.

That left Billy Clanton and Frank McLaury. The air was so filled with smoke that no one could see their targets, so they just kept firing. The noise was deafening. Holliday felt a slug glance off his gunbelt. A bullet bounced off Morgan's armor. Two more bullets ricocheted off Virgil's knee guard; a third thudded home in his thigh.

Billy Clanton, the youngest of the Cowboys, proved to be the bravest. Hit many times by bullets from all three Earps, he stood his ground, then knelt, and finally collapsed but kept shooting.

Morgan, who had fallen to the ground, managed to shoot Frank McLaury in the belly. McLaury decided he'd had enough, and raced out

into Fremont Street. Holliday turned and followed him, only to find that McLaury had stopped and turned, and was aiming his pistol at Holliday's head.

"I've got you now!" yelled McLaury.

"You're a daisy if you do," replied Holliday, crouching and shooting—and a second McLaury was dead at his hands.

He went back into the alleyway, where Wyatt was just finishing off Billy Clanton. And then, as quickly as it began, it ended, with two McLaurys and a Clanton dead, two Earps wounded, Holliday's hip sore but the skin unbroken, and Wyatt the only one to emerge totally unscathed.

Holliday looked around and yelled one last time: "Where the hell is Johnny Ringo?"

He saw Wyatt kneeling down next to Morgan, trying to help him to his feet, and he lent his efforts. Virgil was still standing, but blood was pouring down his leg, and Holliday took off his belt and made a primitive tourniquet out of it.

Once it was clear that Ike Clanton was nowhere in the area and Billy Claiborne wasn't coming out of the photo studio, that the gun-fight was clearly over, Johnny Behan appeared and announced that all three Earps and Holliday were under arrest.

Holliday turned to Wyatt. "You want me to kill him now?"

"You told us you disarmed them," Wyatt said to Behan. "You lied."

"They weren't causing any trouble," said Behan. "I'm arresting you for murder."

"Nobody's arresting us," said Earp. "We're not leaving town. If there's a hearing or a trial, we'll be there." He turned to Holliday. "Doc, I've got to get my brothers to a doctor. If Behan tries to stop us or arrest us, kill him."

Holliday smiled at Behan. "Gladly."

There were no arrests.

Later, after Morgan and Virgil had been treated for their wounds, Wyatt and Holliday sat in the back room of the Oriental.

"Well, at least we took care of the McLaurys," said Earp, "and I don't think Ike will show his face around here for a while."

"It doesn't matter," said Holliday unhappily.

"What are you talking about?" demanded Earp. "We just won the biggest gunfight that ever took place in this town, probably in all of Cochise County!"

"It's trivial. Nobody will ever remember it."

"You're crazy."

"It changes nothing," insisted Holliday bitterly. "Ringo wasn't there."

# 36.

WYATT AND HOLLIDAY TOOK TURNS standing guard at Virgil's house, where Virgil and Morgan had been taken after their brief trip to the doctor's. Tombstone had three newspapers; they all ran midafternoon special editions with the story of the battle on the front page. Two of them had the Earps and Holliday as the aggressors and villains; only the *Epitaph* was on their side. It was being called the Gunfight at the O.K. Corral, despite the fact that it occurred in the alley that led to the corral. One paper reported that every participant except Earp and Holliday was dead; another claimed that three bystanders had been killed.

As soon as they were out of sight, John Behan accused them of resisting arrest and got the court to issue a warrant to bring them in. He had one volunteer—Curly Bill Brocius—and when Brocius accompanied Behan to Virgil Earp's house and saw Holliday sitting on the front porch, he promptly retired from the deputy business, and Behan return to his office empty-handed.

Henry Wiggins came by in late afternoon.

"Mind if I sit a spell with you?" he asked.

"Suit yourself," replied Holliday. "Could be dangerous, though."

"I don't think so," said Wiggins with a smile. "Behan can't deputize anyone, Brocius wants no part of you, and no one knows where Ike Clanton is hiding." He climbed onto the small veranda and sat down next to Holliday. "How are Virgil and Morgan?"

"Could be a lot worse if they hadn't been wearing Ned's armor. Their women are caring for them, changing their dressings and such. I don't think Virg is even going to be limping in two or three days."

"And Morgan?"

"Just a couple of holes—one where the bullet went in, one where it came out. Nothing broken. The armor protected all his vital parts."

"How about yourself?" asked Wiggins. "I heard you got nicked."

"Nothing to speak of," replied Holliday. "Bullet bounced off one of the shells in my holster, right over my hip." He smiled. "I'm surprised the shell didn't fire. Might have taken my toe off."

"And Wyatt's unharmed?"

"He always *was* the luckiest bastard."

"So what happens now?"

"Now we tell our side of things to the Coroner's Jury," answered Holliday. "And then, with a little luck, Tom goes back to working on what he's supposed to be working on."

"It's been an exciting couple of weeks," said Wiggins. "And I've been a witness to it."

"Maybe *you* ought to be writing for the dime novels," suggested Holliday.

"Maybe in my spare time I will," answered Wiggins. "What I've seen can't be any more unbelievable than some of the accounts I've read."

"Just remember when you write it up, I want to be a hundred and sixty pounds and healthy."

"That's a promise."

Holliday looked down the street. "Where the hell's Wyatt? He was just going down the street for a beer."

"He could get it for free at the Oriental," said Wiggins.

"He could get it for free today from a lot of people who didn't much like the McLaurys or the Clantons."

Wiggins studied Holliday for a moment, and then nervously asked a question: "Were you frightened?"

"To be frightened in a gunfight, you've got to be afraid of dying," answered Holliday. "I'm already dying. It's just a matter of dying fast or dying slow."

"There's got to be some way to cure consumption."

"Someday there will be, but not soon enough to do me any good." He smiled. "Back East they call it tuberculosis, and you have to figure anything that hard to spell is going to be even harder to cure."

Wyatt rounded a corner and approached the house.

"Hi, Henry," he said. Then, to Holliday: "I'll take over for the next couple of hours, but I want you here tonight, not gambling."

"Oh, I may still be gambling," said Holliday, getting to his feet. "But with lives instead of money." He turned to Wiggins. "Come along, Henry."

Wiggins fell into step beside Holliday as he climbed down from the veranda and headed south.

"Wyatt's so concerned with his brothers that another matter of some import has slipped his mind," said Holliday.

"What would that be?"

"You'll see soon enough."

In a few more minutes they reached the jail, where they found Masterson in the office, talking with Buntline.

"Hi, Doc," said Masterson.

"Hello, Bat," said Holliday. "This could be the day."

"I'm counting on it."

"But just to be on the safe side, I think you'd better get into the cell," said Buntline. "I'll let you right back out if you're still a man after the sun sets."

"What's this all about?" asked Wiggins.

"Wyatt and I made a deal with a medicine man who has a grudge against the Clantons," said Holliday. "We kill them, and he lifts the spell from Bat."

"But you didn't kill Ike," noted Wiggins.

"We killed Billy, and we killed two other Cowboys, the McLaurys. That's certainly a show of good faith."

Buntline looked out the window. "You'd better go into the cell now, Bat."

Masterson nodded, and walked to the brass cell. He entered it, and Buntline locked the door behind him.

"Now we wait," said Holliday.

"The sun'll be gone in another two minutes," said Buntline. "Then we'll know."

Two minutes passed, then a third, and a fourth, and Masterson remained in human form.

"Well, goddamn, the old bird kept his word!" said Holliday. "Open the cell, Ned."

Buntline unlocked the door. "How do you feel now, Bat?" he asked.

"Hungry," replied Masterson. A strange smile crossed his face, and displayed his elongated canines. "And thirsty."

"Shit!" said Buntline. "What's going on?"

"I think it's Que-Su-La's way of saying we only killed one Clanton, so he's only making Bat partially human at night," said Holliday. "You'd better go back in the cell after all, Bat."

He gently pushed at Masterson, only to be hurled into a corner with almost no effort. Buntline and Wiggins jumped Masterson, with the same result.

"You were my friends," growled Masterson. "Don't become my enemies."

Holliday pulled his gun and fired at Masterson's leg. It had no effect, except to make Masterson turn slowly to face him. "If you do that again, I'll kill you."

"I won't," said Holliday, holstering the gun. "As long as you're going out hunting, see if you can catch Johnny Ringo. I think you're the one man who can stand up to him."

"Ringo's dead," said Masterson, crossing the office and reaching the front door. "I need living prey."

And then he was gone. Holliday rushed to the door, trying to spot which direction he'd gone, but there was no sign of him. At one point he thought he saw a huge bat flying down Toughnut Street, but soon even that was gone.

"Thanks a heap!" muttered Holliday. "We did our best. We'll get Ike before long. You could have given us the benefit of the doubt, damn it."

"Who are you talking to?" asked Buntline, coming outside to join him. "There's nobody here. Maybe you should raise your voice."

"He's a day's ride north of here, and he hears me just fine," said Holliday grimly.

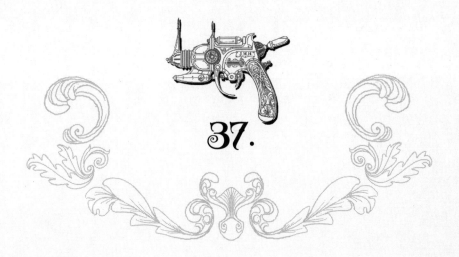

## 37.

"HE WAS *WHERE*?" demanded Holliday.

"Right here," said Kate.

"With you?"

"Good God, no. I find him disgusting. He was with one of the metal whores."

"He couldn't have been hiding," said Holliday. "He can't be killed; he's already dead. So why the hell wasn't he with the others?"

"He left a note for you," said Kate.

She handed him a folded piece of paper. He opened it up and read the neat, precise penmanship:

*I hope you survived. You're mine; I hate to think some illiterate oaf did you in. On the assumption that you lived, I suppose you are wondering why I wasn't with the Clantons and McLaurys. The answer is simple: I work for me, and I take orders from no one else.*

*See you soon.*

*J. R.*

## 38.

THE COWBOYS CAUSED NO TROUBLE for the next three weeks. In fact, the only trouble Holliday and the Earps had was trying to control Masterson. As an enormous bat that operated solely on instinct and had no memory or knowledge of its human existence, he had been content to fly away from people and feed upon cattle and horses. But as a man with a vampire's cravings and needs, he *tried* to obey the law, but the vampire part of him seemed to be slowly winning out. As far as Earp and Holliday could tell, he hadn't killed any citizen of Tombstone yet, but they couldn't be sure he hadn't picked off a couple of travelers or perhaps a ranch hand on an outlying spread.

The "old" Bat, which is to say, the one that existed before the gunfight, had wanted to do the right thing. The "new" Bat had no use for the moral code of what had truly become an alien species.

Holliday had visited Edison the day after the gunfight, looking for something that, if it couldn't counteract the curse, could at least hold Masterson at bay should he approach Kate's whorehouse. Edison replied that he would have to research the European legends, as he had never heard of a vampire in America, and finally, two days later, he sent for Holliday.

"What have you found?" asked Holliday when he arrived in Edison's office.

"I don't think you're going to like it," said Edison. "A lot of this stuff is myth and legend."

"I've got to try *something*," replied Holliday.

Edison sighed. "All right," he said. "First, go to the greengrocer and buy enough garlic to hang over every window and door in the place."

"Garlic?" repeated Holliday, arching an eyebrow.

"I'm not guaranteeing it," said Edison. "I'm just reporting what I've managed to learn."

"All right, garlic. What else?"

"Have every girl wear a cross, preferably on a necklace where he can't miss it. It doesn't have to be expensive. If for some reason one of them can't do that, have her wear it as a pin."

Holliday frowned. "Tom, is this a joke? I mean, Bat's never spent two seconds in a church in all the years I've known him."

"I have no idea if it'll be effective," said Edison, "but I promise you it's not a joke."

"All right. What else?"

"If he attacks you, you can theoretically kill him with a wooden stake through the heart."

"How else?" demanded Holliday. "I'm not likely to be walking around with a wooden stake in my pocket."

Edison shrugged helplessly. "It's not clear whether or not exposure to direct sunlight will kill him, but at the very least it'll be extremely painful wherever the sun hits him."

"Why the hell don't Hook Nose or Geronimo just turn their whole tribe into vampires?" said Holliday.

"I imagine they're considering it," said Edison. "But it does require them to attack at night. In fact, according to what I've found, the only place Bat or any other vampire is safe from you once the sun is out—again, this may or may not be true—is in his own coffin, which must be filled with his native soil."

Holliday frowned. "Soil from *Kansas*?"

"I'm only telling you what I've learned. I am not vouching for its veracity."

"Okay, what else?"

"Theoretically he can't cross over water. Theoretically he has to be in his coffin by sunrise; I think we can ignore that, because he doesn't *have* a coffin, at least not that we know about. Theoretically he leaves no image in the mirror. Theoretically he can't enter a house—I would assume that is a very pliable definition, covering everything from Kate's place to the livery stable—without being invited in. It gets even more far-fetched. Do you want me to continue?"

"No," said Holliday. "You tell me any more and I'll be convinced that you're making it all up, it's so damned unbelievable." He grimaced. "I guess I'll start with the garlic, though I'll feel like a damned fool."

"Don't forget the crosses," added Edison. "Especially if the girl has any intention of leaving the house, even just to pick a flower in the garden or to have tea on the back veranda."

Holliday nodded. "I'll go buy the garlic and the crosses." He frowned. "Kate's not going to like it."

"She'll like Bat less."

"Probably," agreed Holliday without much enthusiasm.

"I'd like to spend the evening there—at least the first few hours of it—and see which of these measures actually do affect him."

"I think you mean: which *if any* of these measures will affect him," replied Holliday with a smile.

"True," answered Edison.

"Well, it won't be dark for a few hours," observed Holliday. "Why don't you take care of whatever business you've got for today while I collect the garlic and the crosses? We can meet at Kate's before sunset."

Edison nodded and walked to the door. "Sounds good."

Holliday felt positively silly buying pounds upon pounds of garlic, but he finally amassed enough to hang over all the windows and doors. He stopped by a jeweler and bought a dozen cheap necklaces with little crosses on them. When he got back to Kate's he enlisted the aid of two of the robotic whores and in twenty minutes they'd put the garlic over every window, even those on the second floor. Ditto for the doors, including a pair of French doors leading to a balcony directly above Kate's office.

Edison showed up just before sunset, with a small metal device in his hand.

"What's that?" asked Holliday.

"The same thing I used on him when he was an enormous bat," answered Edison. "I call it a flash bulb."

"Is there any reason to think it'll work on what he's become?"

Edison shrugged. "I don't know. But I suspect since he hides from the sun all day and only comes out at night, his pupils will be dilated, and this should blind him for five or six seconds, long enough to get away, or at least out of his reach."

"Let's hope you're right," said Holliday. "I've passed out the crosses to all the girls, including the half-and-halfs with the brass limbs."

"I'm not promising anything will work," said Edison. "Remember, this is all based on myth and legend."

"I know. But we have to try *some*thing."

"Do you have some reason to believe he's going to come looking for one of these girls?" asked Edison.

Holliday shook his head. "But he knows there are a bunch of them here, and most of the men will have their pistols hanging on the backs of chairs."

"Okay," said Edison. "It makes sense."

The two men stayed in the parlor until eight o'clock, by which time the sheer number of customers forced them to leave.

"Goodnight, Tom," said Holliday. "Let's hope some of what we're trying works. See you tomorrow."

"If not, we'll do more research and come up with more possibilities," replied Edison. "Don't forget: he's the first one on this continent to carry this particular curse—at least, the first one we know of."

The two men parted, Edison going back to his house, Holliday heading off toward the Oriental. The dentist hadn't gone half a block when he was joined by Masterson.

"The crosses mean nothing to me," said the vampire.

"I didn't think they would," answered Holliday.

"I want you to take the garlic down."

"I can't."

"Damn it, you're the one who made me what I am!"

"We're going to be doing our damnedest to un-make you, Bat," said Holliday.

"Don't bother. I'm very comfortable in this form."

"Until you get hungry."

"I am always hungry."

"But you leave me and Wyatt alone."

"Because of what you were to me, not what you *are*," answered Masterson. He stopped as they came to an alley. "This street is too bright for my taste," he announced. "Don't follow me." He turned and began walking down the unlit alley.

Holliday looked up the street and saw Virgil Earp on patrol.

He yelled and waved, and Earp waved back and began approaching him.

"The games started yet?" asked Holliday.

"A couple of little ones," said Virgil. "The big money hasn't shown up yet. I think most of them are still eating din—"

Suddenly three shots rang out. Holliday looked into the darkness, trying to spot the shooter.

"Damn it!" groaned Virgil, falling to the ground. "I'm hit!"

There was one more shot, and this time Holliday saw the flash of light from a gun barrel that was stationed between two buildings.

"Did you see it, Bat?" he yelled.

"Yes."

"You say you're always thirsty? Run that bastard down and have a swallow!"

Masterson began racing ahead and to his right, where the shots had come from, while Holliday reached Virgil and knelt down beside him.

"It's my own fault," whispered Virgil. "I thought we were done with the trouble. I wasn't wearing my armor."

There was so much blood Holliday couldn't find the wounds. "Where did they get you?"

"One in the shoulder. Another shattered my arm."

"I heard more than two shots."

"Maybe another hit me. I don't know. God, it hurts!"

Virgil passed out while Holliday was cleaning the wounds with a handkerchief, trying to see where to set the tourniquet. As he was doing so, he heard two more shots, and then a hideous scream echoed through the night.

Townspeople began appearing, coming out of their houses and shops, and a few minutes later the still-unconscious Virgil was carried off to the nearest doctor.

Within another five minutes the street was empty again. Holliday stood there, alone and silent, and finally Masterson emerged from the shadows.

"Well?" asked Holliday.

"It was Brocius," announced Masterson.

"And?"

Masterson stopped under an electric streetlight, and Holliday could see the blood smeared on his chest and collar, with more on his lips and jaws.

"And his killing days are over," said Masterson. Then, as an afterthought, he added: "So are his breathing days."

# 39.

I T WAS EARLY AFTERNOON as Holliday walked over to Virgil's house to check on his condition. He found Morgan sitting outside, on the steps leading up to the veranda.

"Hi, Doc."

"Hi, Morg," said Holliday. "How's your brother?"

"It looks like he'll get to keep his arm," answered Morgan. "But he'll probably never be able to use it again."

"How's Allie taking it?"

"She never wanted him to be a lawman in the first place."

"How long have they been married?"

Morgan shrugged. "Seven years, I think. You know what he said to her when the doctor told him the arm was useless?"

"What?"

"That he still had one arm left to put around her, and that was all he needed. That's one hell of a man, my brother."

"Where's your other brother?"

"Out on patrol, probably," said Morgan. "Where's Bat? I want to thank him."

"He's sleeping until sundown," answered Holliday. "I don't think your gratitude would mean much to him these days."

"Even so—"

"If I see him I'll tell him you want to thank him." Holliday paused. "Is Virgil up to having visitors?"

"He was sleeping a few minutes ago. I suppose you could go in and take a look."

"I reckon I will," said Holliday, climbing the broad stairs and entering the small frame house. He walked through the parlor, looked around for the likeliest door to a bedroom, found it, and walked in.

Virgil Earp was lying on his back, his arm and shoulder heavily taped, the smell of alcohol heavy in the air.

"Hi, Doc," he whispered.

"Smells like you've got a distillery here," remarked Holliday with a smile.

"Wish I did. It'd do more good *in* me than *on* me."

"How are you holding up?"

"All right, I guess. I should have ducked—but I never saw him. Wyatt tells me it was Curly Bill."

"It was."

"And Morg says you got him."

"*I* didn't. Bat did."

Virgil smiled. "I wish I could have seen his face when he tried emptying his gun into Bat."

"Must have been a sight," agreed Holliday.

"Wish I could have done it myself—but I'm going to have to teach myself to shoot with my left hand."

"You're out of the shooting business, Virgil," said Holliday. "Leave the killing to me and your brothers."

"It's the only business I know, Doc," said Virgil. "I know I can't try to tame a town like Tombstone, not any more, but there should be some nice, peaceful towns up in Oregon Territory that need a figurehead who knows the law."

"At least you know enough not to think you're staying on here," said Holliday. "Any idea how soon you'll be up and around?"

"Maybe a couple of days."

"That seems kind of fast for the mess your arm and shoulder were in."

"I hate just lying in bed. I'll be up sooner than the doctor thinks."

"Maybe you'd better have Ned Buntline bring over some sheets of his brass," suggested Holliday. "These walls of yours wouldn't stop an arrow, let alone a bullet."

"No one wants me dead except Ike Clanton, and he hasn't got the nerve to show his face in town," answered Virgil. "Besides, I can't afford it. We're going to have to save every penny now, Allie and me."

"Correction: no one wants you dead except Ike Clanton and maybe thirty Cowboys."

"I'm out of the race, Doc," said Virgil with certainty. "They'll be after Wyatt and Morg—and probably you."

A smile crossed Holliday's face.

"What's so funny?" asked Virgil.

"Johnny Ringo considers me his personal property," answered Holliday. "He just might defend me against the Cowboys so that he can kill me later."

"You always did have a strange sense of humor," said Virgil.

"Well, I just came by to make sure you weren't dying. You're not. I'll check on you again tomorrow."

"See you then, Doc," said Virgil, closing his eyes.

Holliday walked out onto the veranda. "He's a tough son of a bitch, your brother," he said.

"They all are," answered Morgan. "Virg, Wyatt, James. Warren's the youngest of us; I wouldn't be surprised if he turns out the toughest of the lot."

"Care for some lunch?" asked Holliday. "My treat."

Morgan shook his head. "I think I'll stay here a little longer. Allie's out shopping, and someone should be here if Virg needs any help."

"I'll see you later, then," said Holliday, walking off toward the Grand Hotel's restaurant.

"I'll try to get by the Oriental sometime tonight, but Josie's new play opens tonight, and Wyatt and I have front-row tickets."

"I hope it's a hit," said Holliday.

He got a few drops of gravy on his shirt while he was eating, so he stopped at Kate's to change shirts—and found out that Johnny Ringo had been there again.

"One of the all-metal whores again?" asked Holliday.

Kate nodded. "He was with Lola this time. I don't know if he prefers them to live women, but they're the only ones that'll let him touch them. Even the half-and-halfs don't want any part of him."

"You wouldn't think a dead man would care about sex," said Holliday.

"He cares about it a lot more than my second wife did," said a voice from behind him, and Holliday turned to find himself facing Ned Buntline, who was carrying a well-worn leather bag in his hand.

"Hi, Ned. What are you doing here—sampling one of your metal ladies of the night?"

"Mimi's leg wasn't performing the way it should have been," answered Buntline, "so I came over to make some adjustments." He turned to Kate. "I hope it'll work right now. One of my meters isn't working correctly. Give me a call if her leg needs more work."

"I wonder," said Holliday. "Can you give Virg a new arm?"

"I'm no surgeon," answered Buntline. "Every one of the young ladies that I've worked on in this establishment had the limbs in question amputated by a qualified surgeon. Once it's removed, I can give Virgil a prosthetic arm. In fact, I offered to, but he says he's sticking with the one God gave him."

"God might have protected him a little better."

"It's all in how you look at it," said Buntline. "God's seen to it that he can live to a ripe old age, which no one seriously expects the marshal of Tombstone to do." He turned toward the front door. "I've got to get back before Tom knocks off for the day. Maybe he can figure out why this damned meter of his went haywire."

"Thanks, Ned," said Kate as he left.

"I'm off to the bedroom," announced Holliday.

"It's a little early in the day for that," said Kate.

"I'm going there to change shirts," he explained patiently.

"Don't tell me you're going to that new play too?"

He shook his head. "No, I'm not. But what's the point of having clean shirts if I don't use them when I need them?"

"What's the point of running a whorehouse if you keep shooting all my customers?" she replied with a smile.

"Okay," said Holliday, heading off to the bedroom. "I'll let Ned live."

"Ned's not a customer," she replied, walking alongside him.

"You mean he doesn't field test Lola and Mimi and the others?" said Holliday. "He never struck me as stupid before."

He removed his shirt and pulled a fresh one out of her dresser drawer.

"I shouldn't see you like this in the light," said Kate. "I forget how skinny you are, and now I'm worried about you again."

"I'm every bit this thin when we're in bed together," said Holliday, getting into the clean shirt.

"There are . . . *distractions* . . . when we're in bed together," she replied.

"You can learn to live with my looks, or I can stop distracting you in bed," said Holliday, buttoning up the shirt.

She walked over and gave him a kiss on the cheek. "I guess I can live with the looks."

He donned his coat and walked through the parlor, tipping his hat to a pair of cyborgs. Then he was outside, and he went over to the Oriental, though he knew it would be a few hours before the big-money games began.

He sat down at an empty table, and the bartender brought him a bottle and a glass without being asked. A few minutes later Henry Wiggins walked in, accompanied by a short, pudgy man who was meticulously dressed and groomed.

"Hi, Doc!"

"Hello, Henry," said Holliday. "Have a seat. Your friend, too."

"Thanks," said Wiggins as they both walked over and seated themselves. "Doc, say hello to Camillus Fly."

"Fly?" repeated Holliday. "You own the photo studio?"

Fly nodded. "I saw the gunfight right outside my window."

"Get any photos?"

"No, alas," said Fly. "It was over too damned fast."

Wiggins signaled to the bartender for two more glasses. "We're celebrating our new partnership tonight."

"I thought you were going to work for Buntline and Edison," noted Holliday.

"I am. But I can't, for example, take a metal whore from town to town with me. I'm no shootist. Someone would steal her—*it*—within a week. Same with many of their other inventions. And what good is showing a potential buyer an electric light that's not attached to the source of electricity? So Camillus is going to photograph all the wonders I'm selling, and make copies so I can leave a presentation book in every place I visit. I don't have the money to commission the photos, but Camillus believes in these inventions too, so he's making the photos in exchange for fifteen percent of my commissions from Ned and Tom."

"Congratulations on your deal," said Holliday, raising his glass to them.

"Thanks," said Fly. "I'd trade it all if I could have taken one clear photo of the gunfight." He shook his head sadly. "But even if I'd known it was coming, there was so much smoke I'd never have gotten a clear image of any of you. I don't know how you hit your targets."

"You make the first shot count," said Holliday with a smile. "The rest are just to impress the onlookers."

"You don't mean that."

"Oh yes I do."

"How's Virgil doing?" asked Wiggins.

"He'll live," said Holliday. "He's not likely to play that new sport—"

"Baseball?"

"That's the one. But he'll live."

"I'm glad to hear it. I've tried to be friendly to him, but those Earps are the most serious, somber, humorless bunch of men. Morgan is a little better, but still—"

"They're in a serious, somber, humorless business," said Holliday.

"So are you."

"But I understand that life is a cosmic joke, and they don't."

"Does anyone in the world share that outlook, I wonder?" said Fly.

"Yes, one man does," said Holliday.

"Who?"

"Johnny Ringo."

They talked for another hour, and then Wiggins and Fly went out for dinner. Holliday took what was left of his bottle to the back room, where he played solitaire in isolated splendor. He looked out at the main room at ten o'clock, didn't see enough big spenders, and decided to walk toward the Bird Cage and hopefully meet Wyatt and Morgan coming back from it.

He walked out into the street, turned when he got to Allen Street, and began approaching the Bird Cage at the corner of Sixth Street. But when he was more than a block away, he looked into the Campbell & Hatch Billiard Parlor and saw Wyatt and Morgan engaged in a game of pool.

He entered and walked over to them. "Play over already?"

"It was a short one," said Morgan.

"How was Josie?"

"Outstanding," said Earp. "I'll be going back to pick her up and take her out for a late dinner, but she'll be an hour getting out of those clothes and that makeup. They've even put a bathtub in her dressing room. Now *that's* star treatment."

Morgan ran the table and held out his hand. "Pay up."

Wyatt pulled out a silver dollar and tossed it to his brother.

"Okay," said Bob Hatch, the co-owner of the pool hall, a lean, balding man with a huge mustache, "now you get to try your luck against the champion."

"Here's my cue," said Wyatt, offering it to him.

"No, thanks," said Hatch. "I've got my own." He displayed it proudly. "I had it made up specially in Chicago."

He racked the balls up, then leaned over and broke. One of the balls went into a pocket, and he took two more shots before he finally missed and turned the table over to Morgan.

"Get ready to part with your money and your crown," said Morgan, surveying the table, then walking around to where he wanted to take his shot. He was lining it up, with his back to the window, when a pair of shots rang out and he plunged forward on the table, blood gushing out of a hole in his back. The second bullet thudded into a wall an inch from Wyatt's head.

"Ike Clanton!" roared Wyatt, racing out into the street.

Hatch grabbed a gun and was about to go out to join Wyatt when Holliday held him back.

"Wyatt doesn't need your help," said Holliday. "More to the point, he doesn't want it. Give me a hand with Morgan."

They turned him onto his back. Holliday signaled for water, and tried to force some between Morgan's lips. Morgan's head rolled to one side, and the water dribbled out.

"He's dead, Doc," said Hatch.

Holliday felt for a pulse and couldn't find any. He saw no reason to listen for a heartbeat.

"Shit!" he muttered.

"You sure we shouldn't go out there?" asked another bystander.

"It was Ike Clanton. Let Wyatt take his revenge."

A few minutes later they heard a gunshot and a scream, then five more shots spaced about ten seconds apart. There were no more screams, only silence.

The Gunfight at the O.K. Corral was finally over.

# 40.

THE NEXT MORNING Holliday walked out the front door of Kate Elder's establishment, shading his eyes from the noontime sun—and almost bumped into Bat Masterson.

"I've been waiting for you," said Masterson with a smile.

"You don't want my blood," said Holliday, with no show of fear. "It can barely make it once around my body without gasping for breath."

"I don't want anyone's!" exclaimed Masterson. "Look at me! It's the middle of the day and I'm standing out here in the sunlight. And look!" He opened his mouth. "No more fangs!"

"Well, son of a bitch!" said Holliday. "Old Que-Su-La kept his word."

"I've already been to the Oriental to thank Wyatt," continued Masterson. "I'm sorry about Morg and Virg—especially Morg."

"If Ike doesn't stick around to back-shoot Morgan, the bastard is probably five hundred miles from here by now, and you stay a vampire forever."

"Even so, I'm sorry."

"Well, I'm glad you're Bat again, rather than *a* bat," replied Holliday. "What are your plans now?"

"The reason I came to Tombstone is gone. Two Clantons are dead and one's crippled, and both McLaurys are dead. I know there are Cowboys left, but they haven't got a leader, and the word I get is that the silver mines are almost played out, so they'll be moving on before too long."

"Who told you the silver mines are almost exhausted?" asked Holliday.

"John Clum, earlier today."

"I hope you weren't there to tell him you're not a vampire any longer," remarked Holliday. "He didn't know you *were* one."

"Actually, I was there about a job."

"Writing for the *Epitaph*?"

Masterson shook his head. "No, I wanted a recommendation. I've had it with the West. I was a writer before; I can be one again. I had him check and see what was available." A happy smile. "I'm going to New York to work as a columnist for the *Morning Telegraph*."

"Never heard of it."

"It's a sporting paper. Mostly horse racing, but it covers prize fighting, and even this newfangled baseball."

"I don't suppose it covers the major poker games," said Holliday.

"Poker's not a sport, Doc."

"It all depends on who you are," commented Holliday wryly.

"Anyway, I'm taking the Bunt Line in about two hours," said Masterson. "It terminates in Dallas. From there I'll take a regular stagecoach to St. Louis, catch a ferry across the river, and finally catch a train to New York. I don't start for a month, so I've got plenty of time to get there."

Holliday extended his hand. "I wish you luck, Bat."

"Thanks, Doc. I'd wish you the same, but you seem to have cleaned up the town already."

"Just about," said Holliday.

"Who's left?"

"Johnny Ringo."

"He makes a frightening picture, but he hasn't actually bothered anyone, has he?"

Holliday reached into his pocket and pulled out a small piece of lead.

"What's that?" asked Masterson.

"I dug it out of the wall after Morg died, while Wyatt was chasing Ike." He handed it to Masterson. "Take a look."

"Looks like a .45 slug."

"It is."

Masterson frowned. "What kind of gun did Ike carry?"

"A single-action cavalry pistol."

"They don't use .45s, do they?"

"No," said Holliday. "But Peace Makers do, and Johnny Ringo carries a Peace Maker."

"Did he kill Morgan too?"

"I stopped by the undertaker's before I went to bed," said Holliday. "He was up all night working on both Morg and Ike, and he showed me the bullet he cut out of Morg's back. It came from a cavalry gun. That means there were two of them: Ike killed Morg, and someone—probably Ringo—took a shot at Wyatt at the same time."

"Then I guess maybe I'd better stick around a few more days, after all," said Masterson.

Holliday shook his head. "Ringo's not here for you. He wants me and Edison, in that order."

"Why you first?"

"Because once he kills Edison, there's every chance that Hook Nose will magic him back into the grave, so he's putting it off as long as he can."

"Then I'll stand side by side with you," insisted Masterson.

"And do what?" asked Holliday. "Empty your gun into a corpse while he takes his time getting you in his sights? Forget about it. Go meet some New York showgirls and write about horse racing, Bat. You've been through enough this month."

"You're sure?"

"I'm sure."

Masterson shook his hand again. "If you ever come back East, you'll always have a place to stay."

"I'll keep it in mind," said Holliday, who elected not to say that of course he was going to die before he could ever go East.

Masterson walked back to his hotel to retrieve his luggage prior to catching the brass coach, and Holliday made his second trip to the undertaker's. This time Earp was there too, staring at the open coffin.

Holliday stopped just inside the door and stood motionless. Earp finally noticed him.

"Hello, Doc."

"Hello, Wyatt."

"Thanks for coming. I'm going to need your help."

"Oh?"

Earp nodded. "I can't run this town, go after the Cowboys, *and* keep an eye on Virg, so I'm sending him and Allie out to our parents' place in Colton, California, on this afternoon's train. I'm sending Morg along with them; he can be buried on their spread."

"Why a train? If you're expecting trouble, why not use one of Ned's horseless coaches?"

"The Bunt Line doesn't go to California. The coaches don't have enough power to run all the way to Colton. The train's the only way."

"All right," said Holliday. "How can I help?"

"Ride shotgun until they're on the train."

"Except for Fin, there are no more Clantons or McLaurys, and Fin's not going anywhere," said Holliday. "Brocius was probably the most dangerous of the Cowboys, and he's dead too. So who are we on the lookout for?"

"Frank Stillwell, Indian Charlie, Pete Spence, Pony Diehl, a handful of others," replied Earp. "I'll kill them all sooner or later, but not before Virg and Morg are safely on that train."

"Where do we meet, and what time?"

"Right here, at three o'clock. I'd like to take Ned's surrey, but we can't fit Morg's coffin in it, so I'll be in an open horse-drawn wagon."

"I'll be here," said Holliday. "Count on it."

"Thanks, Doc."

Earp showed up at three, as he'd said he would. He and two of the undertaker's assistants carried Morgan's coffin to the wagon—Doc wasn't physically strong enough to help—and they headed toward the train station.

The train was late, and didn't arrive until twilight. They loaded the coffin and Virgil's luggage in a freight car. Then, as Earp was helping Virgil and Allie up the stairs to their compartment, a single shot rang out.

"What happened?" demanded Earp, pulling his gun and jumping to the ground.

"Take a look," said Holliday, as the smoke from his pistol dissipated.

Earp walked over and stared down at the body of Frank Stillwell, blood pouring out from the hole in his forehead, his unfired gun in his hand.

"I guess that's one fewer Cowboy for you to hunt down," commented Holliday dryly.

"Thank you, Doc," said Earp. "Would you take the wagon back to the livery stable, please? I think I'd better ride a way with Virg and Allie."

"Happy to," said Holliday.

"I'll buy or borrow a horse and be back tomorrow."

"I'll see you then."

Holliday stayed at the station until the train pulled out, then decided it was time to start preparing for his one bit of unfinished business.

# 41.

OLLIDAY APPROACHED THOMAS EDISON'S HOUSE. As he reached out to knock on the door, it opened—but there was nobody there to greet him.

"In here!" called Edison's voice, and Holliday followed it into his lab.

"Hello, Doc," said Edison. "What do you think of my new invention?"

"The door?"

Edison nodded. "I put a little mechanism under the porch."

"The porch?" repeated Holliday, frowning.

"The veranda," amended Edison. "Anyway, when someone steps onto it, the mechanism signals me. I look out through this little spy-hole"—he pointed to it—"and if I know you, I press this button on the wall, and the door opens."

"And if you don't recognize me?"

"Then the house will collapse of old age before the door opens," said Edison with a smile.

"Even Johnny Ringo couldn't get in?"

"Johnny Ringo can't even come close to the door if I don't want him to."

"Good," said Holliday.

"Why? Have you some information that he's on his way here?"

Holliday shook his head. "He wants both of us, but he wants me first. I think it's about time I had a weapon that will do more than tickle him."

"Ned and I have been theorizing about what might prove effective," said Edison.

"I need more than a theory before I go up against him."

"I have an idea," said Edison, "but it needs more research."

"You tell me what books you need, I'll go out and buy them," said Holliday.

"It's not reference books," replied Edison. "I need data."

Holliday frowned. "What kind of data?"

"About Ringo, of course. You can help."

"Just tell me what you want to know."

Edison looked through the clutter on his lab table, couldn't spot what he wanted, and went rummaging through a cabinet. "Ah! Here it is!" he exclaimed happily, withdrawing a small object about the size of a billfold, but rounded slightly and made of a dull gray metal. There were three tiny dials on it, and a small knob protruding from it.

"What is it?" asked Holliday.

"It's too complicated to explain," answered Edison. "But I think it may provide an answer or two. At least, I hope so."

Holliday took it from him and examined it. "How do I use it?"

"Nothing to it," said Buntline. "Do you see this little thing sticking out of it?"

"Yes."

"It's a key."

Holliday tried to remove it. He couldn't.

Edison smiled. "Try turning it first."

Holliday turned the key, and suddenly it came away in his hand. "One . . . no, two . . . of the dials are moving," he noted.

"I *told* you it was simple," said Edison.

"What does it do?"

"Nothing you have to worry about."

"All right," said Holliday, trying to hide his frustration. "What do *I* do with it?"

"You activate it within fifty feet of Ringo."

"And then what?"

"Then stick around for five or six minutes, and come back here."

"This isn't the weapon I need?"

Edison chuckled. "If it was, I'd tell you to go point it at him and send you out the door."

"But it *will* help you invent the weapon?"

"If I'm right, it'll help me to design it and Ned to make it."

Holliday shrugged. "All right. No one knows where he's staying, now that Ike and Billy Clanton are dead and Fin's been shot up, but I'll pass the word that I'd like to buy him a drink and talk a little literature."

"May I make a suggestion?" said Edison.

"Go ahead."

"If you sit down over drinks with him, he'll see you activate the mechanism. He won't know what it is, but he's bound to be suspicious. He might even take it away from you. With all due respect, you couldn't stop him." Edison paused. "But Ned tells me he's taken to frequenting Kate Elder's place, that he seems to have a fondness for the metal prostitutes. Since you live there, it should be very easy for you to wait until he's in a room with one of them, stand relatively close to it—walls present no problem to this device—and activate it for five minutes. You could have it back to me before he even leaves the house."

"Just turn the key, stand within fifty feet for five minutes, and that's all?"

"Oh—turn it off after the five minutes are up."

"Okay, got it." Holliday inserted the key, turned off the mechanism, and put it in his pocket. "And thanks."

"Don't thank me until we know if my idea works," answered Edison.

Holliday took his leave, and went directly to Kate's house. He entered, ignored the men and women (real and robotic) who were visiting in the parlor, and went straight to Kate's office. She was sitting at her desk with her accounts book, and looked up from it as he entered.

"Is he here?" asked Holliday.

"Is *who* here?"

"Ringo."

"No," she said with a frown. "Is he supposed to be?"

"Is he coming?"

"If he is, he's not doing it with one of *my* girls."

Holliday shook his head impatiently. "Is he due here, damn it?"

"He doesn't make appointments, Doc," said Kate. "He comes by when he feels like it."

"How often?"

"I don't know. Maybe every other day."

"Was he here yesterday?"

"Yes."

"Damn!" muttered Holliday. "I'll be in our room. Let me know the second he shows up, and don't tell him I'm here."

"What the hell's going on?" asked Kate.

"Just do it."

"It could be days."

"Then it'll be days."

He got up, left the office, and walked up the stairs to their room. He sat down on a rocking chair that was next to a small table, turned on the electric light, picked up the book he'd left on the table, and began reading.

Kate sent in his dinner, and later a new bottle of whiskey. He was sound asleep, still in the chair, when she came to bed a couple of hours after midnight, and he was still sleeping when she got up in the morning.

Just before eleven she began shaking him by the shoulder.

"What is it?" he demanded.

"You wanted to know when Ringo got here."

"He's here now?"

"Take a minute and try to wake your brain up. He's here."

"Has he chosen a whore yet?"

"No. He's having a drink in the parlor." She frowned. "I hope he chooses one soon. He walked in, and the two men who were about to pick their bedmates took one look at him and left."

"Then I haven't missed him," said Holliday with a sign of relief.

"You're not going to shoot him?" said Kate.

"It would just make him mad," answered Holliday seriously. "I want you to let me know after he chooses one of the metal girls, and what room they go to."

"I wish I knew what this is all about," she said, but she left the room and went to the parlor.

She was back three minutes later.

"Well?" asked Holliday anxiously.

"He's with Lola."

"I don't care who he's with. I need to know *where* he is."

"First room on the left as you go down the corridor."

"Thanks," said Holliday, walking out of the room. When he reached the parlor he stood facing the wall that separated him from Ringo, pulled out the mechanism, and turned the key. The dials started spinning; he stood motionless for five minutes and then turned the device off. He put it in his pocket, walked to the front door, exited the house, and handed it to Edison a few minutes later.

"Ah!" said Edison. "Let me take a look at it!"

He studied it for perhaps thirty seconds, then looked up at Holliday. "I think we may have something here."

"Good. What now?"

"Now I discuss it with Ned, and if he agrees with me about the principle, we work out how to utilize it. I'll design the weapon, and he'll create it."

"How long will it take?" asked Holliday.

"Maybe two days."

"I suppose I can wait that long."

"It's not how long you have to wait, Doc," said Edison. "It's whether or not the weapon works."

"You'll test it out, and you'll know."

Edison sighed. "I don't think we can test this one."

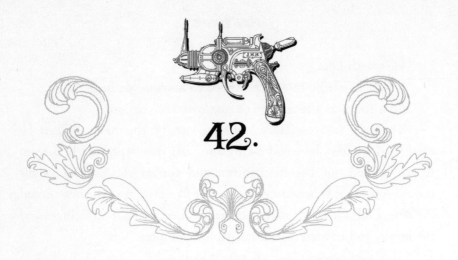

# 42.

**H**OLLIDAY WAS ALWAYS CALM BEFORE A GUNFIGHT, but he was a bundle of nerves the next three days as he anxiously waited for Edison and Buntline to finish work on his weapon.

He spent some time at the Oriental, visiting with Earp, and he began patronizing the bar at the Rose Tree Inn as well. Kate thought sex would take the edge off him, and even encouraged two of her cyborgs to take him to bed together, but he was just as tense and edgy an hour later.

Then, finally, came the word he was waiting for, hand-delivered to him at Kate's establishment:

*Doc—*

    *Come to Ned's place when you get the chance. We've got something to show you.*

                                  *—Tom and Ned*

Holliday was there within five minutes. He was still gasping for breath when Buntline opened the door.

"You didn't have to run," he said with a smile.

"The hell I didn't," replied Holliday, entering the place. He saw Edison sitting at a workbench in Buntline's office. "Hello, Tom. Does it work?"

"We hope so," said Edison.

"If you need more readings or whatever the hell they were, I can get them."

Edison shook his head. "What you got was just fine."

"Then why don't you know if it works?"

"We haven't tried it out," said Buntline.

"You want me to? Just send me out back with it and I'll find a target."

"Don't you remember, Doc?" said Edison. "I told you I didn't think we could test it."

"Are the bullets so expensive that I can't use even a couple of them?" asked Holliday.

"There aren't any bullets," replied Edison.

"A gun with no bullets?" said Holliday, frowning.

"Maybe we'd better explain it to him," said Buntline.

"I think so," said Edison.

"Do you remember the day we met at Kate Elder's?" began Buntline. "I had just finished working on Lola's leg?"

"Yes," said Holliday.

"And I remarked that one of my meters wasn't working right?"

"Yes, I remember."

"I mentioned it to Tom when I got back. He tested it, and it worked fine. So we tried to figure out why it hadn't worked at Kate's place."

"What it is," interjected Edison, "is a device that measures electrical impulses sent from the brain to different parts of the body."

"*Electrical?*" repeated Holliday.

"I've told you before," said Edison. "The brain emits electrical signals."

"Go on," said Holliday.

"We put our heads together, trying to figure out what went wrong with the device, and why it was working perfectly when I got back," continued Buntline, "and then it occurred to me: the only difference between that trip to Kate's and every other one I've made was that Johnny Ringo was there."

"Okay, so he was there," said Holliday. "So what?"

"Think about it, Doc," said Buntline. "He walks. He talks. He shoots. He even fucks. But he's dead, so clearly he's not getting those impulses from *his* brain."

"That's why I sent that strange object back with you," said Edison. "I was pretty much convinced, but I had to make certain. And sure enough, the readings went haywire again. I went over to Kate's about two hours later, after Ringo had left, and the readings were all normal."

"I feel you're telling me something, but I don't quite know what," said Holliday.

"Doc, if *his* brain isn't powering his body, someone else's must be. Who brought him back to life?"

"Hook Nose?" asked Holliday.

"Hook Nose," said Edison, nodding his head.

"Now, theoretically, if you were to kill Hook Nose, Ringo would collapse at the same instant," said Buntline. "But Hook Nose is hundreds of miles away from here, and from what we hear, he's even better protected than Geronimo."

"So the thing to do," added Edison, "armed with the knowledge we have, is to kill Ringo directly."

"Bullets won't do it, of course," said Buntline. "I'll wager even a cannonball won't."

"And the reason they won't," said Edison, "is that they're attacking the body, and the body's already dead."

"But how do you attack the brain, when it also isn't alive?" asked Holliday.

Buntline walked to the end of the table, picked up a small case, and handed it to Holliday. "With *this*," he said proudly.

Holliday opened the case. Inside it was a gun of a design he'd never seen before, snub-nosed, bizarre, and ornate.

"Where the hell are the chambers?" asked Holliday, examining it.

"It doesn't have any," said Edison.

"Then where are the bullets?"

"I thought we were all in agreement that you can't kill Johnny Ringo with bullets," said Buntline.

Holliday examined the short muzzle. "What *does* it shoot?"

"I think *shoot* is the wrong word," said Edison.

"Okay," said Holliday. "Tell me with right words, because as of this minute I don't have a lot of confidence in this thing."

"The reason the butt is so thick is because it holds the most powerful battery Tom could design," explained Buntline. "Now, we know Ringo is being controlled by Hook Nose. Not that Hook Nose is putting words in his mouth, or manipulating his actions as if he was a puppet but he's essentially powering Ringo's brain, allowing it to function as if it's still alive. Do you follow me so far?"

"I follow you," said Holliday. "I'm just not sure I believe you. Go on."

"We used the device you took to Kate's to get an exact reading of the electrical impulses Hook Nose is broadcasting to allow Ringo to act independently. And with this gun Tom has created a field that will disrupt those impulses. It won't damage Hook Nose, but Ringo should react like a marionette whose strings have suddenly all been cut."

"You're sure?" asked Holliday.

"It works in theory," said Edison. "But the problem is, we can't test it out. There's only one thing walking the streets of Tombstone that's being controlled, or enabled if you will, at this frequency. There's simply no other target to test it out on."

Holliday stared at him for a long moment. "If you weren't Tom Edison, I'd say you've been drinking too much, or maybe not enough."

"I can't order you to go up against Johnny Ringo with it," replied Edison. "All I can do is tell you I think it will work."

"I've made a holster for you," said Buntline, pulling it off a shelf and handing it to Holliday. "You'll never be able to fit the Buntline Special in a normal holster."

"The Buntline Special?" repeated Holliday.

"I made it, I get to name it," said Buntline defensively. "Besides, it's using an Edison battery. Fair is fair."

"I don't care what you call it," said Holliday. "I just care that it works."

"So do we."

"How do I know that it's . . . is *loaded* the right word?"

"The battery will power it for up to three minutes," said Edison. "And it'll hold its power for at least two months if you don't use it."

"I take it that it doesn't make a bang," continued Holliday. "Does it buzz, or hiss, or what?"

"It won't make a sound," said Buntline.

"Then how will I know it's working?"

"There's only one way," answered Buntline. "You'll be alive and Ringo won't be."

"He's already dead, damn it."

"All right," said Edison. "You'll be alive and animated, and he'll be dead and unanimated. Is that better?"

"It'll have to do," said Holliday, strapping on the holster. He inserted the Buntline Special into it, drew it and replaced it a few times, and turned to Buntline. "Could be better balanced. It'll take some getting used to."

"Whether it works or it doesn't, you're only going to use it once, Doc. You won't have time to get used to it."

"Whether it works or it doesn't, I'm going to pull the trigger and feel like I'm wishing him to death."

"Speaking of the trigger, there's one last thing," said Buntline.

"Yes?"

"Once you start, keep squeezing the trigger. Let it go the way you do after firing a bullet and the field vanishes."

"Thanks for telling me that unimportant little tidbit," said Holliday sardonically. "Any other trivial little thing I should know?"

"No," said Edison.

"That's everything," added Buntline.

"Then I guess it's time to go hunting," said Holliday, walking out the door.

"Good luck," said Buntline.

"Why do I feel like I'm going to need it?" replied Holliday.

He went back to Kate's in the hope that Ringo was there, but she hadn't seen him for two days. Then he started making the rounds of all the saloons, and had a drink in each, just to be friendly. Either no one had seen Johnny Ringo, or no one was willing to talk about it.

He stopped at the Oriental in late afternoon.

"Is Wyatt in the back?" he asked the bartender.

"No," came the answer. "He's spending more and more of his time with the actress. He'll probably show up after dinner tonight. I mean, how the hell many times can he watch the same play?"

"Then I guess I'm drinking alone," said Holliday.

"Not quite," said a familiar voice from behind him. Holliday turned and found himself facing Johnny Ringo, who stood just inside the swinging doors. "I hear you've been looking for me today."

"I thought you might want to discuss who wrote Shakespeare's plays," said Holliday, carrying his drink to an empty table.

"Five'll get you ten that it was Sir Francis Bacon," said Ringo, sitting down opposite him. "Is there anything else you want to know?"

"Yes. Why did you try to kill Wyatt Earp the other night?"

"I was just trying to make him a little hesitant about bursting through the door before Ike had a decent head start," said Ringo easily. "You don't really think I could miss from that distance, do you?"

"Not really," replied Holliday.

"Now what's the real reason you've been asking after me?"

"I haven't seen you for a while. I was hoping you'd gone back where you came from."

"Too damned hot there," said Ringo with a laugh. "That's an assumption, by the way. I don't remember anything but the grave."

"Seems a reasonable enough assumption to me," said Holliday. "How many men have you killed?"

Ringo shrugged. "I don't keep count. That's for the dime novelists."

Holliday smiled. "You're the only shootist I've met out here who doesn't keep score. Besides me, that is."

"The way I see it," said Ringo, "half of them deserved it, and the other half were going to die sooner or later anyway."

"And at least they don't suffer much if you hit them dead center."

"My feelings exactly!" laughed Ringo. "Damn, but I'm going to be sorry to kill you!"

"Maybe I can spare you that sorrow," said Holliday.

"Come on, Doc—you know you can't kill me."

"I can try."

"I see that fancy gun you're carrying," said Ringo. "It won't do you a bit of good."

"That's possible," agreed Holliday.

"Then let's be friends a few more days before I put you out of your misery."

"It's because you're my friend that I'm going to put you out of yours."

"You're serious about this?" said Ringo.

"Am I smiling?" replied Holliday.

"Then let's step outside and take care of business right now."

"After you," said Holliday, gesturing toward the door.

Ringo walked outside, followed by Holliday. When bypassers saw who was squaring off, suddenly the whole street emptied out, as every last one of them ducked into a store or saloon.

"It's been a long time coming," said Ringo. "Have you been waiting for this as eagerly as I have?"

"Of course," agreed Holliday. "When you're the best, you want to go against the best."

"You might have had a chance against me when I was alive," said Ringo. "You've got no chance today."

"Damn!" said Holliday suddenly.

"What is it?"

"I wish Fly was photographing this."

Ringo laughed, and suddenly went for his gun. Holliday did the same. He was faster by the barest fraction of a second. He squeezed the trigger and held it down, wondering if the gun was working, and bracing himself to receive Ringo's bullet.

But Ringo's shot went wide, and it was clear that he was having trouble controlling his body, which began shaking spasmodically. His gun fell to the ground, he began swaying from side to side, and then, slowly but noticeably, each of his extremities stopped functioning.

Holliday, still squeezing the trigger, began approaching him. Ringo dropped to his knees, his arms hung useless at his sides, and just before he pitched face-forward on the dirt, he smiled at Holliday.

"Thank you, my only friend," he said.

Holliday dragged the body into an alley, gathered some discarded wood and paper, and set fire to it so that it could never be resurrected again.

And five hundred miles away, Hook Nose screamed in fury and frustration.

# 43.

HOLLIDAY HAD NO MORE BUSINESS IN TOMBSTONE—he decided to leave the remaining Cowboys to Earp's tender mercies—and he and Kate packed their things and went to Deadwood, Colorado, where he bought a part interest in a casino and she started up a new one-hundred-percent-human whorehouse. It was almost two months before they had another knock-down drag-out and parted company for good.

Since the Buntline Special had been made for one target and no other, Holliday had no further use for it. He gave it to John Clum, who put it in a glass case and displayed it in the editorial offices of the *Epitaph*.

Earp decided that he wanted a Buntline Special too. He approached Ned Buntline and told him what he wanted in his version. Buntline accommodated him, and a week later he was presented with a pistol that had a standard firing mechanism, but a twelve-inch barrel made of superhardened brass. It wasn't any more accurate than Earp's Peace Maker, but it saved a lot of wear and tear on his fists, allowing him to "buffalo" foes in close quarters by crashing the barrel across their heads, as he had done to Ike Clanton the day before the gunfight.

(Since Holliday's weapon was used once and never again, it was *this* Buntline Special, rather than the original, that became part of the folklore of the West.)

Edison found himself free of distractions, and was able to concentrate on the job the government had given him, and Buntline remained in Tombstone to help him. Henry Wiggins sold enough of their joint inventions to keep them well supplied with money to live on, and to buy raw materials for further experiments.

There came a day, some months later, when a dozen Southern Cheyenne warriors accompanied their leader into the camp of the Apaches. Geronimo, surrounded by his mightiest braves, walked out to meet them.

"I am Woo-Ka-Nay of the Southern Cheyenne," said Hook Nose.

"I am Goyathlay of the Apaches," responded Geronimo.

"I must ask," said Hook Nose. "Were you responsible for the final death of the Ringo thing?"

"I know nothing about it," answered Geronimo. "And I must ask: did you lift the spell from the man-bat I cursed?"

Hook Nose shook his head. "I know nothing of this."

"I believe you," said Geronimo. He paused briefly, then spoke again. "Why have you come to the land of the Apaches?"

"It is time that we stop working at cross purposes," said Hook Nose. "We have been acting solely in our own interests, and where has it gotten us?"

"I agree," replied Geronimo. "The White-Eyes' nation stops at the great river, but *they* do not stop. We must agree to act in concert before it is too late, before there are so many of them that our military and our magic cannot stop them."

"Let us sit in council and determine how best to destroy them," said Hook Nose.

They sat on the ground and ate while their warriors stood guard in a large semicircle, and as darkness fell they moved closer to the fire, talking late into the night as they plotted their eventual victory.

# APPENDIX 1

THERE HAS BEEN QUITE A LOT WRITTEN about Doc Holliday, Johnny Ringo, the Earp brothers, the Clantons, and Tombstone. Surprisingly, a large amount takes place in an alternate reality in which (hard as this is to believe) the United States did not stop at the Mississippi River, but crossed the continent from one ocean to the other.

For those of you who are interested in this "alternate history," here is a bibliography of some of the more interesting books:

Allen Barra, *Inventing Wyatt Earp: His Life and Many Legends*, Carroll & Graf (1998)

Bob Boze Bell, *The Illustrated Life and Times of Doc Holliday*, Tri Star-Boze (1995)

Bob Boze Bell, *The Illustrated Life and Times of Wyatt Earp*, Tri Star-Boze (1993)

Glenn G. Boyer, *I Married Wyatt Earp: The Recollections of Josephine Sarah Marcus Earp*, Longmeadow (1994)

Glenn G. Boyer, *Who Was Big Nose Kate?*, Glenn G. Boyer (1997)

Glenn G. Boyer, *Wyatt Earp's Tombstone Vendetta*, Talei Publishers (1993)

William M. Breakenridge, *Helldorado: Bringing the Law to the Mesquite*, Houghton Mifflin Co. (1928)

Jack Burrows, *John Ringo: The Gunfighter Who Never Was*, University of Arizona Press (1987)

Donald Chaput, *Virgil Earp: Western Peace Officer*, University of Oklahoma Press (1994)

E. Richard Churchill, *Doc Holliday, Bat Masterson & Wyatt Earp: Their Colorado Careers*, Western Reflections (2001)

Jack DeMattos, *Masterson and Roosevelt*, Creative Publishing Co. (1984)

Josephine Earp, *Who Killed John Ringo*, Glenn G. Boyer (1997)

Wyatt Earp and others, *Wyatt Earp Speaks!*, Fern Canyon Press (1998)

Steve Gatto, *Johnny Ringo*, Protar House (2002)

Michael M. Hickey, *John Ringo: The Final Hours*, Talei Publishers (1995)

Pat Jahns, *The Frontier World of Doc Holliday*, Hastings House (1957)

David Johnson, *John Ringo, King of the Cowboys*, Barbed Wire Press (1996)

Stuart N. Lake, *Wyatt Earp: Frontier Marshal*, Houghton Mifflin Co. (1934)

Sylvia D. Lynch, *Aristocracy's Outlaw: The Doc Holliday Story*, Iris Press (1994)

Paula Mitchell Marks, *And Die in the West: The Story of the O.K. Corral Gunfight*, William Morrow & Co. (1989)

John Myers Myers, *Doc Holliday*, Little, Brown & Co. (1955)

John Myers Myers, *Tombstone's Early Years*, E. P. Dutton & Co. (1950)

Gary L. Roberts, *Doc Holliday: The Life and Legend*, John Wiley & Sons (2006)

Karen Holliday Tanner, *Doc Holliday: A Family Portrait*, University of Oklahoma Press (1998)

Casey Tefertiller, *Wyatt Earp: The Life behind the Legend*, John Wiley & Sons (1997)

Ben T. Traywick, *The Clantons of Tombstone*, Red Marie's Bookstore (1996)

Ben T. Traywick, *John Henry: The "Doc" Holliday Story*, Red Marie's Bookstore (1996)

Ben T. Traywick, *Tombstone's Deadliest Gun: John Henry Holliday*, Red Marie's Bookstore (1984)

Frank Waters, *The Earp Brothers of Tombstone*, Clarkson Potter (1960)

# APPENDIX 2

ERE IS THE *TOMBSTONE EPITAPH*'S REPORT on the Gunfight at the O.K. Corral in that other reality in which America extended from the Atlantic to the Pacific:

## YESTERDAY'S TRAGEDY

*Tombstone Daily Epitaph*—October 27, 1881

## THREE MEN HURRIED INTO ETERNITY IN THE DURATION OF A MOMENT

Stormy as were the early days of Tombstone nothing ever occurred equal to the event of yesterday. Since the retirement of Ben Sippy as marshal and the appointment of V. W. Earp to fill the vacancy the town has been noted for its quietness and good order. The fractious and much dreaded Cowboys when they came to town were upon their good behaviour and no unseemly brawls were indulged in, and it was hoped by our citizens that no more such deeds would occur as led to the killing of Marshal White one year ago. It seems that this quiet state of affairs was but the calm that precedes the storm that burst in all its fury yesterday, with this difference in results, that the lightning bolt struck in a different quarter from the one that fell a year ago. This time it struck with its full and awful force upon those who, heretofore, have made the good name of this county a byword and a reproach, instead of upon some officer in discharge of his duty or a peaceable and unoffending citizen.

Since the arrest of Stilwell and Spence for the robbery of the Bisbee stage, there have been oft repeated threats conveyed to the Earp brothers—Virgil, Morgan, and Wyatt—that the friends of the accused, or in other words the Cowboys, would get even with them for the part they had taken in the pursuit and arrest of Stilwell and Spence. The active part of the Earps in going after stage robbers, beginning with the one last spring where Budd Philpot lost his life, and the more recent one near Contention, has made them exceedingly obnoxious to the bad element of this county and put their lives in jeopardy every month.

Sometime Tuesday Ike Clanton came into town and during the evening had some little talk with Doc Holliday and Marshal Earp but nothing to cause either to suspect, further than their general knowledge of the man and the threats that had previously been conveyed to the Marshal, that the gang intended to clean out the Earps, that he was thirsting for blood at this time with one exception and that was that Clanton told the Marshal, in answer to a question, that the McLowrys were in Sonora. Shortly after this occurrence someone came to the Marshal and told him that the McLowrys had been seen a short time before just below town. Marshal Earp, now knowing what might happen and feeling his responsibility for the peace and order of the city, stayed on duty all night and added to the police force his brother Morgan and Holliday. The night passed without any disturbance whatever and at sunrise he went home to rest and sleep. A short time afterwards one of his brothers came to his house and told him that Clanton was hunting him with threats of shooting him on sight. He discredited the report and did not get out of bed. It was not long before another of his brothers came down, and told him the same thing, whereupon he got up, dressed, and went with his brother Morgan uptown. They walked up Allen Street to Fifth, crossed over to Fremont and down to Fourth, where, upon turning up Fourth toward Allen, they came upon Clanton with a Winchester rifle in his hand and a revolver on his hip. The Marshal walked up to him, grabbed the rifle, and hit him a blow on the head at the same time, stunning him so that he was able to disarm him without further trouble. He marched Clanton off to the police court where he entered a complaint against him for carrying deadly weapons, and the court fined Clanton $25 and costs, making $27.50 altogether. This occurrence must have been about 1 o'clock in the afternoon.

## THE AFTER-OCCURRENCE

Close upon the heels of this came the finale, which is best told in the words of R. F. Coleman, who was an eyewitness from the beginning to the end. Mr. Coleman says: "I was in the O.K. Corral at 2:30 p.m., when I saw the two Clantons and the two McLowrys in an earnest conversation across the street in Dunbar's corral. I went up the street and notified Sheriff Behan and told him it was my opinion they meant trouble, and it was his duty, as sheriff, to go and disarm them. I told him they had gone to the West End Corral. I then went and saw Marshal Virgil Earp and notified him to the same effect. I then met Billy Allen and we walked through the O.K. Corral, about fifty yards behind the sheriff. On reaching Fremont Street I saw Virgil Earp, Wyatt Earp, Morgan Earp, and Doc Holliday, in the center of the street, all armed. I had reached Bauer's meat market. Johnny Behan had just left the cowboys, after having a conversation with them. I went along to Fly's photograph gallery, when I heard Virg Earp say, 'Give up your arms or throw up your arms.' There was some reply made by Frank McLowry, when firing became general, over thirty shots being fired. Tom McLowry fell first, but raised and fired again before he died. Bill Clanton fell next, and raised to fire again when Mr. Fly took his revolver from him. Frank McLowry ran a few rods and fell. Morgan Earp was shot through and fell. Doc Holliday was hit in the left hip but kept on firing. Virgil Earp was hit in the third or fourth fire, in the leg which staggered him but he kept up his effective work. Wyatt Earp stood up and fired in rapid succession, as cool as a cucumber, and was not hit. Doc Holliday was as calm as though at target practice and fired rapidly. After the firing was over, Sheriff Behan went up to Wyatt Earp and said, 'I'll have to arrest you.' Wyatt replied: 'I won't be arrested today. I am right here and am not going away. You have deceived me. You told me these men were disarmed; I went to disarm them.'"

This ends Mr. Coleman's story, which in the most essential particulars has been confirmed by others. Marshal Earp says that he and his party met the Clantons and the McLowrys in the alleyway by the McDonald place; he called to them to throw up their hands, that he had come to disarm them. Instantaneously, Bill Clanton and one of the McLowrys fired, and then it became general. Mr. Earp says it was the first shot from Frank McLowry that hit him. In other particulars his statement does not materially differ from the statement above given. Ike Clanton was not armed and ran across to Allen Street and took refuge in the dance hall there. The two McLowrys and Bill Clanton all died within a few minutes after being shot. The Marshal was shot through the calf of the right leg, the ball going clear through. His brother, Morgan, was shot through the shoulders, the ball entering the point of the right shoulder blade, following across the back, shattering off a piece of one vertebra, and passing out the left shoulder in about the same position that it entered the right. The wound is dangerous but not necessarily fatal, and Virgil's is far more painful than dangerous. Doc Holliday was hit upon the scabbard of his pistol, the leather breaking the force of the ball so that no material damage was done other than to make him limp a little in his walk.

Dr. Matthews impaneled a coroner's jury, who went and viewed the bodies as they lay in the cabin in the rear of Dunbar's stables on Fifth Street, and then adjourned until 10 o'clock this morning.


## THE ALARM GIVEN

The moment the word of the shooting reached the Vizina and Tough Nut mines the whistles blew a shrill signal, and the miners came to the surface, armed themselves, and poured into the town like an invading army. A few moments served to bring out all the better portions of the citizens, thoroughly armed and ready for any emergency. Precautions were immediately taken to preserve law and order, even if they had to fight for it. A guard of ten men was stationed around the county jail, and extra policemen put on for the night.

## EARP BROTHERS JUSTIFIED

The feeling among the best class of our citizens is that the Marshal was entirely justified in his efforts to disarm these men, and that being fired upon they had to defend themselves, which they did most bravely. So long as our peace officers make an effort to preserve the peace and put down highway robbery, which the Earp brothers have done, having engaged in the pursuit and capture, where captures have been made of every gang of stage robbers in the county—they will have the support of all good citizens. If the present lesson is not sufficient to teach the cowboy element that they cannot come into the streets of Tombstone, in broad daylight, armed with six-shooters and Henry rifles to hunt down their victims, then the citizens will most assuredly take such steps to preserve the peace as will be forever a bar to such raids.

# APPENDIX 3

T HIS IS A "WHO'S WHO" of the book's participants in that fictional alternate reality where the United States extended to the West Coast.

## Doc Holliday

He was born John Henry Holliday in 1851, and grew up in Georgia. His mother died of tuberculosis when he was fourteen, and that is almost certainly where he contracted the disease. He was college educated, with a minor in the classics, and became a licensed dentist. Because of his disease, he went out West to dryer climates. The disease cost him most of his clientele, so he supplemented his dental income by gambling, and he defended his winnings in the untamed cities of the West by becoming a gunslinger as well.

He saved Wyatt Earp when the latter was surrounded by gunmen in

Dodge City, and the two became close friends. Somewhere along the way he met and had a stormy on-and-off relationship with Big Nose Kate Elder. He was involved in the Gunfight at the O.K. Corral, and is generally considered to have delivered the fatal shots to both Tom and Frank McLaury. He rode with Wyatt Earp on the latter's vendetta against the Cowboys after the shootings of Virgil and Morgan Earp, then moved to Colorado. He died, in bed, of tuberculosis, in 1887. His last words were: "Well, I'll be damned—this is funny." No accurate records were kept in the case of most shootists; depending on which historians you believe, Doc killed anywhere from two to twenty-seven men.

## JOHNNY RINGO

Born in 1850, Ringo was the only college-educated shootist other than Holliday. He was involved in the Mason County Wars, and arrived in Tombstone in 1879, where he joined Ike Clanton's gang and dubbed himself the King of the Cowboys. At one point he and Holliday went into the street to have it out. They were each to put opposite ends of the same bandana in their teeth so they couldn't possibly miss their targets at such close range, but Wyatt Earp broke it up. Ringo participated in some robberies and killings, though he was not involved in the Gunfight at the O.K. Corral. Ringo was found dead on July 14, 1882, in Turkey Creek Canyon, with a bullet in his head. Various historians have credited him with anywhere from zero to sixteen kills.

# WYATT EARP

Quite possibly the most famous lawman of the Old West, Wyatt Earp was born in Illinois in 1848. He was a stagecoach driver in the mid-1860s, and became a lawman in 1870, the same year he married and lost his first wife. He continued his career as a lawman, but also invested in a number of gambling halls and at least one brothel. In 1871 he was arrested for horse stealing; the charges were eventually dropped after he fled town.

By the mid-1870s he had migrated to Kansas, where he served as a lawman in Ellsworth, Wichita, and finally Dodge City, where by his own account (told to his biographer, Stuart Lake, but unconfirmed by any researchers) he arrested Ben Thompson and faced down Clay Allison, two of the more notorious gunmen of the era. He met and befriended Bat Masterson and Doc Holliday while in Dodge.

He moved to Tombstone in 1880 to join brothers James, Virgil, and eventually Morgan, first as saloon owners and eventually as lawmen. He was the only man on either side to emerge unscathed from the Gunfight at the O.K. Corral, and shortly after Morgan's assassination he led a hand-picked and probably illegal posse on what became known as Wyatt Earp's Vendetta Ride against the Cowboys.

He later lived in Colorado and Idaho, never quite making his fortune, then moved to San Diego and finally wound up in Los Angeles, telling his (frequently exaggerated) story to Stuart Lake and trying without success to get Hollywood interested in filming it. He died in 1929.

## KATE ELDER

Big-Nose Kate was born in Hungary in 1850. She came to America as a child, seems to have married a dentist in St. Louis at the age of six-teen, had a baby, and lost both her husband and her child to yellow fever. She got her start as a "sporting woman" by working for Bessie Earp, the wife of James Earp, eldest of the Earp brothers.

She met Wyatt Earp and Doc Holliday in 1876, hooked up with Doc shortly thereafter, and helped him escape from jail in Fort Griffin. She was partial to liquor, and at one point in 1881 Sheriff John Behan got her drunk and had her sign a false accusation that Holliday had robbed a stagecoach. She stayed with Holliday on and off until his death, then married a blacksmith, later divorced him, and lived to the ripe old age of ninety, dying in 1940.

## BAT MASTERSON

He was born in Quebec in 1853. As a teenager, he and two of his brothers left their family farm to become buffalo hunters, and then spent some time in the Indian wars. Bat became sheriff of Dodge City in 1877, where he befriended Wyatt Earp, then was Ford County sheriff until he was voted out of office in 1879. He was in Tombstone until shortly before the Gunfight at the O.K. Corral, and he spent another decade out West as a gambler and sports writer. He wound up his career and his life in New York, where he was a columnist for the *Morning Telegraph*. He died in harness in 1921, expiring at his desk while typing his column.

## Thomas Alva Edison

Born in Milan, Ohio, in 1847, Edison is considered the greatest inventor of his era. He is responsible for the electric light, the motion picture, the carbon telephone transmitter, the fluoroscope, and a host of other inventions. He died in 1931.

## Ned Buntline

Buntline was born Edward Z. C. Judson in 1813, and gained fame as a publisher, editor, and writer (especially of dime novels about the West), and for commissioning Colt's Manufacturing Company to create the Buntline Special. He tried to bring Wild Bill Hickok back East, failed, and then discovered Buffalo Bill Cody, who *did* come East and perform in a play that Buntline wrote. He died in 1886.

## Virgil Earp

Born in 1843, Virgil actually saw some action in the Civil War, fighting for the Union. He worked as a stagecoach driver, did construction work on a railroad, and labored in a sawmill. His first two marriages ended quickly—the records do not say if they were terminated by death or divorce—and he was married a third time, to Allie, in 1874. He moved to Arizona in 1878, was a lawman in Prescott, and then became marshal of the Arizona Territory. He also became the acting town marshal of Tombstone after Marshal Fred White was murdered. He was a participant at the O.K. Corral, where he was wounded in the leg. Two months later he was ambushed on Allen Street, and lost the use of one arm. He later became a railroad detective and the marshal of a small town, and died in 1905.

## Morgan Earp

Born in Iowa in 1851, Morgan became a deputy in Dodge City in 1875, then moved to Montana where he lived until 1880. He then rode shotgun for Wells Fargo, moved to Tombstone to join his brothers, survived the Gunfight at the O.K. Corral with a wounded shoulder, accepted the position of Deputy US Marshal in the winter of 1882, and was assassinated while shooting pool on March 18, 1882.

## Curly Bill Brocius

Born in Indiana in 1845, Brocius was a gunslinger and an outlaw. Purported to be the deadliest shot among the Cowboy faction, he arrived in Tombstone and was later arrested for shooting Marshal Fred White. He beat the charges, and then he and Johnny Ringo went off to Hachita, New Mexico, to kill William and Isaac Haslett (who in turn had killed two of the Cowboys). He was killed by Wyatt Earp, in retribution for Morgan Earp's murder, on March 24, 1882.

## Ike Clanton

Born in Missouri in 1847, he was a horse thief, an occasional gunman (but rarely when someone could shoot back), a gambler, and became the ringleader of the Cowboys after his father was killed by a gang of Mexicans in retaliation for stealing their horses.

He was at the O.K. Corral, but claimed to be unarmed and didn't participate, instead running for cover. He testified against the Earps and Holliday in the aftermath, but lied so blatantly that he actually did more good for the defense than the prosecution.

Ike never bothered to learn a legal trade, and he was shot dead by Detective Jonas V. Brighton in 1887.

## BILLY CLANTON

Born in 1862, Billy was the youngest Clanton brother, and from all historical accounts was a hardworking young man who simply got sucked into his older brothers' schemes. According to all eyewitness accounts he was absolutely fearless in the Gunfight at the O.K. Corral, never ducking or ceasing his efforts despite being riddled with bullets. He died in the Gunfight, at the age of nineteen.

## FRANK McLAURY

Frank McLaury (occasionally spelled "McLowry") was born in New York in 1848. He and his brother Tom moved to Arizona in 1878, where they befriended the Clantons and Curly Bill Brocius, who in turn inspired in them a severe dislike of the Earps. They dealt in stolen cattle from time to time, but were never arrested. They had a series of arguments with Doc Holliday, and were participants in the Gunfight at the O.K. Corral. Frank was killed at the O.K. Corral by Doc Holliday, at the age of thirty-three.

## Tom McLaury

Born in New York in 1853, Tom McLaury moved to Arizona with his brother Frank. They became friends of Curly Bill Brocius and the Clantons, and dealt in stolen cattle on occasion. During a dispute with Wyatt Earp, Tom approached him in a fury and Earp buffaloed him (which is to say, he cracked Frank over the head with his gun barrel), which reinforced a hatred he felt for the Earp clan. It came to a head at the O.K. Corral, where Tom was killed by Doc Holliday, at the age of twenty-eight.

## John Clum

Born in 1851, he became an Indian agent for the San Carlos Apache reservation in Arizona, and was later the editor of the *Tombstone Epitaph* and the mayor of Tombstone. He was a diehard supporter of the Earps and Holliday in their battle against the Cowboys. He died in 1932.

## Geronimo

Born Goyathlay in 1829, he was a Chiricahua Apache medicine man who fought against both the Americans and the Mexicans who tried to grab Apache territory. He was never a chief, but he *was* a military leader, and a very successful one. He finally surrendered in 1886, and was incarcerated—but by 1904 he had become such a celebrity that he actually appeared at the World's Fair, and in 1905 he rode in Theodore Roosevelt's inaugural parade. He died in 1909, at the age of eighty.

## THE REAL BUNTLINE SPECIAL

The Buntline Special, commissioned from Colt by Ned Buntline, possessed a twelve-inch barrel, making it the most distinctive pistol of its time. According to Buntline, he had five made up, and gave them to five lawmen he admired. Four of them (again, according to Buntline) cut the barrels down to the standard seven and a half inches, and Wyatt Earp left his at twelve inches. There is no record at the Colt factory that such an order was ever made or processed, but there are numerous descriptions of Earp wearing it.

# About the Author

Locus, *the trade journal of science fiction, keeps a list of the winners of major science fiction awards on its Web page. Mike Resnick is currently fourth in the all-time standings, ahead of Isaac Asimov, Sir Arthur C. Clarke, Ray Bradbury, and Robert A. Heinlein. He is the leading award-winner among all authors, living and dead, for short science fiction.*

\* \* \* \* \* \*

MIKE RESNICK was born on March 5, 1942. He sold his first article in 1957, his first short story in 1959, and his first book in 1962.

He attended the University of Chicago from 1959 through 1961, won three letters on the fencing team, and met and married Carol. Their daughter, Laura, was born in 1962, and has since become a writer herself, winning two awards for her romance novels and the 1993 Campbell Award for Best New Science Fiction Writer.

Mike and Carol discovered science fiction fandom in 1962, attended their first Worldcon in 1963, and fifty science fiction books into his career, Mike still considers himself a fan and frequently contributes articles to fanzines. He and Carol appeared in five Worldcon masquerades in the 1970s in costumes that she created, and they won four of them.

Mike labored anonymously but profitably from 1964 through 1976, selling more than two hundred novels, three hundred short stories, and two thousand articles, almost all of them under pseudonyms, most of them in the "adult" field. He edited seven different tabloid newspapers and a trio of men's magazines, as well.

In 1968 Mike and Carol became serious breeders and exhibitors of collies, a pursuit they continued through 1981. During that time they bred and/or exhibited twenty-seven champion collies, and they were the country's leading breeders and exhibitors during various years along the way.

This led them to purchase the Briarwood Pet Motel in Cincinnati in 1976. It was the country's second-largest luxury boarding and grooming establishment, and they worked full-time at it for the next few years. By 1980 the kennel was being run by a staff of twenty-one, and Mike was free to return to his first love, science fiction, albeit at a far slower pace than his previous writing. They sold the kennel in 1993.

Mike's first novel in this "second career" was *The Soul Eater*, which was followed shortly by *Birthright: The Book of Man*, *Walpurgis III*, the four-book Tales of the Galactic Midway series, *The Branch*, the four-book Tales of the Velvet Comet series, and *Adventures*, all from Signet. His breakthrough novel was the international bestseller *Santiago*, published by Tor in 1986. Tor has since published *Stalking the Unicorn*, *The Dark Lady*, *Ivory*, *Second Contact*, *Paradise*, *Purgatory*, *Inferno*, the Double

*Bwana/Bully!*, and the collection *Will the Last Person to Leave the Planet Please Shut Off the Sun?* His most recent Tor releases were *A Miracle of Rare Design*, *A Hunger in the Soul*, *The Outpost*, and the *The Return of Santiago*.

Even at his reduced rate, Mike is too prolific for one publisher, and in the 1990s Ace published *Soothsayer*, *Oracle*, and *Prophet*; Questar published *Lucifer Jones*; Bantam brought out the *Locus* bestselling trilogy of *The Widowmaker*, *The Widowmaker Reborn*, and *The Widow- maker Unleashed*; and Del Rey published *Kirinyaga: A Fable of Utopia* and *Lara Croft, Tomb Raider: The Amulet of Power*. His current releases include *A Gathering of Widowmakers* for Meisha Merlin, *Dragon America* for Phobos, and *Lady with an Alien*, *A Club in Montmarte*, and *The World behind the Door* for Watson-Guptill.

Beginning with *Shaggy B.E.M. Stories* in 1988, Mike has also become an anthology editor (and was nominated for a Best Editor Hugo in 1994 and 1995). His list of anthologies in print and in press totals forty-eight, and includes *Alternate Presidents*, *Alternate Kennedys*, *Sherlock Holmes in Orbit*, *By Any Other Fame*, *Dinosaur Fantastic*, and *Christmas Ghosts*, plus the recent *Stars*, coedited with superstar singer Janis Ian.

Mike has always supported the "specialty press," and he has numerous books and collections out in limited editions from such diverse publishers as Phantasia Press, Axolotl Press, Misfit Press, Pulp- house Publishing, Wildside Press, Dark Regions Press, NESFA Press, WSFA Press, Obscura Press, Farthest Star, and others. He recently served a stint as the science fiction editor for BenBella Books, and in 2006 he became the executive editor of *Jim Baen's Universe*.

Mike was never interested in writing short stories early in his career, producing only seven between 1976 and 1986. Then something clicked, and he has written and sold more than 175 stories since 1986, and now spends more time on short fiction than on novels. The writing that has brought him the most acclaim thus far in his career is the Kirinyaga series, which, with sixty-seven major and minor awards and nominations to date, is the most honored series of stories in the history of science fiction.

He also began writing short nonfiction as well. He sold a four-part series, "Forgotten Treasures," to the *Magazine of Fantasy and Science Fiction*, was a regular columnist for *Speculations* ("Ask Bwana") for twelve years, currently appears in every issue of the *SFWA Bulletin* ("The Resnick/Malzberg Dialogues"), and wrote a biweekly column for the late, lamented GalaxyOnline.com.

Carol has always been Mike's uncredited collaborator on his science fiction, but in the past few years they have sold two movie scripts—*Santiago* and *The Widowmaker*, both based on Mike's books—and Carol *is* listed as his collaborator on those.

Readers of Mike's works are aware of his fascination with Africa, and the many uses to which he has put it in his science fiction. Mike and Carol have taken numerous safaris, visiting Kenya (four times), Tanzania, Malawi, Zimbabwe, Egypt, Botswana, and Uganda. Mike edited the Library of African Adventure series for St. Martin's Press, and is currently editing *The Resnick Library of African Adventure* and, with Carol as coeditor, *The Resnick Library of Worldwide Adventure*, for Alexander Books.

Since 1989, Mike has won five Hugo Awards (for "Kirinyaga," "The Manamouki," "Seven Views of Olduvai Gorge," "The 43 Antarean Dynasties," and "Travels with My Cats") and a Nebula Award (for "Seven Views of Olduvai Gorge"), and has been nominated for thirty Hugos, eleven Nebulas, a Clarke (British), and six Seiun-sho (Japanese). He has also won a Seiun-sho, a Prix Tour Eiffel (French), two Prix Ozones (French), ten HOMer Awards, an Alexander Award, a Golden Pagoda Award, a Hayakawa SF Award (Japanese), a Locus Award, three Ignotus Awards (Spanish), a Xatafi-Cyberdark Award (Spanish), a Futura Award (Croatia), an El Melocoton Mechanico (Spanish), two Sfinks Awards (Polish), and a Fantastyka Award (Polish), and has topped the Science Fiction Chronicle Poll six times, the Scifi Weekly Hugo Straw Poll three times, and the Asimov's Readers Poll five times. In 1993 he was awarded the Skylark Award for Lifetime Achievement in Science Fiction, and both in 2001 and in 2004 he was named Fictionwise.com's Author of the Year.

His work has been translated into French, Italian, German, Spanish, Japanese, Korean, Bulgarian, Hungarian, Hebrew, Russian, Latvian, Lithuanian, Polish, Czech, Dutch, Swedish, Romanian, Finnish, Danish, Chinese, and Croatian.

He was recently the subject of Fiona Kelleghan's massive *Mike Resnick: An Annotated Bibliography and Guide to His Work*. Adrienne Gormley is currently preparing a second edition.